LAURIE LEE

Cinderella Spell

By Laurie Lee

Fiction and Literature: Fantasy
Young Adult Fantasy

ISBN: 978-1-0881-3653-9

1

Cinderella's gray service gown swooshed as she crossed the wood-planked floor of the queen's sick chamber. Woven damask drapes lining the slim, long windows kept the room in shadows. Two iron-wrought candelabras fit with six candles cast a soft glow across the thick mattress piled high with fine linen and crafted blankets. Upon the bed, Queen Charlotte lay gaunt against a mountain of pillows. Her once-luxurious ebony hair hung limp, dampened by fever. Even with candlelight across her face, the vivid greens of square pillows and yellow bolster cushions couldn't bring color to her sick pallor.

Cinderella paused beside the bed and allowed a trickle of pleasure to bring a smile to her face before schooling her features. She cleared her throat loud enough to rouse the sick woman struggling before her.

The Queen's dull gray eyes blinked open and she offered a wan smile. "Cinderella? Why are you here?" Her raspy voice reached into the darkness.

Cinderella sat upon the edge of the bed and arranged her skirts. The dark cotton presented a sharp contrast to the cream-colored linen. Cinderella trailed her fingers across both materials before reaching for the queen's hand. "I have come for the key, my lady."

"Key?" The Queen's eyes closed with a sigh. "Rowley is the keeper of keys."

"Except Doorin's Key." Cinderella tilted her head, eager to see the Queen's reaction. "You have been its keeper, have you not?"

The sick woman gasped as she tried to free her hand from Cinderella's grip, but she was too weak. Cinderella kept hold of the queen's cold flesh as she pulled the silver chain that slipped beneath the queen's bedgown. But instead of the key, a silver heart dangled.

Anger burned within Cinderella. "Where is it?"

The Queen seemed to muster her strength. "Beyond your reach."

She tightened her hold on the Queen, but the sight of pain twisting the queen's mouth did not please. "Give me what I want, and the sickness will end." She lowered her eyes, breathed patience, and forced her voice to a sweet and imploring umber. "You will be well once more."

"That door must never be opened. Why ask it of me?"

Cinderella scowled. "You have no knowledge of Doorin's secrets. How can you claim it should never be opened?" She paused until a thought brought a wicked smile to her face. She released the Queen's hand and sat straight. "With your death, the key passes to your son."

The Queen shook her head. "He is protected. The Faere Folk christened him."

Cinderella twisted her hair into a coil and brushed it through her hands over and over. Its dark color faded with each pass of her hand, until her head gleamed with golden hair. "Only until his twenty-first birthday. I have but to wait. I will make him fall in love with me." She grinned. The queen struggled to sit up, and Cinderella read fear in her eyes. "We will dance upon your grave." She stood. In place of the servant clothes she'd been wearing, she fussed with the ruffles of a pale blue silken fabric embroidered with silver thread ball gown. The queen's agitation lifted her spirits, and she giggled.

"No! He will never love you. His heart will belong to a woman of character and faith." Queen Charlotte's denial shuddered to silence as she fought to catch her breath.

Cinderella's laughter filled the chamber. She twirled, catching her image in a large mirror on the far wall. She was a picture of youth and health with bouncing blonde curls and a shapely figure. "Perhaps if you had lived to nurture and guide him as he grows." Cinderella turned from admiring herself in the mirror to gaze once more at the dying queen. She leaned over and placed her hand on the Queen's cheek. "But no." She rocked her head from side to side, taunting the Queen. "You have chosen death."

Queen Charlotte twisted away from her. "Be gone, witch! Darken my chamber no more."

Cinderella slipped into the shadows beyond the candle's glow, but her voice carried. "I will be patient, my lady. Just a while longer. Your son will come to love me, and I will spill his blood in the doorway of Doorin's room."

"Will, my gown!"

King William laughed at his queen's protest, then wrapped one arm around her waist and grabbed his son with his other arm. He growled and pulled the three of them backward into the snow. Cold embraced him, but the sound of Prince Robert's gleeful giggles warmed his heart.

Queen Charlotte pressed her slim hand against his chest. "You've ruined us." But the laughter in her voice belied her severity.

"Pull us up, Son," King William said. But the six-year-old pounced on his chest with ferocious growls.

"Now look, you've turned our boy into a bear," Queen Charlotte laughed as Prince Robert snapped at her fingers.

"I'll save you, my precious," King William wrapped both hands around his son and lifted him above them.

"No, you can't save her." A shadow lurked in his periphery. Though he chuckled at the dangling arms grasping cold air, the shadow moved closer, spreading across the snow. He got up and twirled. Prince Robert squealed and wrapped arms around his neck. Queen Charlotte clung to his side, her feet gliding above the snow. The shadow spun faster, wrapping around them like a snake. The joy of his family warred against the hiss of shadow.

King William lurched from his bed as the dream turned sour. Sweat clung to his skin even though the room was cool. "Charlotte," he muttered her name as he stretched his arm across the other side of the bed. She wasn't there. Hadn't been since she'd taken ill a day after their romp in the snow. "I must go to her." He raked his fingers through his hair. "Bartholomew," he hollered.

The tall, thin, silver-haired man entered from the servant's cove. "Sire, how may I assist you?"

King William gripped a post of the bed. "I must go to the queen."

He bowed. "Of course, Sire. Shall I have a bath drawn for you?"

"No, no. A dressing gown will do. I want to go now." He held his arms out, unmindful of the woolen weave of the fabric being wrapped onto him. Bartholomew buttoned the closure and tied the belt around his waist. He slipped his feet into leather slippers.

Torchmen waited in the hallway to lead the way to the queen's sick chamber. The palace remained quiet as they walked the halls. Something inside him twisted with pain as they reached Charlotte's room.

He blinked against the sting of incense permeating the air as he entered Charlotte's bed chamber. Pain moved to his chest, clutching at the sight of her, pale and wan against the covers. Her dark hair shone with sweat, mirroring the shadows beneath her closed eyes.

How could this be? A week prior, she'd laughed, holding a hand toward him from her seat in the snow. His throat ached, catching what little breath he managed.

"My life, Lord," he prayed. "My life for hers." But his whispered words hit the ceiling and would go no further.

Her chest rose and fell. Mrs. Turney, Robert's old nurse, wrung a towel in a bowl of water and placed the towel across Charlotte's forehead. Her lips parted. William strode to her side. He dipped a smaller cloth in water and put it to her mouth. Precious drops wet her tongue, and the furrow between her brows calmed for a time.

"I am sorry, Majesty." Mrs. Turney's wrinkled face bore testament to her sorrow.

He managed a glimmer of a smile before looking down at his beloved wife. Her eyes shifted. The gray color that had held his attention since they first met at a dignitary's banquet had darkened. He wiped a stray hair from her face. The heat of her skin beneath his fingers put an ache in his belly. "How long are you letting this fever hold you?" He teased as her eyes met his.

She sighed. "Not much longer now."

He choked and turned to the nurse. "A fresh towel."

Charlotte tossed restlessly as her fever-ravished body refused to give up its heat. William pressed the new towel against her forehead, laying another on her chest. She did not calm. Her hand moved, and he took it in his own. She squeezed her fingers around his.

"What do you need?" William kept the tears at bay by sheer will. It was all he could do. Nothing seemed to work against the devilish fever claiming Charlotte's life.

"Promise me," she struggled to speak, but a familiar glint sparked in her gray eyes.

"Anything."

"Take a wife when I am gone."

William leaned closer. "Do not ask it of me."

"You must. For Robert." Her breath rasped between words. "You must. Protect him."

Her pallor turned ashen, and William noticed a drop on her cheek. His tear. Another dampened her face. Helplessness tore at his chest. He shook his head, refusing her request yet again.

Her thin hand brushed against his cheek. He dropped his head to her neck, overwhelmed in his sorrow.

"I am sorry, my love." Her voice managed a whisper, and then her body stilled.

He gathered her body to him and wept, praying death over them both.

LAURIE LEE

2

King William stared at his glass of water as the voice of his beloved whispered from the past. Her request for him to remarry lingered, but he could not make himself to do so.

"My Lord, it's been nearly ten years. I am certain you have been waiting for my little Elouise to grow into the beautiful woman she is today."

"Havish," William called, waving for a guard to remove the offensive woman. His middle-aged advisor hurried into the room, closing the heavy door behind him.

"I don't know how they found out. The street is filled with… with…" He straightened his cravat at the king's raised brow. He cleared his throat. "Women. Mothers, daughters, widows. I am so sorry. I thought we had this visit to the seaside better arranged."

William sighed. "Is there a different exit we can use?"

"There's a patio in the back. Wait there while we clear a path."

The salt air hung heavy in the open space, and he breathed deeply. Though several buildings had been built close together, a gap allowed for view of the beach. William took a step toward the railing before he noticed a tall, thin woman standing there already. "It's not to be born. What are you doing here?"

The woman turned. Her narrow face held both elegance and sorrow. "I often met my husband here."

He relaxed his shoulders. "My pardon. I assumed you were part of the rabble in the front." He searched the area. "You should return inside."

"Is there a reason I cannot enjoy a breath of the sea?"

"My guards are preparing a transport away from the confusion in the street."

The woman paled as her eyes widened. "Your Majesty," she spoke as she swept into a graceful bow.

He offered a brief smile. "My apology to you and your husband. I hope you may enjoy your view once we have left."

She closed her eyes. "Our meeting is in memory. He has been gone four years."

Unlike the widows with their gleaming eyes who showed up nearly everywhere he went, this woman had sorrow as a companion. She turned, went up a short staircase, and through a door into the neighboring building.

In the moment alone, he walked to the edge of the wooden deck and gave in to his own memories.

On the following day, William stood at the window in the most opulent room the seaside village had to offer. Looking out toward waves rolling across the sand proved more appealing than he realized. "Havish, I will take a walk on the boards."

He nodded. "But give us a little time. The women are determined to have an interlude with you."

The king shook his head. "I will speak with our land agent. A summer home in the area will suit me. I will not have to contend with public lodgings."

Havish didn't return for nearly an hour. William rubbed a hand over his mouth to hide his reaction to whisps of hair floating above the man's head as though a great wind had disposed him.

"We are ready, my Lord."

Except they weren't. William felt his ire grow as he noticed a lone woman step out from between two buildings. But the tall, slender woman ignored him and walked to the railing. She did not lean, instead remained straight, looking out to sea. He could have ignored her, but something drove him to walk closer. "Is the sea revealing her secrets?" He spoke in jest, but when she turned toward him with damp cheeks, remorse scolded him. "Forgive me, I should not have interrupted your thoughts."

"Your Majesty." She bowed once more, than glanced both ways on the deserted boardwalk. "I might have known the lack of crowds was not by chance."

"Do you live here, or are you on holiday?"

"This is more a time of memory. We visited the year before his death; my daughter, husband, and I. Now I visit alone."

"Did they die in an accident?"

"They? No, Majesty. My daughter is with her governess."

He nodded. "At least you have her. I am thankful for my son."

The woman smiled. "Prince Robert, I believe. Of course, I have seen his likeness."

"He has more of the queen mother than myself." He tilted his head. "I appreciate the brevity of our conversation. What is your name?"

"I am Countess DeGanne, your Majesty."

"I will resume my walk." He glanced at the soldiers on the far side of the boardwalk. "Shall I leave you to peace and quiet a while longer?"

She almost smiled. "If it pleases you, your Majesty."

Boards creaked beneath his feet as he walked the length. "Ah, Charlotte, my love. I should have brought you to such a place. Surely, the air that drives up from the sea would have healed whatever sickness took you." Gray clouds moved in. He walked a little further.

"My Lord King, um, Majesty," a young soldier drew near.

William faced the lad but remained quiet.

The young man cleared his throat. "Master Havish, Sire, he warns that rain may be coming.

William peered over the water. Indeed, the gathering clouds had taken on a darker hue. He smiled. "Well, I guess the time to return has come sooner than I thought." They turned. The guard walked a few steps behind, and William used a faster pace than earlier. The Countess DeGanne had gone, and he did not think of her.

Sunday, his last day by the sea, William wanted more than a

lavish meal on his own in his rooms. "Havish," he called and his man appeared quickly.

"Sire?"

"I would like to have a meal in the dining room this afternoon. Before Mass, I think. there shouldn't be too many other diners at that time."

"Normally, I am sure there would not. If people know you will be there…"

The king sighed. "I cannot hide from my people forever. Make the arrangement."

"Should I have the room emptied and put a guard on each of the doors?"

"Heavens, no. I would not instill fear. Let us hope there are few patrons at this hour."

Their hopes were not realized.

"Do you desire wine?"

"Allow me to refill your water, Sire."

A bevy of women hovered around his table. He cringed as their voices raked against his nerves and jarred him from peace. One reached in front of him, but a servant swatted her hand with a wooden dowel. The shriek she made did nothing to stop the others.

He closed his eyes. Why had he chosen proximity to the sea instead of his own summer palace? He winced as a high-pitched cackle sounded all too near his ear. "Havish," he bellowed to be heard above the din. He opened his mouth to order the dining room cleared, when he spied a willowy lady entering through the side door.

"Sire?" Havish stood at his elbow, breathing hard.

William jerked his head in the direction of the lady. "Request the Countess DeGanne to join me for supper. Bring another set of dishes."

By the time a second chair had been pulled to the table, Countess DeGanne arrived. King William covered a chuckle with his kerchief as the regal woman looked down her hawk nose at the hovering babble.

"Be gone, you and your foolish sisters." The lady waved her hand, shooing the others from the king's table. Though dark were their looks, the crowd dispersed. The Countess smiled as Havish ushered her into her seat. She turned to face the king. "Thank you, your Majesty, for your kind invitation."

"Thank *you*." His eyes travelled to the stragglers sulking their way to the exit. "Seems you have a talent."

"Forgive them. They are young and do not understand."

"They torment me." A turret of soup with mushrooms and chives was served, but he found himself unable to enjoy the flavorful dish. "You understand, do you not?"

He studied her face as a slight blush crept across her cheeks. She could not be considered beautiful, for age and grief had carved lines in her skin. But her eyes were kind and he found himself able to relax in her company. His gaze moved to the ring she still wore. His own ring felt warm against the skin of his third finger.

"I too have been forged by death." She agreed.

In silent accord, they took of the second course. William ate a slice of cheese with beef, then watched waves strike the shore. Battered sands moved with the force of the water, and yet the beach remained. The ocean tinged the air with salt. Charlotte's request, so impossible ten years before … he glanced at the woman beside him. Perhaps …

William waited for a servant to refill their goblets then leaned closer to the Countess. "Lady DeGanne, you have a daughter?"

A slim smile lit her face. "Marissa. She is twelve."

He took a deep breath, and then plunged. "Let us join our families. I will protect your daughter, and you will teach my son the graces necessary to gain a good wife."

She dropped her fork. "Sire, I cannot."

"Hear me, please." He placed his hand on hers. "I do not speak of love or romance. My heart rests with Charlotte. You, I know, seek no husband. But protection for your daughter is not a small thing. Please, my lady, you understand why I can never be with another. Yet, everywhere I go, I am bombarded with daughters and widows." He shook his head. "It is torment. I want to travel my land in peace."

She turned away from him, but William did not sense refusal. He waited. The sounds of the ocean settled around them. Countess DeGanne took another bite of her pie. A bird shrieked as it flew across the beach.

After a few moments, she placed her fork against the plate, closed her eyes, and a slight sigh whispered from her. She nodded. "I will agree to your proposal. A mother for your son and protection for my daughter."

The burden gripping his chest faded like melting snow. Relief drew a grin on his face. "That is all I ask. In a fortnight, I will send the royal carriage to transport your household to Monmoore Palace."

"As you wish, Sire."

He sighed. "William, please."

They dined in friendly accord until bells called them to Mass.

3

Ogres chased damsels in distress. Marissa was certain their shadowed figures raced just beyond the brocade shades covering the windows of the carriage. The carriage rattled to the side then straightened once more as it journeyed across the ill road. She rose to her knees on the cushioned seat and grabbed hold of the bottom rail of the window. Shadow-play beyond the curtain riveted her attention. She knew, with every fiber of her being, knights and dragons awaited beyond her sight. She frowned at the thick window coverings. With a peek at her mother, accomplishing needlepoint in a rocking carriage, Marissa pulled one corner up and peeked.

A hard rap to her knuckles brought her bottom back to the seat. "A lady does not peek."

Marissa scowled at her mother, the Countess DeGanne, as she rubbed her knuckles. Her mother's thick, brown hair remained twisted in a complicated French knot, even after a day of travel. Her taupe-colored traveling gown remained set about her legs, the skirt swaying with the carriage movement. Marissa's own matching gown boasted wrinkles and a green stain where she'd bumped against a hedge. *If the jay hadn't bounced beneath the branches, I wouldn't have run into the bush.*

Swinging her legs back and forth on the edge of her seat, Marissa turned her attention to the woman sitting beside her mother, her governess turned lady's maid, Mrs. Boyde. The plain brown service gown couldn't hide her creamy skin. Though she held a book, Mrs. Boyde's blue eyes twinkled back at her. Marissa giggled.

She felt her mother's glower and lowered her face to stare at her hands in her lap. *My nails are dirty*. She turned her attention back to the window where mysterious shapes passed them. *A dragon? Knights bounding after it?*

Marissa huffed with impatience. "If we pulled the curtains open, I wouldn't need to peek."

Her mother wrinkled her nose with distaste. "These paths are dusty."

"But the open window would allow air to come in. Please, Mother," she whined, and then tried batting her eyelashes.

Though her mother shook her head, Marissa spied a small smile.

"Oh, very well." Mother waved her hand toward the window dressings. "Mrs. Boyde, would you please." Then she returned her attention to the delicate needlepoint in her lap.

Marissa smiled as her governess leaned past her and unlatched the fabric, rolling it into the straps across the ceiling of the carriage. Marissa contained her giggle as Mrs. Boyde winked. Air moved around them immediately, and they both sighed with relief. Marissa turned her attention to the passing scenery. *No dragons, just lots of trees. Disappointing*. But the scenery looked different than what she knew. Trees were taller. The air was moist but didn't smell like ocean.

"How many days have we travelled? Are we far from home? What if I don't like the palace? What if they don't like us?" Questions flew from her brain through her mouth. She turned for a moment toward her mother. Her mother continued sewing her needle through the fabric, ignoring her. She started to lean out the open window.

"Marissa Rose Clemente DeGanne. If your head exits that window, I will have the curtains lowered again." Her mother's reprimand followed a hand pulling her back into her seat.

"I wanted to see if I can still see home."

Countess DeGanne patted her daughter's arm before releasing her. "You are young. The palace will seem like home in no time."

"I'm not young. I'm twelve." Marissa huffed, flipping her wavy chestnut hair over her shoulder.

"Already?" The countess touched her cheek in a rare display of affection. Its warmth seeped through her skin, and she stilled. Her mother's green eyes were shaped like almonds. Would hers be the same? A small smile, a thumb moving on her cheek. She smiled back.

The carriage rolled to a stop, drawing everyone's attention. Her mother's hand dropped away, and Marissa bounced in her seat. They could hear the driver jump to the ground. Two knocks on the door. *Highwaymen? Are we to be accosted on our way to the palace?*

"Yes," mother answered as she pushed her needlepoint into her valise. The door opened. A young man bowed before addressing the occupants. *Not highwaymen. I could whip this young lad myself.* Mother moved her hand to cover Marissa's chuckle without taking her eyes from the manservant.

"Madame," he began, bowing a second time. 'We have arrived at the edge of the King's grounds. His grounds are extensive, and it will take several more hours to reach Monmoore Palace. The King arranged a light luncheon for you here."

She smiled, sitting taller. "That would be lovely. Show Mrs. Boyde where it is so she may prepare our plates."

"May I help, Mother?" Marissa leaned forward, eager to stretch her legs.

"Help? That is not your…"

"I will watch over her, my Lady." Mrs. Boyde spoke in a quiet voice. "The child desires movement."

The countess hesitated, but then waved her hand, acquiescing. "Fine."

Marissa needed no further word. She leapt from the open doorway, sidetracking the surprised livery servant. She paused for a moment in the middle of the road. Not far ahead, a large stone building with an arch through its middle big enough for the carriage to pass stood guard while flanked by two rows of green hedges. The dirt-crusted road she now stood upon gave way to a cream-colored, raked pavement. She skipped to its edge. Small bits of shells and stones formed the smooth surface. A throat being cleared caught her attention. She followed Mrs. Boyde and others through an opening between the bushes.

A grand table stood in the center of a clearing. White cloth billowed in the afternoon breeze. Servants buzzed around the table, using silver canisters, crystal goblets, and rose-edged china to keep the cloth from taking flight. Marissa stepped to the table, her eyes growing large. She touched the delicate embossed painting of the plate. "It's beautiful," she whispered.

Mrs. Boyde clicked her tongue. "The king seeks to impress."

Something bumped against the back of Marissa's knees, sending her bouncing into the table. Mrs. Boyde caught the china cup before it could roll off as Marissa turned. A young man dressed in a hazel-colored uniform held a high-back chair. He nodded at the seat. She held her gown, as she'd always seen Mother do, and settled. The chair moved forward, and she grabbed the edge of the seat to stay in place. Mrs. Boyde held part of her lower lip with her teeth, a habit Marissa knew meant she was trying not to laugh. She swallowed her own giggles as Mother was led to a larger chair. Two attendants moved her closer to the table. *I can be just as graceful. She is my mother after all.*

The countess smiled at the sumptuous fare provided by the king. Marissa studied her mother, copying the motion of her hands, her choice of silverware. Such delicate movements. She mimicked the bend of her wrist, pinky angled out. She even reached for the decanter of wine, but mother slapped her knuckles again.

"Water, my Dear. Twelve may seem grown to you, but it is not quite old enough." She softened the reprimand with a smile.

Marissa thanked Mrs. Boyde for the water and then plunged her fork through the meat pie. Her nose quivered as she drew the fork into her mouth and brushed her lips across it. The wine sauce had too much tang, but she knew better than to speak of it. They ate in silence, Marissa seated beside her mother with Mrs. Boyde standing to the side. The next course involved long, thin carrots and shallots along with something that looked like a bird. Sweets followed, crusted pavlova in cream sauce. Marissa licked her fingers until Mother swatted her leg beneath the table.

"Will every meal be this fancy?" Marissa asked, her eyes wide as the attendant replaced the china luncheon plate with a silver sherbet dish.

"Hush, child." Her mother whispered from behind her napkin. "You'd think we ate in squalor. This is the king's land."

"Father was important. Did he know the king?"

The countess looked at her and shrugged. "I cannot say. I met His Majesty in Parsea, while we were on holiday."

"May I ask if he knew father? Will I be allowed to talk with him? Will he want to know me?"

Mrs. Boyde drew Marissa's chair back from the table. "Questions upon questions, Child." Marissa bounced to her feet as Mrs. Boyde turned her attention to Mother. "They are ready for you to return to the carriage, my Lady."

"Thank you, Mrs. Boyde. Were you able to clear dust from inside? I fear I will sneeze once we are settled if it has not been cleaned."

"Yes, my Lady. The coach has been refreshed. We opened more windows. I hear the view of the castle is breathtaking."

Marissa skipped to the horses, sneaking each of the matched pair a bit of carrot. Mrs. Boyde led her around to the door and ushered her inside. Silence reigned as they turned expectant eyes to the burgeoning view of the royal grounds.

Two hours later, Marissa gasped at the grand façade coming into view as the carriage rumbled along the paved course. Heavy oaks bent with age curved over the path, blocking her sight. She crawled onto the opposite seat, rising on her knees to lean through an opened window. Her mother didn't try to stop her this time. Spindly towers reaching into the sky broke through the trees.

"It's a castle," she breathed with excitement. Her eyes danced and her smile grew wide as she looked over at her mother.

"Really, Marissa, where did you expect a king to live?"

"Are you going to be queen?" She flipped her attention between the colorful play of sunlight on the still-distant castle and her mother sitting with her hands clasped in her lap.

"No. I will be the king's wife. "

Marissa scrunched her nose. "I don't have to be a princess, do I?"

"Perhaps someday. The king does have a son."

She made another face and shook her head. "Ugh. I won't like him, not one bit."

Her mother frowned. "Bite your tongue, child. It would be very good for you to marry the prince and become a princess. Someday that would make you queen."

Marry a prince? "I don't want to be queen." Her voice emphasized her disgust.

"You are much too young to understand such matters. Trust your mother; I know what is best for you."

Marissa rolled her eyes as the carriage continued along its path.

Monmoore Palace had been built within the curtain wall of an ancient keep. Gray stones from deep within the earth warmed under the spring sun. Marissa bounced on the cushioned seat as the large wood wheels of their carriage clanked across a wooden bridge leading into a lower open courtyard. Green grass spread up a hill to the base of a castle ruin. Against the age-warped pile of rocks, a palace had been built. The cream-colored stones appeared as sunlight to the darker rock's shadow. Towers rose, creating the jagged elevation she'd viewed from a distance.

Marissa climbed across Mrs. Boyde's lap to gape through the window on the other side of the carriage.

"Marissa." Her mother's stern voice carried a warning.

The young girl glanced at her mother before returning her attention to the view of weathered stone and well-worn courtyards. The stench of the still waters beneath the bridge wafted through the open window. Marissa jerked back, her nose wrinkled in dismay. "That is not the ocean."

Lady DeGanne pressed a finger against her nose and frowned at her daughter. "It is different, I grant you, but ocean breezes were not always pleasant. You will grow to love it, I surmise."

"Can my room be at the top of the tower? Will I be able to see outside the wall?" Marissa leaned her head back as far as she could to view the highest turret. "Have they fought battles? Will I be trained as a soldier? I could stand on the parapet with a bow and arrow. Just think, there will be ghosts, and dark creatures from a bygone era." Excitement buzzed through her blood and her attention flew from her mother, to Mrs. Boyde, and back to the castle.

Mrs. Boyde laughed. "That's all we need, you, running around in one of those towers. I suppose the family has rooms in the new palace wing. Plenty of people to keep an eye on you. Time you learned to behave as a young lady ought to behave."

Lady DeGanne chuckled. "That is your greatest challenge, I fear, Mrs. Boyde. My daughter is too like her father. Civility may be beyond her."

The thought of father stilled her a moment. "Am I like Father? Does it make you sad to look at me?"

"Not in the least. You are his greatest legacy." Lady DeGanne turned away as the carriage rumbled to a stop. They had arrived.

4

Marissa smirked as she slipped into the library, losing her tutor in the twisted hallways and galleys within the living quarters of the palace. Not even a week since their arrival and Mother already insisted she continue with her studies. She hadn't met the king, nor his son. She hadn't met anyone other than the pale, dull tutor. She refused to be melancholy, instead turning her attention to the cases of books standing floor to ceiling. The faces of ancient men frowned down on her from the painted ceiling. She ignored them, twisting her braid. *The shelves formed a bit of a ladder, she could...*

"I wouldn't recommend it. It's a nasty fall when you lose your grip."

Marissa yelped and spun around, finding herself facing a young man at one of the desks forming a study area in the center of the room. *The prince?* She narrowed her eyes and studied him a full minute. "You look ordinary enough, so you must not be the prince." She offered a bright smile.

"Oh?" His dark brows lifted. "What must the prince look like? Haven't you met him?"

"Goodness, no." She skipped closer, her braids bouncing off her back. "Why would I want to meet him? He'll be nine feet tall with his nose in the air another six inches. "

The young man offered a perplexed look. "Why is he so tall?"

"Well, I'm sure he thinks he is, being royal and everything." Marissa leaned on the edge of the desk, peering at the open book the young man had been studying.

"Aren't you royal now as well?"

"I'm ordinary as can be, no matter what Mother says. She would love to have me fall in love with the prince, but I refuse." She stomped her foot emphatically.

"You're all of what, twelve? Too young to fall in love."

Her lips thinned. "I'll be thirteen in a month."

He nodded, smiling. "Hm, that means you'll be this short of grown up." He held his thumb and forefinger apart, measuring an inch. "Maybe you could be the prince's friend."

"Why would he want me for a friend?"

"Because he's lonely, living in this drafty old castle without a friend in the world." The young man stood. "He was sincerely wishing you would accept him."

Suspicion caused her to furrow her brow. "He told you this?" He remained silent, his gaze steady as a horrifying thought came to Marissa's mind. She stomped her foot again. "It isn't fair. I was determined you would be a horrible creature and I would have nothing to do with you."

"I'm not horrible?"

She couldn't ignore his hopeful look. She smiled and shook her head. "No, you aren't. Although you should have let me know right away who you were." She tried to stop a grin, but failed. "Well, maybe not. I wouldn't have talked with you long enough to like you."

"You like me now?"

"In a *friend* sort of way." She emphasized friend.

He laughed. "You are almost thirteen and I'm halfway to being seventeen. Friends it will have to be." He rubbed his chin. "But what about six years from now?"

Marissa shook her head. "I'll be too flighty to get serious about anyone. You'll have to wait at least ten. Hopefully you will be married before then."

He stuck out his hand. "Prince Robert of Camden." He bowed over her hand.

She shook her head with an exasperated sigh. "Marissa DeGanne, of nowhere and never will be."

They both laughed. Robert waved at a seat across the desk from him. Marissa sat.

"What do you think of the parade for Saturday?" He asked.

Marissa was more interested in the oversized book on his side of the desk. She moved from the chair to crawl on her knees so she could lean across the desk, flipping to the next page in his book.

He asked again.

She raised her brows as she looked up at him. 'Parade?"

He nodded. "The kingdom wants to see the new queen."

Marissa shook her head. "Mother isn't queen, she's the king's wife."

Robert shrugged. "Whatever she chooses to call herself, our people wish to see her. And you, of course."

"Me? Why would anyone be interested in me?"

"You're right." He grinned. "Since I'll be in the carriage with you, no one will pay you any heed anyway." He ruffled her hair.

Marissa swatted at his arm, giggling.

"Marissa DeGanne."

The firm voice of her mother caused Marisssa to flop back in the chair. Robert's eyes widened as Marissa dropped her hands in her lap, smoothing her skirt. She faced her mother. "Yes?"

"Where have you been?"

She swallowed. "Professor Renois was speaking of artists. I've been here in the library with Robert." She turned the oversized book a bit to the left. "Look what we found."

"Prince Robert?" Lady DeGanne smiled at the young man.

"We've agreed to be friends and there's no need to worry about his title." Marissa knew by the slight throb of a vein at her mother's temple she would receive stronger discipline once they were alone.

Lady DeGanne smiled at the prince instead. "I hope she has not disturbed your studies."

"Quite the opposite. She is a delightful partner." He pointed at something on the page. "She's pointed out details I've never noticed before."

"Marissa is more interested in her imagination than what can be found in books."

Marissa rolled her eyes, but at least she hadn't been dragged from the library yet. "Perhaps my studies should take place here." She waved her arms. "Professor Renois should be able to find something on every subject here."

It was Robert's turn to frown, but Marissa ignored him.

"Renois is your tutor, Marissa. Prince Robert should not be

disturbed by him."

"Why?" Marissa turned from Robert to her mother. "Does he get someone better?"

"Professors of university come to the palace."

Marissa stood. "Then I should be here. Did you hear that mother? From the university?"

"I will speak with King William, but, until I say otherwise, you will work with Professor Renois. You will not leave him scouring hallways in search of you."

Robert's grin made Marissa want to laugh, but to do so would be reckless. She bit her lips instead, took a deep breath, and nodded. "Yes, Mother." She took a few steps toward the door, then turned to Robert. "Shall we meet after dinner? What sort of games do you have?"

"How about you and your mother come to the peach parlor after dinner? I'll send Rowley to show you the way."

Marissa waited for her mother to respond, then added her own, "That would be delightful." With a final grin at Robert, she followed her mother.

"Did you know there will be a parade on Saturday?" Marissa walked through the door her mother held for her.

"You have a fitting this afternoon."

"A fitting for what?"

"A gown for the parade and ceremony first. There will be others. Day dresses, evening frocks." She gave a sharp glance. "School uniform."

"Did something happen to my things? I thought Mrs. Boyde unpacked the trunks."

"This is a different time and a new place."

She crossed her arms. "I don't want to look like a princess."

"No matter your clothes, my dear, you will always be Marissa. Monmoore Palace is part of who you are now. Accept the responsibility that comes with living in the palace, rather than fight it. Life will be much happier."

They reached the set of rooms used for tutoring. A man in a blue uniform opened the door. Marissa could see Professor Renois hovering like a thunder cloud beside where she should be sitting. A thick black book that didn't look as interesting as the one Robert had on his desk rested by her writing slate.

"I will fetch you after luncheon. Seeing how your escapade took so much time, we'll have a light tray brought to you here."

Marissa groaned, but moved into the room even though she wanted to run and find Robert again. The door closed as she slunk into her seat.

LAURIE LEE

5

"Keep still." Mrs. Boyde grunted as she tugged Marisa's undergarment of stiff linen and tied the ribbons. "Ow," Marissa complained, but the ribbons did not loosen. The pale dress of silk with a hint of hazel color floated down over her head to settle at her feet. She frowned. What did she need with something so fancy?

"You almost look like a princess.' Mrs. Boyde teased as she secured the column of painted buttons. "No need to worry, I won't give you away."

"I don't want to be a princess." Marissa frowned. The girl in the mirror did not look like herself. This other girl had glossy curls and dainty feet wrapped in silk slippers peeking out from beneath the skirt. At least the gown was straight. She was too young for a bustle or the dreaded bone crusher that gave a different sort of silhouette. "Will you be in the carriage with us?"

She shook her head. "I have this mess to clean up."

Marissa noticed a shadow cross Mrs. Boyde's face. "What's wrong?"

"Wrong?" Their eyes met in the mirror and held a moment. "You see things you should not."

"What do you mean?"

But Mrs. Boyde finished tying a wide ribbon and stood back, admiring her work. "There. I've never seen you look more beautiful."

"It isn't me." The fine material made her hands sweat.

"Oh, Mars." The nickname reflected love as she took her young charge by the hands. "It isn't the dress that makes you beautiful, it's you who makes the dress. You are no longer a child and we must do a better job of grooming you to be the young woman you are destined to become." Mrs. Boyde turned away, leading her charge downstairs.

Marissa followed, but she couldn't forget the shadowed look. Memory of it caused an unsettled feeling in her stomach.

Grand did not begin to describe the procession awaiting in the lower yard of the palace. The king's horse stood proud and tall, its black coat gleaming in the sun. With its head high, Marissa imagined he commanded awe of all the others moving around the green lawn. The palomino standing nearby had hazel ribbons plaided with its white mane and tail. Both horses were draped with royal blankets in hazel and blue. An open carriage pulled by twin champagne roans with white manes stood further to the left.

Archers, pikemen, and bannermen lined the promenade. Nearby, knights in light armor controlled their horses with soft words. Beneath the chapel arch at the far side of the palace stood the bishop who had overseen the small wedding that had taken place the previous week. Two monks, two nuns, and four young friars carrying trumpets displaying banners in the same fabric as the king's horse stood with the bishop. On the other side of the yard, a man with captain's bars on his uniform paced. The red tuft of his helmet fell like a braid down his back. Marissa edged closer to Mrs. Boyde at the cacophony of color and pomp that met her. Her heart thudded in her chest, and an unfamiliar fear made her want to throw up.

"Not as bad as it seems." Robert nudged her arm.

She gulped. "I don't know what to do."

"What to do?" He looked at her and the twinkle in his eye caused her insides to unwind. "We sit in a carriage, wave a few times." He smiled. "Chat. Argue over whether the bird in the old woman's hat is alive."

The blast of a trumpet caused Marissa to jump. Excitement buzzed through the air as the king and her mother arrived. Rows of people dropped down in a bow. Marissa copied their movements. She peaked at her mother and widened her eyes. The long rose-pink cape contrasted with her thick dark hair. The dress beneath seemed to shimmer with silver, as did the stars in her hair. The king appeared splendid as well. His silver coat with puffed sleeves added breadth to his shoulders. His trimmed beard also twinkled with silver. His lips widened when he saw his son. He left the line to shake his hand. With a laugh, he lifted Marissa in his arms.

"How do you like our little parade thus far?" He pointed at the horses pulling a carriage toward them. "Picked them just for you." His voice lowered. "I hear they are unicorns in disguise."

Marissa settled against her new father, even though she thought she was too old to be carried. The merry glint in his eyes made her believe he cared. She offered a kiss to his cheek as he deposited her in the silk-lined carriage. The eruption of applause caused her to blush, and she plopped in her seat as Robert jumped beside her.

The collection of clergy started the procession. The king and Mother followed. Marissa hadn't noticed them mount their horses. Mother looked like a queen, sitting side-saddled while somehow managing to appear straight and tall. Her cape draped over the horse's rump. Even though the animal pranced, she remained in place. Marissa straightened her back, trying to figure out a way to arrange her dress.

Robert leaned in. "Stand up and give a wave. Before you sit, pull your skirt."

Marissa followed his advice, pleased to see her mother nod with a gentle smile. The trick worked, and she settled more comfortably as the carriage rolled forward.

"Once we cross into the market, we'll see the crowds. The trumpet heralds the coming of the king. People may toss flowers."

His predictions proved true. As they turned yet another corner, Marissa looked down at the roses piled over her feet. Then she noticed an arch crossing the road. She peered up as the carriage passed beneath. Carved angels, forever frozen into the tray ceiling, looked down on her. She smiled with whimsy, but then a shadow crossed over. The chill that followed the lack of sunlight seemed colder than it should be. Something menacing lurked. She twisted to see, but the sun returned, and the feeling faded. Still, she looked behind. The captain noticed something as well. His hand moved stealthily to the hilt of his sword as he focused sharp eyes into the crowd. Marissa strained to see what he noticed. A blur of cold eyes and blond curls jolted her where she sat. She looked at Robert, who had noticed nothing, then back into the crowd. Whatever had startled her was no longer visible.

Cinderella slipped through the crowd until she reached the edge closest to the road where the parade would turn on its way back to the castle.

"Horses are coming. I can't believe we're this close to the parade route," a young woman babbled.

Cinderella set herself between two larger men. The sound of clomping hooves led to her first sighting of the caravan. The crowd surged around her. A soft-spoken spell and imperceiveable touch kept the men from blocking her view.

King William's horse pranced behind the church relics. Cinderella narrowed her eyes as he passed. "Fickle man. Where's your love for your queen?" The king's sallow face had filled. His smile seemed easy as he spoke with his bride. She scoffed at the pair of them. "Too easily swayed by another woman."

The other woman pressed next to Cinderella. "Not a beauty, is she?"

Cinderella shrugged. "She sits her horse well enough. One of the manor mistresses could give her a few hints on adding some curves to her chest and hips."

The young woman giggled. "She's about as enticing as a street beggar. Does she resemble the first queen?"

"Not at all. I wonder what caused his taste to change."

She tilted her head. "You speak as though you knew her. Perhaps the queen is watching over them, protecting them from the grave."

Cinderella laughed. "The dead have no power in this world." A carriage rumbled along the cobbled brick road behind the king and his bride. Her attention turned to the prince.

"When did the prince turn into a young man?" The woman asked with a sigh.

Prince Robert sat on one side of the open carriage. Cinderella watched him. "He's maturing."

"He'll have wide shoulders like the king. His face… dd his mother have dark hair and pale features?"

"From what I remember," Cinderella nodded. "He looks less

rustic than his father. I bet he breaks plenty of hearts."

"Or wins the best heart. Who's that with him?"

Prince Robert leaned across the carriage to speak with someone. A young woman, practically still a girl, sat across from him. His smile and his laugh were received and reflected in the guileless face of the girl. She was a charmer, Cinderella scowled, clenching her fists.

"He doesn't have a sister, does he?" The young woman asked.

"No, he does not. Whoever this little girl is, best not get in my way."

"What do you mean? Get in your way?"

"I've always fancied the prince could fall in love with me, if we should meet at the right time." Cinderella touched the woman, and any questions forming faded away. With the distracting stranger silenced, she breathed as the carriage turned the corner to follow the king beneath an ancient archway. The girl turned to look behind. One moment longer, and Cinderella could lock eyes with her.

But Someone else was seeking her power. As Cinderella summoned a spell to alight on the girl in the carriage, she felt an opposite, competing power. The whisper of recognition flared to burning pain. Cinderella gasped, turning away before she could complete her attack.

More carriages followed in the parade, but the dignitaries were of no interest to Cinderella. She placed her hand on her companion's arm.

The woman shook her head, and then smiled. "Is it over? I was dazzled."

"Royalty can have that impact." Cinderella slipped away. A few blocks brought her to a tree-lined street of houses and shops. She stopped at a windowpane of glass in a door reflecting the morning sunlight. With no one on the street to witness her departure, she could call on the magic mirror to return her to the great hall. She lifted the pouch of sacred sand from a secret pocket. It would only take a few grains to connect the reflection of the shop window with the magic mirror. She drew her fingers across the reflection in the glass. "Mirror on the wall, return me to the great hall." She closed her eyes, stealing herself against the whorl that twisted her stomach.

When she opened her eyes, she no longer stood on a street in the capital. She was home, an old manor house, far removed from the King's city. Instead of looking at glass reflecting sunlight, she stared at her reflection in the full length, gilded mirror. The reflection she saw was of her masqueraded-self, long blond curls framing a youthful face. The serviceable gown could not hide her shapely body.

Cinderella blinked, and released the masquerade. This time her reflection was taller, thick dark hair framing a beautiful face that had lost its youthful roundness. Cinderella smiled at herself.

She touched the mirror. "Mirror on the wall, answer at my call. Who prevented my will on the girl?"

Her image and the reflection of the hall faded. Another took its place. Cinderella recognized the parade route. Horses flew past, then the scene slowed. A shadow grew from the right side, crossing over the mirror before the carriage rolled into full view.

She frowned. "What does this mean? Show me Doorin's key." Though the shadow turned to gray and swirled like mists at the edge of the sea, what Cinderella desired most to see did not materialize. "These shadows are similar. Are these protections around the prince because of the faerie blessings at his christening?" The mirror gave no reply. She huffed. "What do we do against the protectors? I need a way around them."

The mists blew away. For a moment, the reflection was that of a world with a tempest of sand. Cinderella hid her shudder at the scene. It changed a moment later to the King's palace. She recognized the hallway with the queen's bedchamber.

A small eight-legged creature crawled from behind the mirror. It stood a moment on an azure blue tile, a smear of dark on the pristine. Then it crawled to the mirror, passing through its silvery sheen, until it clung to the ceiling in the castle. Fascinated, Cinderella watched it spin a strand of web. "What will this be able to do?"

In the next scene, webs drooped from corners and across doorways. The view moved to the open door of the queen's bedchamber. The plain woman she'd seen beside the king sat listlessly staring out a window. Webs turned her dark hair gray, yet she didn't seem to realize they were there. The spiders could weave spells of forgetfulness through the castle. Anyone or anything protecting the prince would be useless against such.

The plan to get herself to the palace began to form. Pleasure stirred in her chest. "Show me my prince." The mirror's scene returned to the open carriage. Robert's dark curly hair brushed forward in a breeze. Laughter spilled from the vehicle. The slim girl bounced on the cushioned seat as flowers rained on them. "Stepsister, I presume. Don't bother getting attached, dear girl. Robert will be *my* prince." He was too young yet, but time would change that soon enough.

As they reached the end of the parade through town, Marissa wiggled her toes among the flowers. Not all were roses.

"Asters symbolize love," Mrs. Boyde piced up a patch of purple flowers with yellow centers. "As do the chrysanthemums." She reached further. "This daffodil would not be easy to find. Somenone tended it in a hothouse."

"What about this?" Marissa picked up a white flower. Just moving it brought a sweet smell.

"Ah, gardenia. They smell almost as good as jasmine. I'm surprised someone would have tossed a yellow hyacinth. No one need be jealous of you." Mrs. Boyde tossed out the offending plant.

"I remember the yarrow was tossed by a group of children. They were sweet."

"If we're done with the lesson," Prince Robert stood beside Mrs. Boyde, "how about I lift you out?"

Marissa scooted onto the seat of the carriage. She wrapped her right hand around Robert's wrist, then noticed a flower stand out from the others. "What's this?" It's petals were a silvery white with a pink and red center. Marissa picked it up, but Mrs. Boyde took it from her.

"This is a star flower. I placed it there this morning."

"I've never seen a flower like it."

"It comes from a rare garden, requested special for today." She touched the soft tufts in the center, some of which had turned red. "It served its purpose." She stepped to the side, waving at Robert. "Lift her from the melee."

Robert did so, and Marissa giggled at his touch. He smiled. "What do you think of your fair, new home?"

"I did not expect so many people. Will we get to visit the town often?"

Mrs. Boyde took her hand. "I think not. You'll be groomed into a proper lady. You won't have time to roam the village or countryside."

Marissa rolled her eyes, making Robert chuckle, before allowing Mrs. Boyde to lead her back into the palace. "I don't want to be a lady."

6

Six years didn't change much. Marissa sighed as she replaced Diocese' sermons beside a vase etched with icons. She glanced at library shelves looming overhead. Six years of opportunity gone. Mrs. Boyde would give her a royal scolding if she attempted to climb the shelves now. A door slammed, and she twirled around. Robert offered a dark glare, brows furrowed and fists clenched, before crossing to a high-back cushioned chair set in front of a large fireplace. Marissa waited for some explanation, but all she saw was a foot swing up and down in an agitated manner. She rolled her eyes and joined him, sitting in an adjacent chair. While she remained straight, with her slippered feet peaking from beneath her gray and blue day dress, Robert leaned against one arm of the chair, legs crossed at the knee as he continued to rock the right one with irritation. The years had filled him out, but he looked much the same as he had when they first met in the library. Marissa smiled at the memory.

His frown deepened. "What are you happy about?"

"Thinking of our first meeting. Wishing I had climbed the shelves before I became too proper a lady to make the attempt."

"You? Proper?" He scoffed, and then sighed.

"What has disturbed your cheery outlook?" It was a fair question. She rarely noticed any sort of blot on his attitude whether they stormed horses along paths in the palace woods or argued over the value of farming rituals.

"Father has lost his mind."

Marissa leaned forward. "What do you mean? What has happened?"

He waved his hand. "He isn't ill, just unreasonable. He's insisting on a ball."

"A ball?" Marissa brightened. "What's the problem with a ball? I love to dance."

"I have to pick a wife."

"What?" Had she misheard him?

"He says I am too old not to have marriage plans in the works. Either I choose a bride at the ball or he'll choose one for me."

Marissa opened her mouth, but her voice seemed taken away.

Robert rubbed his forehead. "I made friends at University but no one I want to spend the rest of my life with. How could any of them be queen?"

"You've misunderstood him. He would never…"

He shrugged. "I thought so too, but father explained himself. A bride by midnight."

"Isn't there anyone you might fancy? I could invite Lade Teresa. Or Sereh. You enjoyed her company when she was here."

Robert wished a fire would fall over in the grate. Or a shelf breaking would pull him from the seat beside Marissa, because her name was the first one to come to mind with the question asked. Ridiculous. Mars was a dear friend; they could mean nothing else to each other … or so she had reminded him for years.

Why did father insist on this plan? Twenty-two wasn't too old to be without a wife. But invitations had already been sent. He'd held a stack of replies, and a basket of kerchief's causing an uncomfortable smell in the cubicle beside the king's office.

And who was Sereh? He couldn't remember. Mars befriended a few of the livelier courtesans.

"What prompted his decision?"

Robert shrugged. "Hadn't heard anything, but invitations are out and responses are already coming in." He turned to Marissa. "How could he have done this without consulting me first? Why now, of all times? I've been training with Standish for skirmishes in the marshes next month."

"I haven't heard about training."

He grinned. "You think Lady DeGanne would let you run around in the mud? She gave me looks for months when we started fencing together."

"I have as much right to know how to defend myself as anyone else in the realm."

"Having the right and your mother accepting unladylike behavior are two different matters." The weight on his chest seemed lighter. Imagining Lady DeGanne's face made his lips twitch.

Marissa pulled her legs beneath her and leaned against the arm rest. "Stepfather is a reasonable man. Try to consider his proposal. I'm certain, in the end, he will accept whatever choice you make."

"I know what choice you will make." Cinderella brushed her finger over the image of Robert that appeared in the mirror. The surface shimmered. For a moment, a different image appeared behind that of Robert lounging in front of the fire. Dry twisted limbs and oceans of sand caused her to jerk her hand away. "I don't like your alien landscapes," Cinderella hissed. The mirror turned gray, then faded into a real reflection. Though Cinderella stood in her own home, she'd reverted to her masquerade of a young woman. The curls and youthful facade pleased her for the moment. Darkness in the reflection of her eyes did not. She turned away, leaving the great hall and the magic mirror. She opened a small door hidden in paneling at the top of the main stairs. The servant steps looped around and down to the old kitchen. Before reaching the kitchen, she entered into a butler's pantry, passing cabinets filled with china. The open door on the far side led into a workroom. High windows let in plenty of light. Shelves filled with jars and canisters were arranged in four rows on two walls. On the counter beneath them, among other items, stood a smoky jug, the inside of which crawled with spiders. An invitation to the ball leaned against a shallow bowl where crow feathers curled into ashes. "I have set the stage, my prince." Cinderella admired all she had done in preparation.

With no other preparations needed, she wanted to leave. A

sparkle gleamed in a shard of glass. As she looked, the reflection grew, and she recognized a dusty attic. She frowned. Why did it seem familiar? Before she could pull herself from the mirror's control, she plunged back in time.

7

Ella stood in the attic of the old manor house. Rafters and tresses crisscrossed the angled roofline. Light from windows and broken boards in the roof shed beams of light across the floor. Tiny bits of dust kicked up by her movement sparkled, not usually worth her attention, but there was also something silver glinting from a deserted corner as she turned to leave the attic. A drop of blood from the spider she'd pinned to the wooden rafter poised on her finger. Her small feet took another step, and then slowed. She turned her head. A ratted quilt covering an object near a dark corner had slipped. The afternoon sun streaming through a round window nearby highlighted the shimmering surface. Ella raised her long skirt with one hand, sucked the blood from her finger on the other hand and turned. The quilt covered something twice her height. She tilted her head. An unfamiliar thump in her chest made her pause. Run. Turn. But Ella ignored the voices in her head and reached with her left hand to pull the covering away. The shower of dust that flowed around her didn't matter. The quilt fell to the floor, revealing an ornate silver mirror.

The eyes of the little girl staring back at her widened. Ella stretched her hand and touched her reflection. The wavy brown hair of the girl in the mirror had been braided. Her serviceable dress was too dull and dark. She should be brighter, softer. Something that could turn heads. She touched the mirror, tracing her fingers along the edge where glass melded into the frame.

But the image changed in an instant, from a young girl in an attic to a harsh sandstorm blowing around twisting bare branches of a half-buried tree. Her heart thumped again. Ella jerked her hand away from the mirror and ran from the room, sown the stairs, and through the battered door. Even after she returned to the carpeted hallway lit with sunlight streaming through the windows of the manor, fear shivered her skin.

"A spell is not child's play," Grandmother slapped the spider from Ella's hand.

"I'm not playing. You said we can make spells for protection."

"From what?" Grandmother scoffed.

Ella didn't want to share her secret from the attic. She ran, and pouted, and waited for another day.

The air turned cold as the season changed. Workers went to the attic to prep fireplaces for winter's use. She hovered in the hallway, hiding behind curtains, as they came down. They spoke in hushed voices and wiped uselessly at their dirt-encrusted fingers, yet none of them seemed alarmed. Her foot tapped the floor as she peered up the stairs. Ignoring the urge to go up, she slammed the door and waited.

It wasn't until spring, when a cat attacked a bat and left it for dead on the front stoop, that she made up her mind. The creature was close to death and she wanted to add it to others. Bat wings thrashed against the palms of her hands. Ella looked from the dying creature to the dark stairs leading into the attic. She shouldn't. She didn't want to. But as warm blood dripped through her fingers and splattered on the faded carpet beneath her feet, she knew she had to go. She lifted her foot to the first riser leading upstairs.

Once she reached the top, she crept to her usual corner. Afternoon sunlight offered a soft look upon the carcasses hanging on a p9ost. She blew to move particles of dust that had settled on the dried features. She pulled the nail from her pocket, set the bat in place, and drove the nail through its cooling body into the wood. The bony finger on one of its wings twitched before drooping.

Ella shifted her eyes to the right. She could feel herself being watched. The year it took to return hadn't quelled her fear, yet something greater had grown, curiosity. She focused her attention on a box fallen over in the corner. She listened to the sounds of boards creaking beneath her feet as she walked to the box. She looked down. Her bare feet were gray with dust. She wiggled her toes. A slight turn, and the gilded frame came into view. Warmth reached out to her, like a kind hand pressing against her cheek. She lifted her face.

It was her in the mirror, with awkward limbs of a thirteen-year-old sticking out from her short dress. As she watched, the surroundings of the attic softened, changing to a grand ballroom. Ella pulled at the sides of her plain gown. She changed. Her reflected image wore a rose gown with ruffled sleeves and pearl drops across the bodice, and the length of the gown and sleeves fit. She twirled. The reflected girl in the ballgown mimicked her movements. She stilled, and as she watched, the girl in the mirror morphed into a beautiful young woman. Her cheek bones were high and well defined, as were her breasts. A shadowy cleavage hinted at her full figure. Ella twirled again, and the woman followed.

A silver necklace with a key bob appeared around the neck of her future self. Excitement stirred, and Ella touched the silver surface. She needed the key. It was somehow tied to her destiny.

Something thumped on the floor near her foot. She looked down at a torn book with burnt edges. When she looked back, all reflection in the mirror had ceased, leaving a fog to fill the frame. Ella knelt to retrieve the book, keeping her eyes on the strange mirror. She would not wait a year before returning to explore further.

The book belonged to a man named Doorin. Though she did not recognize the name, when she spoke his name aloud, the hairs on her arms tingled. His was a powerful name. Why had someone tried to burn his book, and how had a mirror been able to save it? She hid the ancient text in a cupboard in her sitting room, but it became as a living thing to her, calling, desiring her to take it from its secret place.

When she did, she gripped it tight with both hands and her blood would pound. Her feet felt as though they wanted to dance.

Grandmother looked long and hard, but Ella kept knowledge of the book to herself.

A few weeks later, when she knew she would have the day to herself, Ella raced through the attic to stand breathless before the mirror. "Who is Doorin?" There was no voice to answer, but the image in the mirror changed.

A man moved about in a large room. He stepped over something. Ella's mouth opened as she realized the body of a younger man, a teen perhaps, lay on the floor. His wasn't the only one. Another body he pushed out of the way. Others entered the room. He directed, waving hands furiously, to move the large object from the center table.

She stared at Doorin. His golden-brown hair was pulled back in a ponytail. A thin circlet around his head marked him as a member of the royal family, but not the king. His eyes were a dazzling vivid hue of green. For a moment she wondered if he could see her.

Light shadows twisted into the room like angry spirits. They caused a binding Doorin could not break. Fire flashed through the workroom. A smaller mirror than the one that had been removed toppled to the ground. A key, the key she'd seen around her neck, was used to lock the room, and its keyhole disappeared. The light shadows set a powerful shield on the door, empowering the key. The scene changed to a king's chamber. A woman wearing a white gold crown designed by intertwined flowers with jeweled centers held her hand to an older woman sheathed in white. The queen allowed her hand to be pricked and blood dropped upon the key. Rather than slide away, blood soaked into the metal. The key was then set upon a delicate chain and placed around the queen's neck.

The images faded to nothing. Ella stood wondering at all she had seen.

Cinderella stood before the mirror, memories returning meant to remind her whose power allowed her to work as she did. She closed her eyes and willed the turmoil and shaking within to cease. The terrible beauty of the mirror had taught her it needed the key to open Doorin's room. Queen Charlotte had chosen death rather than release her control of the key. Her plan for Robert would fare much better.

Blood pulsing with desire to gain her prince, she traced her fingers across the smooth surface. "Mirror on the wall, make me fairest of them all." Images of others who would be attending the prince's ball flashed across the surface. The mist that poured from the mirror no longer elicited fear. Excitement threatened to burst through her control. The royal family could not stop her. They accepted the idea of the ball as their own. The force that had assailed her at the parade had not shown itself again. Nothing worked against the webs flowing into the palace. Cinderella grinned when the need for the prince to choose a bride became their thought, as it had been hers. Protection of the Faere broke at the end of his twenty-first year. Now he was hers for the taking.

The mist rose, wrapping around her like lover's hands caressing her body. When it faded away, the soft taffeta was not as she'd expected. Its color was subdued, a robin's egg hue, one expected on an innocent young woman. Part of her hair had been swept above her temples and set with pearl studs while waves flowed down her back. Yes. Simple would be far lovelier than the gaudy designs of the other women seeking the prince's hand. "I do believe the prince is mine for the taking." Cinderella rolled her shoulders.

"Even though you already have a husband?"

Cinderella turned at the man's petulant remark. "Crow." Her name for him was an apt depiction of his appearance, as his skin as well as his gentleman's robe, shone as black satin. She crossed the room, pulling at the belt around his waist and placing both hands on his thick chest. "Robert of Camden will not hold that distinction for long, my dear." She moved her hands to his cheeks, pulling him down so her mouth could dance against his. He pulled her closer. She watched his dark eyes as he laid claim to what he thought was his. He pleased her with his body, yet it was his other form that had kept her from destroying him long before.

LAURIE LEE

8

Marissa watched Sereh hold a gold brocade gown to her chest, swishing back and forth to show the gleam of gold thread across the bodice. "Gold is one of his favorites, you say?" Sereh's deep brown eyes met hers in the mirror.

Robert seemed to compliment her when she wore gold, so Marissa nodded. "You will look splendid. You should have a number of suiters by the end of the festivities." It was true. With Sereh's dark skin tone and tilted eyes, she had an exotic air most men would find attractive.

Sereh sighed, letting the dress droop. "My interest remains with Prince Robert."

Marissa responded with a smile of encouragement. Sereh hadn't made an impression on Robert yet. No reason why the ball would change things. The thought should not make her smile. But it did.

Would any of the others capture his interest? Marissa didn't want to consider the possibility. Better to focus on other eligible men in attendance. Lord Bainwych sent a card requesting two dances. Stephen and Denver were like puppies following her around. Perhaps one of them would suit Sereh?

Sereh switched the gold gown for one of soft green that highlighted her eyes. Marissa nodded. "The perfect dress. That color compliments you."

"But will Robert like it?" Sereh whined.

Marissa shrugged. "For truth, I've never noticed an affection."

Sereh dropped the dress on the floor and Marissa held her hand up. "That doesn't matter. The color flatters you. The ball is meant for the prince to choose a wife, not a gown."

But Sereh was already moving on, selecting a bright blue monstrosity. Marisa shook her head, wrinkling her nose. Next came a deeper blue. Sereh traced a finger along the satin fabric. "Everyone knows the prince favors navy."

Marissa held up a finger. "And half the court will be wearing that exact shade." Three more dresses were soon discarded.

Marissa heard a distant bell. She jumped to her feet, grabbing Sereh's hand. "I have lessons. I'm sure you will find the best ball gown. Remember, dinner at eight, ladies only." She ran from the room.

What had possessed her to invite Sereh to stay in the palace?

"Marissa DeGanne, Mistress Eloise informs me you have not been to your fitting."

The sound of Mother's voice caused her heart to plummet. Marissa turned. "Fitting?"

"For your ball gown."

Marissa frowned. "I have plenty of gowns suitable for a royal engagement. We've been through this already."

Lady DeGanne offered a thin smile. "You care for Robert. Why would you not attempt to draw his hand?"

"We are friends." How was she to make her mother understand? "He and I even discussed it once." She held up her hand to stop her mother's protest. "Not when I was twelve."

Lady DeGanne's lips tightened as she stood straighter. "If you do not wish to capture the attention of the prince as a suitor, you still have a responsibility as a member of the royal household. You will be fitted."

Marissa lowered her eyes and managed to nod. "Yes, mother." It would mean standing still and getting pricked by pins. She wanted to argue, but mother turned into the yellow sitting room, leaving her alone in the hallway.

Within the hour, Bentley, one of the younger lads on staff, managed to find Marissa and take her to Mistress Eloise.

"Finally, the illusive princess." Eloise spoke with a strong accent.

"I'm not a princess." She tried once again to get the petite woman with a mass of black curls pulled up with ribbons to understand, but Eloise refused to be turned.

"You are the prince's particular friend." She patted Marissa's cheek. "You will know beyond doubt how best to entice him." Eloise's dark eyes glittered as she pulled Marissa toward a bundle of cloth bolts.

Marissa clutched her hand to her mouth to stop any desire to insult the brash colors popping out among the more traditional whites and rosy hues. Orange? Who would wear such a hideous color to a ball? And what term could be used for the green resembling split pea soup?

"Which will Robert prefer best?" Eloise waited, brows raised.

I don't want to pick for Robert. Marissa didn't dare say the words aloud, but she passed over the navy and white print which would have made a lovely full skirt.

"More guests tonight?" Lady DeGanne glanced over the edge of her wine glass.

Sereh blanched, but Marissa tapped her hand, reassuring her. "You remember Sereh. She stayed with us most of last summer." Marissa watched Mother's perfectly arched brow lift.

"Did she? I do not recall." She placed her glass on the table and waved her hand. "So many young ladies come and go."

"Mother." Marissa gave a hard look, and then turned to smile at Sereh. "Did you choose the gown you will wear to the ball?"

Sereh picked up a thin silver fork and used it to tug on the oyster inside a half shell.

"Oh, dear." Lady DeGanne groaned. "You shouldn't use that fork." She pressed a hand against her throat. "Oysters come from the sea. Are you trying to poison yourself?"

The clatter of silverware disrupted the dining room even more as Sereh dropped the offending tool. "Oh, my goodness, I meant no disrespect."

Marissa put an arm around her shoulder to calm Sereh. "Simple mistake to make. Here, let them take care of the mess. Can't stand the slimy things myself. I prefer we start with a simple salad platter."

Sereh relaxed. "I prefer the days cook sends up slices of cheese and round soda toast. Have you had them? She claims to have gotten the recipe on a trip in France."

"Sounds better than saying it's what the doctor ordered for your father's sour stomach."

Marissa rolled her eyes at her mother, but the woman seemed to be enjoying her oysters. The next course arrived. Sereh had no trouble selecting the soup spoon. "Which gown did you say?" Marissa returned to the conversation.

Sereh offered a smile between sips of the squash nutmeg. "Thought I'd wait to see your gown before making a final decision."

"Impossible." Lady DeGanne interrupted. "Marissa's gown will not be ready until the day of the ball. You must give your choice to the lady maids at least three days before. Five would be better. You cannot expect them to press a dozen gowns the day of the event."

Sereh turned from Marissa to Lady DeGanne, then back to Marissa. "I... of course not. I thought since we are to be companions, it would be best to be in compliment of each other."

"Sweet girl. I am sure whatever gown you choose will captivate a young officer." Lady DeGanne paused as soup was replaced with a cold meat tray. "But you must realize, Marissa is the king's daughter. As such, hers will be beyond any other in attendance."

"Step-daughter." Marissa seethed.

"Of course." Sereh gushed. "I hadn't considered..." she toyed with the meat on her plate without eating any of it. "I do prefer the blue. I'll order new ribbons for the waist."

"You will be spectacular." Marissa reassured. "Have you tried the roast? It has a savory flavor."

Sereh obliged, eating one of the small cubes. "Delicious." She ate more.

By the time desert arrived in a golden dish lined with cherries, Marissa was ready to exile both her mother and Sereh. The blend of sweet and tart delighted her mouth, but her stomach churned. *Perhaps I need soda bread*, she sighed, then smiled at her friend. "I fear if I eat another bite, I shan't be able to do a thing this next week."

"Nonsense. You'll have dance lessons every day this week. A few more fittings will be necessary. The rectory's wife will expect you to accompany her on visits since I cannot." Lady DeGanne motioned at Sereh. "Sophia can go with you."

"It's Sereh." Sereh tried to correct, but Lady DeGanne ignored her, preferring to list a few more chores Marissa would do.

"Mother, if I keep to your schedule, I'll be exhausted by the time the ball gets here."

She smiled. "I'll speak to Mrs. Boyde to make sure you are not over-taxed. Of course, I want you at your best. You're expected to dance with Robert."

"I'll make sure he holds a cotillion for Sereh as well."

"If it's possible. There are so many young ladies expected, he can't dance with them all."

"Sereh will have her chance soon after me." Marissa assured. "Shall we play cards in the parlor?"

Sereh nodded emphatically, but Lady DeGanne declined. "I'll have your glasses of sherry delivered to you."

With an inward sigh of relief, Marissa removed herself from the dining table.

LAURIE LEE

9

The night of the ball, Marissa waited until she heard Sereh's steps in the hallway. She gave the gold lace a final tug and exited the room. Sereh swung around, her blue gown flowing around her. She gasped. "Your gown…" Sereh put her hand against her throat. "I've never seen fabric that color."

"Mother insisted on unique."

"You're stunning. I feel as though I should bow."

Marissa rolled her eyes. "Don't. One thing I've always appreciated about you. You treat me as a person, not as royal."

"It will be hard for the prince to notice anyone else."

She shook her head. "We are here for his engagement."

Sereh swirled, flecks of jewels in her bodice caught the light. Her dark hair was swept into a French knot held with sapphire clips. "You are dazzling as well." Marissa grinned.

"Enough for a prince's hand?"

"Are you certain you would like him?"

Sereh frowned. "He's a prince. What more do I need to know?"

Marissa held her tongue. Robert enjoyed challenge. Sereh's tendency to bend to whoever's will would grate on his nerves. She grabbed Sereh's elbow. "Shall we spy out the ballroom? I know a perfect perch." She didn't wait for a response but turned the opposite direction down the hall, pulling Sereh with her. She took a turn into a smaller room storing covered bits of furniture. She pushed on a panel of the wall and pulled Sereh into a narrow walkway. Marissa opened the door at the end, took a few steps up, and led Sereh onto a dark platform.

Sereh gripped Marissa's arm. "What are you doing?"

"Wait until you see this." She slid a frame from the wall and an oblong opening allowed light to brighten the space. There were three more such openings, but Marissa didn't need to go further. "Look." Part of the grand ballroom of Monmoore Palace lay before them.

Chandeliers of black iron burned reservoirs of oil, adding a smoky haze along the coffered ceiling. Columns decorated with green vines stood like sentinels opposite them. A little beyond, open French doors lined the outer wall, showing the fade of afternoon. The marble floor shone.

"What is that?" Sereh pointed out the medallion inlaid in the center of the ballroom.

"It is the King's coat. The hothouse has been brought in." Arrangements of flowers, ornamental bushes, and trees were scattered around the large space, creating manageable areas for activity.

A bell rang. "Called to supper." Marissa picked up the frame from the ground, sliding it along the wall until it hooked into place, throwing them into darkness again.

"Isn't it early to be eating?"

"We have a long evening ahead of us. Dinner won't be until the midnight hour." Marissa led the way, trying to pull her skirt from Sereh's feet as her friend kept a tight grip on her arm. She led them through the room to the hallway.

"There you are."

Marissa turned around with a gasp, and then grinned. "Were you looking for me?"

Mrs. Boyde raised a brow. She waved a passing servant to them. "Please, take Miss Sereh to the ladies dining hall. Marissa will join them when I am finished with her."

Marissa said nothing as Sereh was led from the guest wing. She turned to Mrs. Boyde as her friend disappeared around a corner. "Is something wrong?"

"Not at all. I have a gift for you. Something your father commissioned. This evening is a special occasion. I think now is the perfect time for it."

"Father?" Marissa started to ask, but then she stared at the silver necklace Mrs. Boyde held between her hands. An intricate swirl of roses and birds, eyes twinkling, hung in the air. "How could this be from Father?" Marissa touched the delicate design with one finger. The cold feel of silver caused a chill to run down her back.

"It is from one of his travels." Mrs. Boyde made a turning motion with her finger, and Marissa obeyed so she could lock it around her neck. "He gave it to me for keeping until you were old enough for such a bauble. Would have given it to you himself if he could."

The necklace lay against the bare skin above her bodice. She covered it with her hand, blinking moisture from her eyes. Father? All that remained of his memory was a vague shape of a large man with blue eyes and a laugh that made anyone nearby want to laugh in response. The memory washed over her, causing a warm glow to radiate through her soul. Mrs. Boyde turned her about, placing hands on her shoulder and giving her a once over. "I always knew you would be beautiful." She took a breath and stepped back. "There. You will be fine."

Marissa grabbed her hands. "Join us for dinner."

She patted Marissa's cheek as she gave her a gentle smile. "That is not the way of this world. I will hear about your adventures tomorrow."

Marissa studied the group of ladies chattering around the table. *How could Mrs. Boyde be anything less than one of these?* She shook off the thoughts. The necklace rested against her chest. She could feel the touch of silver on her skin, yet, none of the others seemed to take notice. Could they not see the delicate design? Did they not notice the glitter of diamond eyes? Sereh pulled her attention. Within moments, Marissa herself forgot about the talisman around her neck.

Cinderella twirled in front of the mirror. The gown settled against her legs.

Crow moved like a shadow behind her. "Does any of the real

you remain?" His dark eyes met her soft blues in the reflection. The image shimmered, and then revealed the taller woman with jet black hair falling in waves around her shoulders. Instead of the rounded face of youth, her real face had high cheekbones, arched brows, and wide lips with natural berry color.

Crow slipped his dark hands across her pale shoulders, but Cinderella moved away from him. His features darkened, while desire and jealousy sparked his eyes. "Why must you do this?"

Cinderella spoke to the mirror. "Reveal Doorin's key."

The mirror's reflection altered again, a haze rising and filling the space. Cinderella dragged her finger across the mirror. "The key will not come to view until I have wed the prince. Then, just as it took blood to seal the guard, his blood must be spilled to allow the key to unlock Doorin's rooms."

She turned to him and rested a hand against his cheek. "I will need you, need your help. Others will oppose us. You are my eyes and ears."

"I have vowed my life to you."

"Your loyalty will be repaid, my love. Now leave me. I must prepare the spell that will enchant our prince."

When she stood alone, she faced the mirror again. "What must I do?"

The reflection of the room returned. Beside her were a pair of clear shoes. Light sparkled from them, caught up in facets of glass. The shoes were not on the floor, they were in the mirror. Cinderella crouched and reached her hands for them. The mirror became shifting sands. Pain scratched across her flesh and she tried to pull away. She was pulled deeper instead. The cut of sand seared through her arms and hands as though she were being flayed. Screams echoed in the air around her. Her fingers curled and she somehow managed to grip the shoes. The pull of the sands shifted, and she fell back.

Pain washed through her and she expected to see her hands had been torn apart. She scurried away, holding the shoes against her chest. She swallowed against the heave of her stomach. Pain waned. She gulped, willing her breath to calm to normal. Tightening her grip on the shoes, she pushed herself to her feet. The mirror revealed a woman with pale features and fear-skimmed eyes. She blinked then looked at the glass slippers in her arms.

Light from the sconces caused shimmers of jewels to appear in the glass. The edges were smooth. Cinderella ran her fingers across the arch of the slipper. The glass felt soft. Moving to a wooden chair, she placed the shoes on the ground and steadied herself as she slipped one foot and then the other into the delicate shoes. Her feet warmed, glass molding to her shape. The fit was perfect.

Three steps towards the door and Cinderella wanted to keep the shoes forever. Nothing had ever felt as comfortable. With one hand against the door jam, she turned back to look at the mirror. "How will these help with the prince?"

The image shifted to the prince holding a glass slipper. But then the slipper turned into a spider crouched in his hands, webs draping around the prince. Yes, she could feel it. Threads of a web already starting to spread. Her chest throbbed. Not with fear, but with hunger. Prince Robert would not be able to resist her. Everything she desired, she was to have.

LAURIE LEE

10

The view from the hidden room did not convey the elegant transformation of the ballroom. Marissa weaved through a throng of lords and ladies, Sereh hurrying to stay by her side. They slipped through the opening to the ballroom, side-swiping the bellowing caller at the top of the stairs. The mutterings of those in attendance made it almost impossible to hear him. Marissa found an opening where she and Sereh could glance through the gathering crowds.

With both hands gripping Marissa's arm, Sereh peered in one direction and then another. Disappointment settled across her face. "Where is Robert? If he hopes to announce an engagement by midnight, he at least must dance with some of the ladies," she gushed, drifting her gaze with longing across the crowd of nobles, their daughters, and the sea of servants moving silently among them.

Marissa was aware of the attraction of jewel tones and sparkling garnish adorning the elegant contestants for Robert, Prince Regent of Camden. She glanced at her own gown of silk taffeta with pearl-edged double sleeves. Though the unusual golden color suited her, its flounces in silk and ivory lace tickled her arms. She returned her attention to Sereh. She lowered her voice and raised her brows. "What if he does not wish to announce an engagement?"

Sereh widened her eyes with concern. "No engagement?"

Marissa forced a feigned look of dread on her face. "Perhaps not. Stepfather gave him little choice in the matter, but …"

Her friend gasped. "Only you would refer to the king in a cavalier fashion."

Marissa shook her head, laughing at her friend. "King he may be, but he is also my stepfather. I call him whichever suits me at the time."

A deep, gravel voice came from behind them. "And in a crowd of subjects would it not suit to refer to me as Your Grace?"

Marissa glared at Sereh, who had turned pale, before pivoting to greet King William with a gentle kiss on his cheek. His serious tone may have her friend shaking where she stood, but Marissa knew him better. "You are a most beloved stepfather, and that should mean more than any title." She placed her hand in his and pressed her cheek against his arm.

"It does." He agreed, tapping her nose. "For you are an excellent stepdaughter." He looked through the growing crowd. "Unlike my son, flesh and blood though he may be. All of this for his involvement," he swept his arm around the sparkling auditorium, "and yet he is unaccounted for."

"I'm certain Robert is working his way to the reception hall. Would you like me to find him and hurry the process?" *Just like Robert to be late for such an important event.*

"I would greatly appreciate it. Tell him if he fails to appear in a timely manner, he will find himself engaged to his stepsister, for that is the only female I know with whom he is acquainted."

Her heart thudded. *Engaged to Robert?* "Heaven forbid, Sire, I have no more interest in being queen than mother has in my not being queen." Marissa loved her mother, yet her desire for class and prestige had not passed to her daughter.

King William laughed again before pushing her away. "Have off, before you shock the nobles with your commoner ideas."

"As you wish. I will find your truant son." She kissed his cheek.

Sereh made to follow Marissa, but the king took her hand and wrapped her arm with his. "Who is this pleasant young friend?"

"Sereh of Fonsby."

"Lord Pritchard's granddaughter? How delightful."

"She's been visiting for several weeks."

He patted her arm. "I must introduce you to the French dignitaries. Your grandfather is a favorite of them. Do you see him often?" The king led Sereh away. Marissa narrowed her eyes. Could the king and her mother be conspiring against her? She shook off the notion and edged her way back through the throng of people.

Musicians on a balcony above the southern terrace played lilting harmonies, basking the room in cheerful waltzes and stringed ballads. Dancers forayed below them, digging out an area for turns and shifts, courting each other with fine conversations and dazzling costumes. Around the space reserved for dancing gossiped mothers and guardians, pressing each other knowingly, yet with decorum, all the while keeping their charges within sight. The northeast terrace had been set with tables for cards and conversations. Marissa delighted in the activity. The king's assistants had done well organizing the festive atmosphere for the prince's engagement party. She made her way beyond the terraces and anterooms. With no sighting of the prince, she moved inside the palace. Not far beyond, she found Prince Robert contemplating the wall of books in his father's public library.

"You are here. Aren't you coming to your own party?" Marissa exclaimed, earning herself a dark look from the handsome man. She contemplated his attire. Buff pantaloons graced his muscled legs while the royal green brocade jacket lent a sparkle to his hazel eyes.

"Wouldn't miss it for the world. It isn't every day a man is engaged to a woman he hasn't yet met." His sour tone matched the drawn look on his face.

She rebuked him. "Perhaps if you consent to mingle with the throng of women parading through the reception hall, you would find one to catch your eye and give you cause not to resent your father's heavy hand."

"Heavy hand? He sent a full entourage across the land with invitations for all available titled ladies. Half of them probably buried their husbands in the past six months."

"And the other half have sped their daughters to marriageable age." Marissa giggled. Robert's laugh joined her. *There was something about him tonight.* She linked her arm with his and drew him from the library. "Are you ready, sir, to whirl me onto the dance floor so I may enjoy the splendor of the evening rather than pass my time among dusty books?" She gazed up at him, teasingly blinking her eyelids.

Robert shook his head and tapped her nose. "Mayhap you will be the one to swoon at the foot of a gentleman, and Father will make an announcement for the two of you."

"What man could compare to you? I've been hopelessly

spoiled." She admired her friend with a smile but faltered for a moment. Her heart skipped a beat. *What was she thinking? This was Robert.* She shook the thought from her mind and pulled him toward the ballroom.

Robert walked beside the young beauty who had been his friend and confidant since her arrival at Monmoore. *Why did Marissa's eyes darken? Had it been a trick of the light?* They turned a corner, and noise from the ball wafted over him. His stomach soured, and he swallowed the bile trying to rise into his throat. Marissa took his hand, twining her fingers with his. Her skin looked pale in contrast to his own.

"Courage, friend," she smirked.

It brought a smile to his face. It was a term he used when they fenced against one another. "To the battle?" He replied on cue.

"A battle would be easier to face, sir, but face this you must."

She pulled him with her, not allowing his feet to slow, nor providing the opportunity to turn tail and run. The ballroom was packed. She tried to release his hand, but he tightened his grip. Her brown eyes sparkled with amusement as she looked up at him. He smiled back. With her, at least, he could have courage.

She rolled her eyes. "Fine. I will take the first dance."

The sea of bodies seemed to part as they moved toward the other dancers. The set paused, allowing them to join the line, and then they continued. Robert fell into step with Marissa at his side.

He enjoyed whirling around the floor. The first set ended, and he begged another, a full set. Marissa made a good partner and the easy banter between them boosted his confidence. He glimpsed the chaotic rumble of nobles as they turned to the beat of the orchestra's strains. The press of bodies was impressive. Everyone appreciated the open terrace doors throughout the ballroom allowing fresh, cool air to alleviate the heat of the crowd. He tried not to notice the women, but several of them were ramrod straight without a curve to be seen. Marissa mouthed "child" for his delight, causing him to laugh. They were tall and short. Skinny and fat. Chubby and clumsy or plain and graceless. Some were even tall and graceful. But none captured his attention, drawing him beyond the safety of his stepsister.

She pulled him into a private corner and scowled. "You have to dance with them, Robert. Put on your royal mask and give them what they came for."

"You really want me to offer one of them my hand in marriage?" Looking at Marissa now, beautiful with tiny beads of sweat touching her hairline, he didn't think it was possible. He didn't want to be this close to anyone … else.

Marissa blinked, and he could read confusion in her face. She darted a glance at the opening of their alcove. She closed her eyes and seemed to shake herself. When her brown eyes were once more set on him, he could tell a mask had been put in place. Calm. Determined, as usual.

"No, I want you to see if you could love one of them. If you go the evening without making a proposal, your father will have to accept your decision."

"What of you?" He joked, but his heart pulsed at the thought.

"I'm safe and familiar." She backed against the wall, putting space between them. "It's time for you to step out of your comfort zone."

The music stopped, and they heard dancers clapping with appreciation.

"Choose a different partner. I'll see you at the end of the evening." Marissa leaned into him to kiss his cheek. He turned, and their lips met for the briefest of kisses. They lingered a moment. When she drew back, her eyes were wide. His own thoughts were muddled. Had he meant to? Or had it been an accident? She staggered back, and he reached for her.

"I thought I recognized my son." The king's voice boomed. The ball invaded their alcove, and Marissa slipped away. Robert pulled himself together as his father squeezed his shoulder. *Ridiculous, thinking such thoughts of Mars. She was right, though. Father would have to accept his decision, even if it meant there wouldn't be an announcement tonight.* He let himself be pulled into the fray.

Though Robert recognized Marissa's friend, her name escaped his memory. The dance brought them back together, her tiny hand upon his. He felt nothing for her. Marissa's hand had been warmth. The moment his lips touched hers had sent… something through him. The girl's eyes widened, and he smiled at her. Her cheeks flushed, but then it was warm. The set wound down, and he bowed over her hand, kissing the air above it. For some reason, he had no desire to touch his lips to any other woman. The girl gave a pretty curtsy.

"I would ask for another dance, but duty demands otherwise." He released her, taking a step backward.

"Perhaps later." Her voice had a high, nasal sound to it.

"It would be a pleasure." He bowed again and turned with a sigh. A paragon of a woman already headed in his direction, daughter in tow. He pasted a smile on his face and went to meet her.

The orchestra drew the final chord as long as it could, but Robert was compelled to hand his dance partner to the next victim on her list. His trampled toe throbbed, but his attention lingered still on thoughts of Marissa. Although the kiss had happened by accident, he couldn't forget. It wasn't that his partners so far were limpid and dull, but none compared to his feisty young stepsister. None made him want to forget her. What was Father thinking, demanding he end his bachelor days and choose a wife? He'd be turning twenty-three in a few months. He wasn't ready for a serious relationship, and if his reaction to a simple kiss with Marissa caused such fervor within him, perhaps he needed time to consider her more than friend.

A moment of despair threatened to overwhelm him, but then a spark in his periphery captured his attention. The air itself changed, luring him to turn, earnestly gazing through the melee. His attention settled on a demure young woman conversing with an older gentleman. Her simple-cut gown shimmered like the palest blue snow flowers. Blond hair curled down her back. It seemed the most natural thing in the world for him to walk to her side and hold out his hand in invitation. Luminous blue eyes looked up at him, surprise gracing her lovely face. Then she smiled. His thoughts vanished. He was a moth drawn to her light. When her hand touched his, the noise of the ballroom melted away.

They danced. This wasn't the graceful banter he enjoyed with Marissa. This dance took his breath away and left him wondering if heaven were anything more than this moment. No words passed between them, but their eyes held. He couldn't turn from her. He didn't want to. The orchestra ended one set and began another. Still they danced.

Minutes, maybe hours passed. A final chord of music resonated through the air. Robert slowed to a stop. One of his hands rested at her side, the other held hers. Her warm skin caused him to tingle. They kept an appropriate distance between them, but he wanted to pull her closer. He wanted to drown in the blue of her eyes. How had his thoughts been turned so quickly from Marissa? He tried to back up a step but couldn't make his feet move. She blinked, a nervous laugh breaking the spell. Breath moved into his lungs.

"My lord."

Her voice had a musical essence. Others wandered around them, but he didn't give them attention. His focus remained on her. "My name is Robert." *Was that his voice?*

Her eyes widened, a look of surprise glittering in the blue. "Robert. Prince, I don't know what happened."

He laughed, the same overwhelming sense he experienced. "We danced."

She withdrew her hand from his and pulled out a fan, waving it toward her face. The movement of air caused her scent to drift across him. "Yes, that I noticed."

"Would you like a drink?"

"Water, please. And air."

He turned her to the right, nodding at the open doors. "Wait on the terrace, I will meet you there." He bowed over her hand, holding it a moment longer than necessary. He wanted to lift her hand to his lips, wondering if her skin were as delicate as it seemed, but he released her.

The full rush of the crowded ballroom washed over him as he forced himself from her side, increasing his sense of loss. His thoughts poured over her as he strode to the closest servant. How was it possible such a woman existed? Had his father known this would happen? She was beautiful yet innocent. Would she be waiting for him on the balcony or would she disappear as though she were naught but a dream? He motioned for a tray of drinks and followed his heart through the French doors. Could he have fallen in love?

She found him before his eyes adjusted to the deepening shadows. "You are real," the woman greeted him with a shy smile. Her voice sounded like a melody of songbirds.

"As are you. I was afraid you would have disappeared." He

reached for her hand. "Your fingers are cold." He wrapped his hands round hers, an excuse to move closer.

"This night has been magical. I feel as though I'm in a waking dream. The ballroom is beautiful. The music … it's like nothing I've heard before."

"It was ordinary until you arrived. I feel as though I'm lost and yet somehow, I've found myself." He laughed. Marissa would mock his ramblings, but he couldn't stop the words that tumbled from his mouth. Something about her enchanted him. "Who are you? Where do you come from? Who are you with? Where are your parents?" *What else could he know of her*?

"Slow down," she laughed, her eyes twinkling in the starlight. "I live in the Belton Provence. You would never believe what I had to go through to get here." She looked away, color in her cheeks deepening. "I thought this was all mammon, but since meeting you … I feel … I can't …" Her eyes darkened with emotion when she returned her gaze to him.

Robert understood what she seemed unable to express. "I know. My stepsister Marissa would think us mad."

She placed one hand on his chest, and he thought his heart would burst. "It must be madness. How else could this be?"

"Maybe we are mad. Perhaps madness has taken over our senses and we will never be free of it. I don't care."

"I don't want to be free either." She nodded in agreement. Her eyes held him captive.

He pulled her closer. "Please, your name?" he begged.

"They call me Cinderella." She whispered.

The way she looked at him made him feel breathless and powerful. He repeated her name as his hand crept to her cheek, caressing her soft skin. "Would you do me the honor of becoming my wife?" He felt no qualms for asking. She was much more than he thought possible.

She stared, her eyes round with wonder.

Robert held both her hands. "My father orchestrated the evening to find my bride. Somehow, he knew you were out there, and this was the only way to find you."

She shook her head, and the swirl of her hair captivated him.

"But I'm nobody," she protested. "There's barely a name to our family to get me here. Belton has to be the smallest province in the country. I have nothing to offer a king's son." She tried to pull away, but he held her tighter.

"Something greater than either of us is at work. I wouldn't care if you had nothing at all or if you owned the largest castle between Monmoore and the ocean. None of that has to do with you and the way I feel. Say yes. Say you will marry me. I will bring you to the king. He can announce our engagement tonight."

She shook her head, and a single tear dripped down her pale cheek. "Dance with me," she whispered, her voice breaking. "I am bound in a way that I cannot give us our heart's desire. Not yet. Dance with me, tell your father of us on the morrow. You must find me. When you do, we can be together for always."

He didn't understand her tears, but he couldn't deny her request. She moved her hand to his cheek. He drew her closer and sealed his promise with a kiss. A warm rush of love swept him under like a crashing wave. He was lost, his fate sealed. They returned to the open floor, swirling through the crowd without noticing the others. They were for each other only.

LAURIE LEE

11

Marissa shook herself yet again. Foolish thoughts. The kiss was naught but an accident.

A friend of her mother took her hands. "Marissa, darling. You are a beauty." The woman leaned in and kissed both cheeks.

"Lady VanCleif. Good to see you."

"With so many eligible ladies in attendance, I thought it proper to force my son to attend."

A young man stepped to his mother's side. Marissa bowed. "Sir Scott, thank you for allowing your mother to force your attendance. We have a great need of men among such a crowd."

Though half a dozen years older, Sir Scott had an easy grin that matched the red thatch of hair covering his head. "A service I am pleased to offer, though I can scarce believe your stepbrother would release such a beauty as yourself."

"He insisted I dance with him, give him a feel for those ladies he should attend. I'm afraid the night does not hold enough hours to dance with them all."

He bowed. "Would you do me the honor of this dance before another fellow comes to carry you away?"

"I would be delighted."

He smiled, took Marissa's hand, and then nodded at his mother. "Will you be alright if I leave you here?"

She thwacked his arm with her fan. "I am quite capable of conducting myself at a ball." She looked at Marissa. "Enjoy yourself, my dear."

Sir Scott swept her away, though they chose to wait for the next set.

Marissa kept her hand hooked through his elbow. "Your mother is a sweet woman."

"I have been blessed in both my parents. Do you not feel the same?"

Her lips took on a wry twist. "Lady DeGanne is a force to recon with, even by me at times."

"She brought you here. I must say, most of us at University thought Robert would look no further for his bride."

"We are friends, that is all." *Liar.* She gave herself a mental shake. *Why did that voice have to contradict now*? She gazed at Sir Scott's handsome features. "What did you study at University?"

"I found myself interested in business."

"Perhaps you can tell me more later." Marissa pointed in the direction of the dancers. "The next set is beginning."

He patted her hand. "Would you do me the honor of being my dinner partner, if you wish to hear more?"

Marissa's smile widened. "I am honored, yes."

He moved them into position in the line of dancers, releasing her. The feel of his fingers on her skin did not elicit any other response than one of camaraderie. Was this to be the way of it? She looked at the man standing across from her, but who she wanted to see was Robert. *No, no, no.* She forced her thoughts away from her stepbrother as the music began.

The full set lasted almost half an hour. Sir Scott breathed deeply as they neared an open doorway. "The throng is thick this evening. Might I get you a glass of something?"

Marissa rested her hand on his arm. "Water would be delightful. Shall I wait here for you?"

His smile brought a twinkle to his eyes. She couldn't hear his response, and then he walked away. A throng indeed. He labeled the garrulous gathering well. An unfamiliar man wearing a blue velvet suit with a long feather draping back from his hat sauntered past. Marissa shook her head. The woman at his side wore a gown with a stiff skirt that swung back and forth like a bell as she walked.

Something crawled on her arm and Marissa swept it away with a shiver. Cold blew across her back, wrapping around her. For a moment, her heart thudded with fear, her breath catching in her throat. She raised a hand, fingers brushing against the silver necklace she'd forgotten she was wearing. Warmth spread and the tight hold on her chest relaxed. She gasped, searching for what had caused such an unpleasant feeling. Nothing seemed amiss.

"Right where I left you." Sir Scott appeared at her side, offering a glass.

She blinked at him and gave another glance through the area.

"Are you well? Has the air become too cold?"

Marissa gave herself a mental shake. "For a moment. I appreciate the water." She offered a sweet smile before drinking. The water did refresh, wetting her dry tongue.

"Shall we dance again? This set just begun." Sir Scott took her empty glass along with his and gave them to a passing servant.

Marissa nodded, placing her hand on his forearm. The tone of conversation changed as they walked toward the group of dancers. She couldn't hear what they were saying, but excitement buzzed through the air. It wasn't until the crowd parted and she saw Prince Robert pass through a stream of light. He wasn't alone. He hadn't been the entire evening, but this was different. The woman with him gazed up in perfect rapture. He looked down equally enthralled. They twirled away, and those nearest her burst into discussions.

Someone tugged on her sleeve. "Who is she?" Sereh blinked tears. "This was to be our dance. How can he…" She waved at the floor.

"But you already danced." Marissa thought she had seen them together.

"He offered another." Sereh scowled in the direction of the dancers. "And then he noticed her."

Marissa held on to Sir Scott as the crowd thickened. He leaned close. "Do you want to join this set of dancers?"

"Yes, yes." She squeezed his arm and nodded in case he couldn't hear her. She turned to Sereh. "I will try to find out. He would not be so ignoble as to ignore a promise."

They joined the line of couples. Sir Scott proved an excellent partner, and yet it was every passing of Robert that grabbed her attention, that fed the fluttering in her chest and weighted the sinking feel in her stomach. *Who is this woman?*

The prince danced with the stranger. It was as if they were the only ones on the floor. Their eyes held, their bodies moved in tandem, following the steps while being wholly absorbed. Marissa twisted her neck to try to get a better look at her. She caught a hint of golden curls and a simple gown of soft rose. Sir Scott took her hand and they spun in the opposite direction.

"Prince Robert has caused quite the stir. Was this not the purpose of the evening?" Sir Scott drew Marissa toward a seating area after the end of the set.

"Do you know her? She did not look familiar."

He offered a wan smile. "I'm afraid my attention is more attuned to a different woman this evening."

Her? "You are kind, Sir …"

"Please, just Scott. We have known each other long enough to be on a first name basis?"

"You do me great honor, Scott."

"And may I call you Marissa?" He tucked loose hair behind her ear.

"You may."

He offered her a seat, and then pointed at a table with refreshment. "I'll be right back."

Marissa turned her chair in such a way as to allow her to spy the next set opening. Robert and his lady friend were at the front of the line of dancers. They looked like lovers. She frowned. *I should be happy for him.* The touch of metal around her neck calmed her thoughts. *But I'm not.*

"Exquisite workmanship. Who gave it to you?" Scott took a seat beside her.

"What?" Then she noticed his attention on her necklace. "This? I've worn it all evening."

He offered a small silver tray with two drinks and almond cookies. "Indeed? I had not noticed. Your eyes must have more sparkle."

Marissa felt her cheeks heat. "Sir … I mean Scott. Your flattery is appealing."

"Then I shall continue."

Conversations around them lowered. The two of them glanced at the dancing. Scott shook his head. "Prince Robert holds to his beauty. He's causing a stir." A woman wearing a deep blue gown sobbed as she hurried past. "And tears."

Marissa frowned. "Did you hear people talking? Does anyone

know her?"

"Someone seemed to think her a third or fourth cousin of French royalty, but the French are not blonde, and no name was offered, not even a family name."

"A mystery." Her shoe tapped against the marble floor as the prince swirled the unfamiliar woman. The heightened color of her pale skin was expected since they'd been dancing for so long. Her petite hand against his blue blazer gave an appearance of possession.

Scott draped his arm across the back of her seat, leaning closer. "The night is young. We will know all we need to know during the midnight supper."

"You mean to keep the princess to yourself, VanCleif?" Another young man stepped in front of them, blocking Marissa's view.

Her lips twitched. By his rosy cheeks, he'd gone for something stronger than water.

Scott didn't move. "I suppose if someone worthy came along I could part with her until supper."

Marissa tilted her head. "You don't think Tennison a worthy dance partner?"

Scott looked horrified. "Do you cherish your toes?"

Marissa grinned, looking from Scott to Tennison. "He has a good point. Millicent Stol had to sit out an entire evening."

Tennison rolled his eyes. "Am I never to be forgiven?"

"Not yet." She held up her card. "I will challenge you to a game of whist."

He bowed. "You are gracious, my lady."

Scott laughed after Tennison sauntered away. "You are brave. I hear he's worse at cards than dancing."

Marissa slapped his arm with the fan dangling from her wrist. "The way he's been drinking, he won't make it through dinner. I think I'm safe from cards."

"Thinking women are not approved by many." His eyes twinkled, revealing his thoughts on the matter.

"You believe different."

He tapped her glass with his. "Indeed, I do."

"There you are! I've been looking everywhere." Sereh rushed up behind them.

Scott relinquished his seat with a flourishing bow.

Marissa wanted to shake her friend. "What is this? You've been crying, and now you have smudges of dirt on your face." She drew a handkerchief from the pouch sewn into her gown. "Have you learned anything of interest? I admit we have not." While she talked, Marissa dipped the edge of the kerchief in water and then dabbed at Sereh's cheeks.

"He won't look on anyone else." Sereh grabbed her hands.

Marissa took a deep breath. "I know you had hoped for something more. I am sorry." She stood, pulling Sereh with her. "There are other worthy men. Do you know the VanCleifs? This is Sir Scott." Marissa gave him a glance. "Scott, this is Sereh."

He bowed. "A pleasure. I understand your heart must be broken, but would you do me the honor of a dance? Or a service, a plate perhaps?"

Sereh managed a watery smile. "Another opportunity to dance?"

Scott offered his arm. "You must dance. I insist."

She fluttered, cheeks turning pink, and acquiesced.

Marissa sat as they moved away. *He is everything a man ought to be to engage my interest, but I don't even mind he's gone off with Sereh.* Her lips tingled. If Robert's kiss had been on purpose, if they had allowed it to deepen, would Robert be by her side at this moment?

Not much later, another young man approached. "A f-f-f-ine ball, i-i-isn't it?"

"Clayton, how are you? I haven't seen you since Robert returned from University." Marissa held her hand toward him. The young man clicked his heals and bent to kiss the air an inch above her skin. "How are your sisters?"

"B-b-big, though not b-b-big enough for the b-b-ball." He breathed. "Would you d-d-d …"

Marissa stood, allowing him to take hold of her hand. "I would enjoy a dance, Clayton."

Though he lacked the presence of Scott and Robert, Clayton held his own as a kind, attentive partner. His being shorter allowed Marissa to see Robert and his lady returning from a balcony. They joined the set, but he never glanced in her direction. The other woman did. Marissa felt a chill scrape down her back. The unfamiliar attitude made her want to stomp her foot. *I am pleased for Robert. She's a beautiful woman. They have a connection, which is what stepfather wanted.*

"What did you s-say?" Clayton quizzed as the turn brought them together.

Marissa blinked. "Robert has found a lovely young lady. Do you know her?"

He shook his head. "Pity. Any n-n-number of us would d-d-dance with her if w-we could."

"If only men could gossip as well as women." Marissa sighed. "She doesn't seem inclined to girl-talk."

Sereh and Scott joined their corner. Sereh seemed relaxed, her smile natural as she allowed Scott to twirl her to the opposite side of the corner. Clayton took Sereh next, the two of them faltering before he set her in the opposite corner. Scott crossed to Marissa, twirling her in the same manner as Sereh. He raised his brows. Ah, he noticed as well. They both smiled before the set continued and they moved to different boxes.

Then it was Robert and the woman. Neither of them said a word. They watched each other, even when being moved by a different partner. Marissa kept a smile pasted on her face, but her insides twisted with unfamiliar turmoil. The set continued. Robert and his companion went to a different square.

The night dragged. Marissa laughed, danced, spent a moment reassuring Sereh and the other young ladies. Through it all, she was acutely aware of Robert and the mysterious lady no one had yet been able to name.

Robert was spoiling her fun. She wanted to stomp her foot and hit him. Hard. Midnight approached, how many hours had he spent at that woman's side? The music stopped. Marissa saluted the musicians, then turned to see the woman exiting to the balcony. Robert chased down a servant and went after her. With a fervent pardon to Sir Scott, and a request for refreshing liquid, she chose to follow.

LAURIE LEE

12

"You won't forget your promise?" Cinderella looked deep into his eyes, as though determining his worth and stability.

The first toll of midnight rang through the gardens. "Nothing, not a moment will I be able to banish from my mind. You are everything I've ever wanted."

Her eyes closed at the second ring, and she rested her head on his chest for a moment. His heart pounded, as though it wanted to burst free. The third stroke of midnight had her pulling away. "Then I will see you again, I know it." With a precious smile, she kissed him on the lips and turned from him. He needed to reach for her, keep her from disappearing into the night, but his arms remained motionless at his side. He could hear the clink of her dancing slippers on the stone steps, further and further. Every toll of the clock carried her further from his side. Weakness assailed him, and he leaned against the balcony.

Marissa saw a touch of lace disappearing around the stairwell. Unease twisted her stomach as she searched the dimly lit terrace. She sighed with relief when Robert's broad shoulders came into view. He stood alone, slumped against the stone wall at the edge of the terrace. For a moment, her desire was to return to the warmth of his arms, whirling through the ballroom and sharing laughter with her best friend.

She shook her head to clear it. This wasn't about her. This was about the dainty blonde woman who seemed to captivate the prince. Marissa walked to Robert. She placed her hand on his arm, and then followed the direction of his focus. Even in the dark of night, light illuminated the strange woman as she walked between two rows of carriages. She stumbled for a moment and Marissa felt Robert's arm stiffen.

She turned to him. What caused his fascination? "Where is she going?"

He offered no response, attention fixed on the disappearing young lady.

"Robert," Marissa said again, but still nothing. She shook his arm, and he dragged his attention from the lower hall and looked at her with bleary eyes. Marissa frowned. "What is wrong with you?"

"Marissa?" He seemed confused for a moment, and then he sighed. "She has gone."

"Who? Who is she?" She looked down again, but the mysterious woman had vanished.

He shrugged. "I don't know. But it doesn't matter. I love her."

"Love? It's been what, three hours?"

"You wouldn't understand, Mars." He jerked his arm away. "It's nothing you've experienced. Nothing like us."

Marissa blinked, turning her face so he couldn't see the hurt inflicted by his sharp tone. "I'm sorry." She swallowed her pain. "To whose family does she belong?"

"She did not say."

Marissa clenched her hands to keep from biting her nails. "You don't know her family?"

"Her name is Cinderella." His voice resonated with wonder.

"Cinderella who?"

He shrugged.

"You must know a surname. You can't go to the king and tell him you want to marry Cinderella. Your father will not stand on the dais and announce his only son, Prince Robert of Camden, is engaged to … to Cinderella."

"I can. I will." He glared. "If I tell him I love her, he will be satisfied."

She grunted in frustration. "Follow her, look to the emblem on her carriage. Find out what you can of her people. What manner of woman entices a man to love her and runs away?"

He grabbed her arms, his look earnest. "Mine. She is perfect for me. "

Marissa bit her bottom lip to keep from rolling her eyes. She watched as he blinked, and his glance focused on her mouth. *Did he remember?* But a veil dropped over him, and his arms released her. He slipped past to follow the path Cinderella had taken. Marissa shook her head, wrapping her arms around herself to ward off the chill. A shiver stole down her back and a lone tear trailed the smooth pale skin of her cheek.

Robert raced down the stairs. The hallway was empty, and he noticed nothing amiss in the shadows. It was too far, running to the end of the hallway then back around to the carriages. He jumped the hedge.

"Ey, ladd."

He ignored the old man brushing a chestnut horse. She had escaped through the rows of carriages. He pushed the horse out of the way. The path was empty. She couldn't be far, hadn't been that long since she parted ways with him. Her groom would still be helping her. He ran along the line. Groomsmen and livery mingled, hollering as he disturbed their games, but there was no sign of Cinderella.

The shelled pathway turned to uneven stone. He fell to his knees, cobbles shooting pain through his hands and legs. It didn't matter. Breath refused to move from his lungs. *She was gone. How had he missed her? Where had she gone?* He doubled over, felt the cold touch of stone against his forehead. Her image filled his thoughts. The soft dress billowing as they twirled across the ballroom. Her peach lips against the glass flute filled with champagne. Her face bathed in moonlight. A sob shook his body, then he noticed a glitter.

A sparkle lit the corner of his eye, as he had seen at the ball. Hope flared to life and he surged to his feet, turning. But it wasn't Cinderella. What had called him? He looked down. Moonlight gleamed on a slipper, a dainty thing forged in glass. It was hers, he was sure of it. A piece of herself left behind for him. He touched it, but it had already turned cold. How had she danced the night in such a thing? He lifted the slipper. It was like a jewel, glittering with hues of rose and dandelions. *I will find you*. His words echoed in his head. His promise. She needed him. He cradled the slipper against his heart. This was how he would find her.

13

Dawn kissed the eastern edge of the sky when the last of the guests wound their way to their rooms or sauntered to their carriages. The royal family didn't watch their going. The king, his son, and Marissa were in the king's office. Mahogany wood desk and bookcases added to the air of elegance brought on by the subdued pattern of linen wallpaper and wainscoting the color of champagne. Prince Robert sat on the edge of a hard, straight-back chair. His father lounged in a more-comfortable stuffed chair that matched the walls. Marissa slouched on a bench, leaning her head against a tapestry while watching Robert and his father argue.

"Why did she leave?" King William asked a third time, his voice projecting his irritation.

"She didn't explain. But you noticed? I could not take my eyes from her. The moment she entered the room, I felt alive."

Marissa pressed a hand against her temple. The fervent look in Robert's eyes evoked a pounding in her head. The king's fist hit the desk, causing her to jump.

"If she knew she procured your affection, she should have stayed. Why run?"

"You wanted a match, I made a match." Robert's steely voice chilled the room.

The king shook his head. Age and weariness showed in the sloop of his shoulders and the pull in his frown. "Not just a match, Robert. I want you to be happy, to be loved as I was loved by your mother."

"I do love her, Father. More than I can express." He reached out to touch his father's arm. "I am grateful—if you hadn't insisted on this ball, we may never have crossed paths."

"Too bad," Marissa muttered soft enough that the others couldn't hear, then she admonished her attitude. *What right do I have to think negative thoughts about the prince and his new love?* She toyed with her necklace. The king focused his attention on Marissa, causing her to sit straighter. Her cheeks flushed.

"You saw her?" he asked.

"Everyone saw her. She was the only woman he danced with once she arrived."

"None of the other guests knew her? No one recognized her?" King William's forehead wrinkled.

Marissa sighed. "None that I could find. She did not leave with anyone. Robert tried to find her, but …"

Robert jumped to his feet. "It matters not. Cinderella is the woman I love. She is the woman I will marry. I have vowed to find her. When I do, I will bring her to the palace. You will love her, Father. She is everything that is sweet and kind."

The king tried to smile, to reassure the prince, but Marissa thought it looked more like a grimace. She stood, eager to retire herself. "We are tired." She waved at the heavy curtains that couldn't block out the morning glow. "Morning light has come. Let us retire to our chambers and sleep. We will think and reason better when our minds are rested."

"You make a fine point, my dear. Robert," He turned to his son, "we will find Cinderella. The more I hear of her, the more I long to meet her."

Robert rubbed the bristles beginning to cover his cheeks and chin. Marissa quelled the unexpected desire to offer comfort and turned her back on the pain in his eyes. *What is wrong with me?* She muttered something unintelligible and removed herself from the king's office.

14

Light still shone through the heavy curtains of her room as Marissa stretched. Sleep had been sweet. Somewhere in her dreams, Robert's lips moved against hers. She pressed into the down-stuffed mattress fitted with soft linen sheets, wanting to return to her dreams. Warmth spread through her body. She turned her face into a pillow. *What am I thinking? Robert is a dear friend, a brother. Stepbrother, no relation.* She growled at her racing thoughts, threw the covers to the side and sat up. "This is not helping, Mars." She launched herself from the bed. Cold water on her face helped clear her thoughts. Any considerations of her dearest friend were pointless. She forced herself to think of Robert and Cinderella twirling through the ballroom. That was the threat needing to be thwarted. *Threat?* She groaned once more.

The door slammed against the wall. Marissa jumped, her yelp echoing through the room. Heart thumping in her chest, she glared at her mother standing in the doorway.

"I don't like this." The older woman glided into the room, her smooth motions at odds with the fire of her voice. "What is the meaning of this?" Her green eyes blazed as she hissed.

Marissa huffed, but her mother continued to rant. "He was meant for you. Prince Robert has always been meant for you."

Marissa looked down at the hand gripping her arm, and then frowned. "Robert and I are friends. We consider each other brother and sister. I will never enter any other relationship with him. You know this because I've told you countless times."

Lady DeGanne shook her head sadly. "But it's supposed to be you. He cares for you, and you care for him, even if you're afraid to admit such a thing to yourself." She flailed her arms. "You could be queen."

"I don't want to be queen. It is enough to have grown up as a king's daughter. I am the prince's friend, nothing more."

"You are a fool, Marissa. Yes, you are young, but if you do nothing, Robert will find the woman and he will be out of your reach forever."

"Mother." Marissa glared, fighting tears.

"I'm sorry." Lady DeGanne bent her slender body onto a settee. "I am furious with you. You will do nothing, allowing this … this woman we know nothing about to lure the prince into marriage. Be honest. Can you tell me your heart will feel nothing when he weds?"

"Robert has chosen." She crossed her arms. *What right did she have to push so hard?* "He will do everything he can to find Cinderella."

"Which leaves you forty days to convince him you are the better woman."

"I'm not." Marissa shook her head, frustrated with herself and her determined mother. Forty days? The traditional engagement period, of course. A headache flared to life. She rubbed her forehead. Cinderella would live in the palace, chaperoned by the mothers. Her own mother, in this case. She gave her mother a hard look. "You will do nothing to interfere."

"How could I not? I'm supposed to accept a nobody over my own daughter?"

"I will leave, I swear it. Robert with Cinderella is enough to deal with, not you as well."

Anger melted away and her mother beamed with pleasure. "You do care."

"I said nothing of the sort." Marissa protested, but her mother didn't notice. She rose, swept her skirts into order, and sailed from the room.

Marissa groaned, and fell back on the bed. *Has morning changed Robert's feelings?* Marissa stared at the ceiling, but the swirls of puffy clouds painted against soft blue gave no answer. *I will find him myself and gage if his senses have recovered.* She rang the bell for assistance with her morning gown.

15

In the hours between dawn and noon, an army of workers had restored the castle to its traditional splendor. The one remnant remaining of the ball included a blood-red cloth covering a single table, upon which sat a glass slipper. Marissa clenched her abdomen as something inside her ached. Beside the table, in a tall, gilded chair, Prince Robert slept. One leg propped against the seat allowed his hand to reach toward the slipper. He leaned to the side. Stubble had grown into a shadow covering the lower portion of his face. There was nothing peaceful about his sleep. His body twitched, and his hand closed into a fist, as though trying to pull away from something unseen.

Marissa ran to his side, turning her back on the offensive reminder of the previous evening. She knelt beside the chair, taking his hand in her own. His struggle ceased, and he opened his eyes.

"Marissa," he greeted her with a smile.

"Good morning. Well, afternoon." Her eyes searched his. Encouraged by the clarity she saw in him, her smiled brightened.

His hand warmed her cheek. "It seems we have gone from night to night." He frowned. "The ball was last night, was it not? My memories make no sense."

"The day has not darkened yet." She squeezed his hand, leaning closer. "Do you remember her?"

"Who?"

Cold washed through the room before she could answer. Robert straightened in the seat and his attention moved to the slipper.

Kneeling beside him, she watched as he seemed to be dragged toward the object. His touch slipped away from hers. She didn't bother hiding her distress, Robert's attention had been engaged by the sparkling slipper.

He moved to the table, touching the detestable shoe with his fingers. "Cinderella."

Leaving the ball, as Cinderella walked between the rows of carriages, she could feel the gaze of the prince. He watched. She didn't need to turn around to know for certain. Pleasure of the night filled her. Though young, the prince held himself with the stature of royalty. The bearing of his mother shone through him.

She stumbled, and the delicate shoe fitted to her foot slipped off. She gasped. Broken? But when she saw it, the glass slipper gleamed in torchlight from a lantern hanging on a nearby carriage. It was meant to stay. She moved on, hobbling a few steps. When she turned from the view of the prince, she leaned against a vehicle and removed the other slipper.

A large window reflected her image. She slipped her finger into the pouch of sand. "Mirror on the wall, return me to the great hall." A slight tremor of unease caused her hand to shake as she touched the reflection. She closed her eyes. The next moment she found herself home.

The long mirror stood in its majesty. Cinderella placed the single shoe on the floor a hand's width from the mirror's frame. She caught a glimpse of her reflection as she stood. The blond curls were charmingly disarrayed. Tiredness drooped her eyes and paled her lips. She stiffened her shoulders. There were things to check and preparations to be finalized. She couldn't stop herself from smiling, nor the gleam of victory from sparking her eyes.

"A very good night." She told her image in the mirror.

"Now sleep. Preparations will be ready tomorrow." Her reflection answered.

She padded across the floor runner in her bare feet, pulling herself up the stairs to her bedroom. The inky shadow on the far side of the bed moved. She ignored Crow. After exchanging her ball gown for a sleeping tunic, she slipped beneath the cool covers of the bed. Though she didn't mind Crow's arm wrapping around her, the flashes of images behind her closed eyes as she settled for sleep were of Prince Robert.

When she woke, Crow had gone. Sunlight peeked through the thick curtains over the window. She breathed, allowing her thoughts to spread. The spell weaved its workings. She could feel it, every movement like a brush of air across her skin. "I must see," she declared as she pulled herself from the bed. Food didn't matter. She wrapped herself in clothes and returned to the deep room where the mirror waited.

"Mirror on the wall, reveal my prince at my call." She stood before it. Her reflection faded and the image of the prince asleep in a chair came to view. The touch of her finger on his hand through the glass caused his fingers to pull into a fist. "The spell works." She allowed herself to smile. Then the image widened as a young woman approached. Cinderella frowned. "What do you think you are doing, Dearie?"

The woman crouched beside the chair, taking hold of Robert's hand. He relaxed, tension flowing from him. Cinderella couldn't hear their words, but she didn't need to. The gentle breath of webs razed against her skin, leaving angry red welts on her arm. This woman would be a problem. How had the prince attached himself to her?

"Can you not strengthen the spell?" Cinderella demanded of the mirror. The glass slipper glittered on a dais in the room with the prince. Robert's attention fell away from the mysterious woman. His body tensed. The woman stepped away, hurt reflecting on her face. Cinderella tapped the woman through the mirror. "Robert is my prince, whomever you are. Don't get in my way."

She took a step away, turning toward the door. "Crow!" Cinderella hollered. The black man stepped into the room. She turned toward him. "You must go. Get her away from him. Distract her so my spell has time to weave throughout the palace."

He glanced at the image in the mirror. "What is she compared to you? The girl is no threat."

Cinderella pressed one hand against his cheek. "You speak truth. She will not be." Her voice hardened into a snarl. "Now, go."

He hissed, pulling away from her, but it was too late. The man faded, and a large crow squawked in his place. His wings beat the air, but Cinderella kept hold of his feet. "To the palace. Whatever it takes." She released him, and he flew away. She turned to look at the young woman in the mirror, and growled in a low, menacing voice. "Don't come between me and my prize."

The image changed from the palace to Cinderella's bedroom. Her reflection carried the other slipper and hid it in a closet. It then withdrew a suitcase and dowdy clothes and placed them by her foot. Cinderella looked at the floor. The shoe remained where she'd placed it.

She took it with her and moved to her bedroom. Excitement stirred as she opened the closet. The secret compartment held her book of spells, but she wasn't here for that now. She picked up the suitcase and placed the glass slipper on the shelf in its stead. She pulled the pale dress from her body, letting it fall to the floor where she could step on it. She raised the lid of the case and took a service gown, giving it a shake before slipping it over her head. A kerchief covered the blond curls while pulling her hair away from her face. Nothing of herself remained. Satisfied, she lifted the case by its handles and carried it to the room with the mirror.

She set the trunk in front of it. "I will need the little mirror." It appeared, resting against the front of the case. She snatched it from the mirror, but this time no pain seared her flesh. Once the hand-held mirror had been placed inside, Cinderella lifted the case and stood ready. "Show me the manor." Fields illuminated by moonlight sped by until a large country manor with wings on either end came into focus. "Take me to my room." Images in the mirror shifted as though they reflected the eyes of one who walked the path to the front door. They turned to the left, taking a narrow hall leading to the back of the house. The servant stairs were through an old, battered door. At the top of the stairs, it turned and moved three doors. When they stopped inside a small room, Cinderella closed her eyes and shifted through.

The slight nauseous feeling came and went, just as it had when she traveled to and from the palace. She opened her eyes. After placing the case in a corner, she first removed the small hand-held mirror and affixed it to the wall. The servant's room was the size of a closet. A simple straw bed pushed against the wall allowed room for a small table with a cracked pot and wash basin. She looked at her smooth hands, then flexed her fingers. Spots of skin darkened. Bruises and callouses rose across her knuckles and on the pads beneath her fingers. Working hands. She grinned. The spell strengthened, she could feel its slivers of thread spreading. All that remained was for the prince to find her.

A knock sounded at the door. "Morning is wasting."

She looked at the dark window and raised her brows. Morning? She didn't bother arguing. Life at the manor was an act to be played.

16

The image of blue eyes burned in Robert's mind. "Find me." He could hear her voice calling to him. The room around him faded until the cold feel of glass controlled his senses. He hadn't realized he'd picked it from the table. Need caused his hand to tremble, and he tightened his grip. Dropping the connection between himself and Cinderella—he couldn't bear the thought.

"This is how I will find her." He spoke with force, a part of him recognized Marissa standing beside him. "I will find her and return her to our home as the princess she is and the queen she will be."

"I pray it will be as you will it," Marissa answered.

Her soft voice washed over him. A memory hovered just beyond Cinderella, but the glass in his hands grew warm.

"Find me." Her whispers tore at his heart, drenched in desperation. "Please, you must find me before it is too late."

He rushed from the room, determined to set the search into action.

Anger and hurt warred within Marissa. She didn't follow Robert. By the next morning, the tension of emotion had her pacing her room. At the first sign of dawn, she grabbed her cloak and hurried to the stables. The embroidered rug was heavy, but Marissa wrapped both arms around it and carried it to Soliloquy's stall. Her dapple-gray mare shook her head as Marissa approached. The groom had connected the pillion that set both feet on one side of the horse. Marissa unhooked the buckle, letting the pillion fall to the hay-covered floor of the barn. She draped the rug across Soliloquy's back instead. The mare chatted. Marissa rubbed her hand along the coarse hair covering her neck. Tension eased from her shoulders, allowing her to relax. She pulled a light saddle from the empty stall to her right. Robert had taught her the proper way to latch the saddle to keep from falling. Once they were ready, Marissa led Soliloquy through the back side-door. The trail curved away from the palace and ancient keep. A few minutes' walk brought them to a stand of trees. Marissa stopped beside a tree stump. She rubbed her hand along Soliloquy's back. "Don't move."

With a glance back to be certain no one followed, she pushed herself from the stump and across the horse's back. Standing with her feet in the stirrups, she arranged her skirts and settled. She'd insisted Robert teach her to ride a horse the same way he did, even though her mother would whip both their backsides if they were caught. Marissa shook her head. Enough thoughts about Robert. She pressed her knees, signaling Soliloquy to trot.

Air moved around her. The scent of trees springing back from winter's chill surrounded her. She slowed to a walk to cross the stone bridge. Water bubbled and rolled through the creek bed, fed by melting snow and spring rains. No rain today, though. She smiled at the feel of warmth on her back. She signaled Soliloquy to speed up. The horse obeyed, its muscles moving. Marissa leaned forward, resting her cheek against the solid neck.

The moment her cheek touched, a loud squawk dove over her. The scream of a large black bird startled horse and rider. Marissa gasped, wrapping her hands around Soliloquy's neck as the horse bounced and chatted against the attack.

"Easy Girl, easy." Marissa rubbed one hand along the neck as she pulled open the leather satchel attached to the saddle. She felt for the short whip. Another squawk, and she snapped the whip through the air above her with a shout. The bird disappeared into the crown of trees. The horse shivered, and Marissa used a quiet voice to calm her. When she felt Soliloquy still, she turned them toward home.

"Thought I might find you roaming out here." Mrs. Boyde, properly seated in a pillion on her bay gelding, crossed onto her path.

"I needed air." Marissa checked behind, but there was no sign of the black bird that had tried to attack them.

"It is a beautiful morning. Don't mind if I join you." She positioned her horse to the right of Marissa so they could face one another.

Marissa noticed the look at her skirts spread across Soliloquy, and the fact her governess-turned lady's maid said nothing caused her to want to giggle.

Mrs. Boyde grinned. "I've heard little about the ball. Other than cries of Sereh and several of the young ladies."

"You haven't heard the story of Cinderella and the glass slipper?"

"A glass slipper?"

Marissa shrugged. "Robert claims the shoe he found was worn by her."

"How did she lose a shoe?"

"I found him at midnight on the back terrace. She was running away. We saw her trip. When I asked him what her name was, all he could tell me was Cinderella. No family name. Oh, Belton Province. She did tell him that."

"She must have been staying with someone nearby. It would take more than a week in fair weather to travel from Belton Province."

"If so, we haven't found them. She was *the* topic of conversation during dinner. No one had seen her before."

"Very odd. What will Robert do?"

"There's a meeting today to discuss how he will search for her." Marissa moved ahead to cross the stone bridge first.

"You should go." Mrs. Boyde resumed her place beside Soliloquy.

"Me? Whatever for?"

"You are his friend. He may have lost his head over this Cinderella, but you can make sure the search is something that will work."

Marissa chewed her bottom lip. *I am curious.* "I think I will. I had to sit and listen to him and stepfather argue into the morning after the ball. Anywhere I went yesterday, it was Cinderella this, and Cinderella that," she snarled as she pulled Soliloquy to a stop beside the stump.

Mrs. Boyde raised her brows. "Aren't you riding to the stables?"

Marissa breathed, turning her face to the warm sun before allowing her lips to twitch. "I prefer to walk the rest of the way." She pulled herself from the horse, then stretched her legs to work out the ache from riding. "I need to ride more."

Mrs. Boyde pointed at the clouds hanging along the horizon. "I don't think the weather will agree with you for a few days."

An older groom approached as Marissa and Mrs. Boyde entered the stables. He addressed the women with a heavy accent. "Thought I saw ye earlier. Ye know not to ride aloon, Miss Marissa. Wot were ye thinking?"

Mrs. Boyde laughed. "Mr. Rickers, she should know better than to try to get a horse from your stables without you knowing. I went after her."

"Good thing." He took the leads for both horses. "Too many strangers aboot, after det ball. Don't worry, I'll take care of des two." He looked at Marissa. "Ye take someone wit ye next time ye ride, or dis saddle'll disappear."

"I'm sorry, but I didn't go far." *And the only thing to attack was a stupid bird.* "I'll take one of the lads with me next time."

"Give him your word." Mrs. Boyde offered a steady gaze.

Marissa tried to ignore her, but she could not. "Fine. I promise someone will be with me when I take Soliloquy."

Mr. Rickers nodded. "Want ye ta be safe."

"Thank you, I will be."

Mrs. Boyde patted her arm, tucking her elbow through Marissa's, and led the two of them from the stables toward the palace. Once they were clear of the building, she spoke before Marissa could complain about being followed. "You will check on the meeting? I admit, I'm curious what Robert will do to find this woman he thinks he's fallen in love with."

The distraction worked.

Robert paced from the window with burgundy drapes pooling on the floor to the French doors leading into the library. Tiredness tugged at him. The weight across his shoulders increased.

"Robert, sit down before you wear a hole in the floor." Marissa admonished.

He glanced at her. The pain in his chest grew until he looked at the slipper ensconced in a glass case. "We have to find her. She said Belton Province, but what if they stopped before returning? It is the furthest of the provinces."

Captain Standish pointed at the slipper. "Our crafters need two more days to replicate the shoe. We'll have a dozen at least, in case any should be broken."

"Then what?" Marissa sighed with exasperation. "Knock on every villa, mansion, and estate house between here and the borderlands?"

"If we must." Robert stood still, anger causing his fists to curl. "Every eligible woman should try the shoe."

Marissa held up her hands. "It could take months, possibly a year. There has to be a better way."

"How?"

Marissa looked at King William. "How did the announcements for the ball go out?"

Father opened his mouth, and then frowned. He thought for a moment. "I don't actually know. They sort of just happened."

"The criers went out, didn't they?" Marissa walked to the map on the wall. "What if you sent criers ahead of soldiers, letting the people know ladies needed to try on the slipper?" She turned around. "They could set up in town centers, have the ladies come to them. Everyone tries on the shoe. If no one fits, the soldiers move to the next town."

That could work. Robert felt the first glimmer of hope. He strode to Marissa's side, taking her hands. His mind blanked, and the turmoil faded. He opened his mouth, but for a moment, he wondered what if he chose Marissa instead? Forget the search. "Mars?"

Something crashed against the window. Marissa jumped. Robert pulled back, turning to look, and his eyes rested on the slipper. The need to find Cinderella struck like a physical blow.

"Bloody bird," Captain Standish turned away from the window. "Are you certain you want to go now? We've been working drills for a campaign."

"We can postpone the skirmishes. The soldiers will get terrain training instead."

"What do we do if we find her? When?" Captain Standish corrected himself.

"Bring her here." King William struck the armrest of his chair. "Let her explain why she left my son."

"She is not a prisoner." Robert couldn't bear the thought she might be mistreated. "Take a royal carriage with you. The shoes can be stored in a compartment beneath the seats. Convey Cinderella and her family. Be sure they lack nothing."

"What of the real glass slipper?" Marissa asked.

"It remains here." He didn't want to look away from it.

"Is that wise? Yes, our best craftsmen work to make replicas, but nothing will match the original as well. Even if someone can fit their foot, you won't know for certain until she tries the real slipper."

He felt torn. What Mars said was true, and yet the thought of parting with the remaining piece of Cinderella? How could he bare it?

"I agree." Captain Standish nodded.

"You would have to go with it. Guard it with your life." Robert wanted him to say it wasn't possible, then the slipper would have to stay.

Captain Standish tugged on his short beard. King William studied them both. "This is important, not just for my son, but for our country. I think you must go. If we have dire need, the pigeons are trained to cover distances."

"Cinderella's glass slipper goes with him?" Marissa seemed a bit too eager.

"Perhaps I should go as well."

"No." Standish, Father, and Marissa objected.

Captain Standish took the lead. "This venture is already going to cause a stir in every city and town we visit. Adding you in the mix would make it dangerous."

"I don't know that I can wait here and do nothing." The thought of not knowing … it wasn't to be born. His breath stuck in his throat.

King William pointed out the window. "You have military training. Our tenants need to be evaluated after winter. There is work for you here."

Work didn't appeal. He wanted Marissa. No, he *desired* Cinderella. He looked at Marissa. Where had the first thought come from? He'd found love, true love. Whatever these stray thoughts about his stepsister were, they needed to stop. He focused on the glass slipper. He focused on Cinderella.

LAURIE LEE

17

Cinderella didn't need the light of morning to know a week had passed. She stood ready in the open doorway of her room as the wing manager banged a gong, pulling the others from sleep. She trailed with them down the back steps, listening for the squeak which sometimes resulted in the tiny scurry of footsteps behind the wall. Today there was nothing, and she continued down to the lower kitchen. The group sat around a table set with mismatched chairs. A bowl of oatmeal slid in front of her. Weak coffee complimented the tasteless break of fast.

"Oy got sheger." The girl beside her announced to the quiet group. "Wot yer give fer a pinch?"

"If you got sugar, it's because you taken it from somewhere. You lose a hand if they get you."

"Oy not a stealer." She frowned at the older man. "Gil who stayed, she gave it ter me. I takin' nothin."

"What cha want fer it?" The old lady with the keys asked, as she pulled a small satchel from a pocket deep within her dress.

"Not gonna waste sugar on you, old witch." The large man beside her nabbed the satchel.

"What are ye doin? Thief, thief," she screeched, reaching across him to try to grasp her bag from his far hand. The bowl of oatmeal in front of him spilled across his lap and onto the floor. He flew from his seat, backhanding the older woman.

Cinderella looked down as chaos erupted around the table. Discord flavored her oatmeal, and she ate while the others bickered and fought.

Breakfast ended, and work began. Cinderella crouched in front of the fireplace. She scooped through the ashes piled against burnt shells of wood.

"Cinder among all the ashes. Seems fitting." Heavy footsteps were followed by a deep voice and a throaty laugh.

Cinderella glanced up at the man looming over her. His was a full figure, the edges of his face beginning to blur. "I'm working, sir."

"I have another job in mind for you." He swept a hand across her hair. Cinderella made to stand but he pushed against her shoulder. "We can do this here. No one will disturb us."

"I don't want trouble, sir." Cinderella lifted the pail, holding it between them.

He knocked it from her hands. "I'm more interested in what I want. Right now, that would be you." He grabbed at her hair and Cinderella hissed at the feel of a pin scraping against her scalp.

She grabbed his wrist. The blaze of anger on his face soon paled, and his fingers released her. Cinderella stood, keeping her grip on his arm sharp. "I don't like what you have in mind. Is this how you treat your staff?"

Veins in the man's face bulged through his skin. His mouth opened and closed several times, resembling a fish, but he remained silent.

Cinderella glared. "What is your name?"

"Richards," he wheezed.

"Richards, you should be grateful I have a purpose for you." Cinderella sent power through his veins. The predatory glare of his eyes dulled until a vacant look remained. She released his arm. He remained facing her, waiting for instruction. "Return to your post. I will call when I have need of you." He turned, obedient, and walked away. Cinderella returned to the task of shoveling ash into the cast-iron bucket.

"I don't know what's come over Richards, but I hope it stays." A young servant girl dropped her bag of laundry beside the heated pool.

"That lecherous sod?" Milly grunted as she moved sheets through the purple-colored water.

Cinderella pulled sheets from the other side of the pool and fed them into the wringer that would rinse the bluing. "What happened?"

"I keep out of his way, ever since…" She blushed as she looked around the room. "Well, you know how he is. I turned the corner, and he's standing at the door. Just standing there, staring. Thought my heart was going to burst out of my chest. But he stood, didn't turn or nothing."

"It's this backward province. He wouldn't behave that way elsewhere." Milly looked at Cinderella. "You grew up gentry."

"I barely remember life before my stepmother. It was my father's house. He wouldn't have allowed me to be mistreated."

"How'd you end up here?" The girl stared.

Milly threw a bag of the mistress' dirty linens. "If you can't work and chatter, then keep silent."

"Stepmother thought I was competition when it came to finding mates for her daughters."

Milly laughed. "Competition? If she could see you now, she'd know how wrong she was."

Cinderella did not give in to the tingle of irritation.

The girl moved closer when Milly turned her back. "Ignore her. She thinks she's in charge. Everyone takes what they can."

"But not you?" Cinderella grabbed her arm. The girl struggled, gasping at the pain of Cinderella's grip. Until she, like Richards, went blank. Cinderella released her. "Get Richards and meet in my chamber."

The girl turned and walked away as Milly entered the cleaning room. "Where's she going?"

"I sent her on an errand."

"You? What right…"

Cinderella glanced at Milly. The woman silenced, returning to her duty of paddling the sheets and linens through the bluing formula.

Cinderella finished wringing sheets, then took the back stairs to her chamber. Both Richards and the servant girl stood inside the door. The girl stared in the mirror while the man stood with his arms hanging at his side. Cinderella walked behind the girl. "What's your name?"

"Abigail."

"Have you ever been anywhere besides Belton Province, Abigail?"

She shook her head. Cinderella looked into the mirror. "Take them to Monmoore Palace. A soldier and a chamber maid."

The mirror dripped down the wall and formed an oval large enough for the two to pass through.

"In you go." Cinderella stepped out of the way, allowing Abigail to pass first with Richards following. Both crossed into the mirror. Their steps faltered, and bodies arched. Though silence remained in the room, Cinderella could see their mouths open in voiceless screams. The clothing they wore blasted away in bits and pieces, wind-blown sand tearing at them. The wind stopped, and Abigail fell to her knees, naked and bloody. Then wind came once more, this time from all directions, pummeling them. Cinderella lost sight for a moment, and then the air cleared. They lay on the ground dressed in the livery of the King's court. Richards pushed himself, crawling forward, looking toward something Cinderella could not see.

Cinderella tried to turn away, but she was caught, watching, until both figures completed their journey through the mirror. Her heart thudded, desiring and repelled by the power contained within the mirror. Silver slid up the wall, until the small mirror returned to its original shape.

18

Elizabeth Boyde felt the chill of a cold finger down her back. She closed her eyes. The evil in Monmoore deepened. She thinned her lips, noting her pale reflection in the mirror. "Been too still for too long." She spoke to herself, but Guardians were never unwatchful. She glanced upward. "Might have warned me a witch had her focus here."

She opened the narrow center drawer of the dresser, reached around to the back of the drawer and tugged at a latch. The bottom of the drawer popped open. Elizabeth selected a small opaline pearl from the compartment, closed the lid, and returned the drawer to its rightful place. She dropped the pearl into her pocket.

The knock on her door was not unexpected. Lily, a young serving girl from the kitchens, gave an awkward curtsy. "Lady Marissa asked me to fetch you, Mrs. Boyde. Something about a promise to go horseback riding when there was no one else."

Elizabeth smiled. "Thank you, Lily. I will go at once." Elizabeth stood in the doorway until the girl turned the corner. When she was alone in the hall, she touched a line of silver imbedded in the wood door frame. She'd placed the silver thread from her homeland once she knew the child would remain at the palace. With a touch, her presence would be masked from the witch. She closed the door, traced her finger along the line that blended with the natural grain of the wood, and then stepped back.

As she walked to join Marissa, she frowned at the webs dripped in the corners of the hallway and stairs, although few others would notice. Spells rising to encase the palace were delicate in nature. The witch meant to lure her prey through complacency. By engineering the ball and then running away, Cinderella provided time for her webs to spread.

Marissa leaned out the door of her bed chambers. "There you are, Mrs. Boyde. The sun is up, and this air indoors is stifling."

Elizabeth faced her beloved charge, grinning. "Eager to escape, are you?"

"You required my promise. Seems fitting I should call for your company."

Elizabeth waved her arm, indicating Marissa should lead the way. The patter of their feet on the woven runner fit companionable silence.

The request by Marissa's father for a Guardian came when Marissa was five years of age. For eleven years, Elizabeth had been Marissa's governess, confidant and friend. She'd comforted the broken child at the death of her beloved father when Lady DeGanne couldn't manage. She reigned in the escapades before Lady DeGanne ordered her whipped. Elizabeth peered at Marissa. They could be taken for mother and daughter. Marissa was close to her height. They were both slender, though not possessing the regal stature of Lady DeGanne. Marissa's hair was darker, and she wore it braided to keep the wind from blowing it about as she rode.

They used the grand staircase to get to the foyer. It was on the bottom step Elizabeth felt cold fingers stretching around her once more. She reached into her pocket, pinching the pearl until she felt it break, then rubbing her fingers through the powder.

A large man filled the box station beside the door. He wore the king's livery, and his hair was trimmed to frame his pudgy face. His eyes were blank, and yet something swirled in their depth.

"The door, good man." Marissa's voice reflected her surprise he had yet to move.

With stiff motion, as though unsure what to do, he stepped from the station and pushed through the normal-sized door built into the massive eighteen-foot-high doors. Elizabeth waited until he turned his back on her and then reached out with the hand that had been in her pocket and marked his shirt with powder. "Marissa, dear. Go to the stables and let me speak with this servant. Have them bring our horses here."

Marissa did not need to be asked twice. She tugged on her skirt and took off with a quick walk. Elizabeth smiled. The younger Marissa would have run. Her smile stopped when she turned back to the stranger. Pain seared his face. Moments he battled, and then blanched. He hurried to the station, grabbing the bucket kept for body relief and vomited. He sagged against the side of the box as he wiped his hand across his mouth.

Elizabeth narrowed her eyes as she studied him. Cruelty had been part of him once, but whatever happened drove it from him. "Can you manage this post?" She asked him.

He looked around before nodding.

"If the other one comes, do not reveal yourself." Elizabeth felt certain a second watcher from the witch lurked within Monmoore.

The sound of horses echoed through the open door. Elizabeth rubbed her hands together before pulling on her soft leather gloves for riding. "I will speak with you later." She nodded at the man.

He blinked, lips tight. "Thank you, Mistress."

Elizabeth pulled herself onto the pillion, arranging her skirt after hooking her feet in the stirrups.

"I don't recall seeing him before. Is he new?" Marissa asked. Even though she'd spread her skirts and twisted to the side, Marissa used the regular saddle Robert had procured for her.

Lady Grace, Elizabeth's gray mare, shook her head. Elizabeth clicked her tongue, and the horse moved forward.

Marissa drew her horse alongside. "The air is fresh." She took a deep breath. "Much better than the stuffy palace."

"Find Robert. He usually entertains you on days like today."

She grimaced. "He's no fun. Sat and stared at the bloody shoe all day until they left with it. Now he looks like a sod who's lost his prized dog."

Elizabeth frowned at her. "Not the language a lady uses."

"At least it is gone for a while. Do you think they will find her?"

"Oh, yes." Elizabeth nodded. *This has all been contrived for her purpose.* The witch planned well. Her spell worked like threads of a web. When Cinderella returned to Monmoore, there would be no resistance to her plans. Elizabeth watched Marissa. Or so Cinderella thought. But two things now existed in Monmoore against the spell. Marissa loved the prince, even if the girl refused to admit her feelings. And a Guardian lived among them. Two, if the captain chose to reclaim his position.

Marissa's horse brayed, stopping. Marissa held her seat. She pointed into the trees. "It's that bird, again. Tried to get Soliloquy to drop me."

Though Elizabeth could not see the creature, something menacing lurked among the branches. "We'll keep to the open field. Perhaps the bird is protecting a nearby nest." They turned onto the lane that led them around the keep to the upper field. The ancient ruin seemed more like a shadow in the overcast afternoon. Turning the corner, they heard the clash of sword on shield. The field was being used by Captain Standish and his men.

"Shall we watch?" Elizabeth asked, but Marissa was already stopping and didn't bother to answer her.

She pointed to a skirmish taking place close to the rocks of the keep. "There's Robert. Why let him fight when he's distracted? Look, he isn't even holding his shield in the proper form."

They both winced as he took a hit to the shoulder. He fell. The other soldier reached a hand to help him to his feet.

Marissa pulled her horse around. "If this is love, I want nothing to do with it. Or him." She spurred Soliloquy. Elizabeth pushed Lady Gray to follow.

19

Do something. Marissa tied the kerchief over her hair as she thanked the two maids for lighting torches in the attic. Memories of hide and seek with Robert tried to surface, but she pushed them away. "Not going to think about you. There are interesting pieces here and its time we made a list." Marissa stepped around a pile of blankets. She remembered a hand-carved walnut table sitting beneath a window. She pushed a pair of glazed chairs out of the way and found what she sought. She pulled on a bronze handle to open the large drawer. The quill pen and parchment remained as she'd left them years before. Marissa reached into her pocket for the jar of fresh gal ink and set the supplies on the table. A mystical beast carved into one of the fluted columns of the table legs gazed up at her. She shook herself, ignoring the urge to throw a blanket across the feet as she had when she was younger.

In this attic, brightest of the three on this level of the palace, Robert had told her all he remembered of his mother. Six paintings of the beautiful queen leaned against the wall, near the back corner. Marissa had spent long hours copying the poses of the elegant woman. She made a notation on the parchment before walking to the back corner. A black chest with gold rivets was set near the paintings. Marissa knelt in front of it. There was no lock. She pulled the lid up. Hinges screeched at being forced to move, but the single item within caught her attention. The thin silver sword was too long to lay flat in the chest. Its hilt, also silver, was wrapped with a leather cord. She traced a finger along delicate scrolls on the blade. "Why would someone leave you here?" Nothing in the chest gave clue to the identity of the owner. "Would be a shame to keep you in an abandoned chest." She lifted the sword from the chest and stood. Light reflecting from the blade bounced on the papered wall of the attic. "Captain Standish will know what to do with you."

She closed the lid, tossed a blanket on the floor near the door, and placed the sword upon it. She returned to the table to mark the chest on the parchment list. "What other treasures will we find, I wonder?"

Shadows crossed the room as she continued to work. An ornate high back bench hid a pair of brass candlesticks. She pushed the bench against the wall and tugged the chest in front of it. Pulling a sheet from a wardrobe, dust sprinkled over her, causing a sneeze. She wiped her face against the sleeve of her brocade dress. Moving the oak wardrobe proved challenging. Marissa huffed, leaning against the narrow side as she pushed herself backward. The thing scraped the floor as it moved, but Marissa blew hair from her face and kept pushing. Her heart thumped by the time she set the wardrobe in place against the wall beside the bench. A drop of sweat rolled down her cheek. She wiped it away as she added to her list.

She continued to scribble notes, recording furniture, ornate statues, and the contents of each chest. She dragged each object across the attic to form a new pile.

"Very industrious of you, Marissa."

Marissa looked up from the parchment, and a large smile lit her face. "Mrs. Boyde. What brings you up here?"

"Do you mean aside from the sound of a small army and bits of ceiling falling around me as I try to dust your chambers?"

"It *is* an old castle." The common excuse Marissa used for many of her antics led to the expected smile.

"Find anything interesting?"

Marissa pointed to a corner near the stairs. "That old sword. I plan to take it to Captain Standish. I'm not sure why anyone would bury it up here."

"A sword? Not the sort of thing one stores in an attic." Mrs. Boyde gave it a cursory glance, and then returned her attention to Marissa. "How can I help you?"

"You have enough work of your own."

"I'm not just a maid or your governess, Marissa. Nor am I

referring to this chore you assigned yourself. What troubles you child?"

Marissa faced the woman. Though she had no doubt of her mother's love, it was this woman who provided the daily nurturing necessary for a child to grow into a young woman. But she couldn't explain her actions to herself, let alone another person. She shrugged.

Mrs. Boyde shook her head. "Robert's not much better off than you. The pair of you have gotten yourselves into a pickle, haven't you?"

"What's wrong with Robert?"

"Perhaps you should see for yourself. I'd wash the dirt from your face and hair first, or he may not recognize you."

Marissa looked at her soot-smudged hands. "I have been busy."

"Come. I'll have the chamber maid draw you a bath. Then later, you can pull Robert from his despondency."

Marissa grabbed the sword and a brocade blanket as she followed Mrs. Boyde down the stairs.

LAURIE LEE

20

Two weeks after the ball, news reached Belton Province. An envoy of the king arrived in a few days.

"What do they mean, we have to try on a slipper?" Millie pushed against the press of people eager to see the announcement nailed to the town square post.

"What does it say?" Cinderella feigned ignorance.

A young man in king's livery held a scroll. "By order of King William, his royal majesty of the Kingdom and Northern Isles, all eligible ladies are hereby ordered to attend the slippering to take place here, five mornings hence. Neither rank nor duty will prevent any female from attending the slippering. Twenty lashes will be laid on any who impair the King's command."

"Oy heard bout this." Tanisa mumbled to the small group gathered with Millie and Cinderella. "Prince fell in love at the ball." She opened her gray eyes wide. "Someone or something tore her away. This must be how he means ta find her."

Millie scoffed. "But maids and scullery girls? Does he think one of us made it to the ball? They'll get more than a whipping if they find its one like us." Millie shook her head.

Tanisa grinned. "It'll be fun ta go. Watch da ladies en all."

"Perhaps the king will provide cake and punch for us while we wait." Cinderella teased.

Tanisa's face brightened. "Do ya think so?"

Millie slapped her on the back of the head. "Imbecile. Best take a chunk of bread and cheese with you, the king won't provide for the likes of us."

The others moved away, their excited voices dropping as they moved. Cinderella remained to examine the poster. The king's signature looked like the scrawl of an old man bound by duty. Prince Robert's appeared fresh, with thick black strokes. What would it be like to love him? To garner his affection without the trappings of spells? She stretched her hand to touch his writing, then fisted her fingers and dropped her arm to her side. What was the love of a man compared to the power of Doorin? Humans were weak. Magic remained strong, not even time could unravel its grip. Joy broiled her blood. Cinderella moved across the lane to rejoin the servants with whom she worked. She didn't notice the jarring bumps and jolts of the wagon as they returned to the estate.

On the fifth morning, cold breakfast filled the table as everyone rushed through their chores.

"We're all to go to town," an excited scullery maid exclaimed, bouncing as she ran to Cinderella. Cinderella chewed her toast. Weeks of self-imposed drudgery were soon to be ending.

"All of us," Tanisa squealed. "Sir Anler isn't pleased, but what can he do? It's ta King's directive."

"Dress in your Lord's Day finest," one of the overseers called out in a deep, loud voice. "The wagons will be hitched and prepared to depart in an hour's time."

The young women screeched and ran for their chambers. Cinderella finished her meal, and then skipped across the cobbles. Ah, the delight of a well-laid plan. She retired to her meager chamber to dress.

21

"Robert?" Marissa stared at her friend. In the few weeks that had passed, the Prince seemed overcome by a heavy weight. His ashen face was slimmer. His mouth pulled down in a frown. She crossed the veranda and grasped his hand. Unease churned within her as she noted its coldness. "You mustn't let yourself lose hope."

"Hope? What is that? I live in despair." He struggled to remove his hand from hers as though she pained him.

Marissa refused to release him. "She told you Belton Province. The soldiers and herald will have arrived by now."

"You will love her once she is here."

"I desire to understand her first, but I have no doubt she will become as a sister to me." Robert's hand warmed, and she took hold of his other hand. She could feel him relax.

He looked at their entwined fingers and tightened his hold. "I do not understand this madness," he whispered.

"None of us do. "

He breathed deep, and then turned his attention to the objects leaning against the door. "What is that?"

Marissa turned. She had forgotten about dropping the sword when she saw Robert. "I found it in the attic. I thought to give it to Captain Standish." Marissa ran to the sword and picked it up, laying it across both her hands to show it off. "Have you seen it before?"

Robert shook his head. He grabbed the hilt. "It's been ages since I practiced with Captain Standish." He brandished the sword as Marissa looked on.

"Perhaps a good fencing match is what you need? Something to relieve the angst as you wait?"

"You and I used to fence." A ghost of a smile cracked the severe lines that had taken root in his face.

Marissa laughed at that. "I'm sure the Master of Defense would provide better sport."

"Are you no longer quick on your feet? You may not have had my strength, but I lacked your dexterity and nimbleness. Have you become less in your old age?"

"Ha, sir, never remark on a lady's age nor her ability." Hands on her hips, she stomped her foot in protest to his comment. "I will meet you in the yard and we shall see what you have gained or lost since last we crossed swords."

Robert laughed, pleased with the prospect.

Marissa wasted no time in changing into an appropriate outfit for whelping a mouthy prince.

Both donned the protective gear. Robert held a capped rapier to Marissa. The hiss of blades moving through air preceded the first clash of metal upon metal as the match began. A few faltered steps ending with a whack to her backside and Marissa remembered how to parry and attack. She was faster, dancing out of his reach. Robert loosened up, his laughter filled the yard as Marissa managed to escape yet again.

Marissa dropped against the short retaining wall. Laughter and breathlessness shook her as she laid the sword across her chest. "Surrender," she cried out. "Mercy."

Robert held his hand to her, offering assistance. She allowed him to pull her to her feet. He didn't retreat, and they stood together. He lifted her mask with his other hand. Her heart pounded as he tucked a strand of hair behind her ear. He still wore his mask, preventing her from seeing his face. She couldn't read his expression.

"This is a fine blade," the fencing master called from somewhere. "Let's test it in a match." Robert pulled away from her and Marissa allowed a soldier to help her over the wall. She remained, watching the two men thrust and parry. Her breathing didn't improve. She could see Robert's muscles moving beneath his sweat-coated white shirt. Grunts, shuffling feet, murmurs of the growing crowd...they filled the air around her, and Marissa shook her head. What was she thinking?

Horse hooves thundered into the yard. "My Lord, a message has arrived." The announcement had Marissa running for the palace. There wouldn't be time for a bath.

22

Cinderella followed the other women from the manor as they entered the town square. A large tent had been set up near the well. King's soldiers and messengers hurried about their tasks. A line of women from the Belton Province snaked its way around the corner of the smithy. Rather than wait in the lengthy line, Cinderella pushed her way through the crowd to watch the proceedings under the tent. A narrow table stood near the entrance. A soldier sat, with vellum paper and gall ink with feather pen at the ready to record the name of each female. A heavy chair had been set in the shade of the tent. Its ornate mahogany wood carvings and rich velvet seat cushion intimidated the scullery maid perched at its edge. The frightened woman looked at her master standing nearby and then at the soldier kneeling at her feet. She smiled with delight when the shoe would not fit. She thanked the man who tied her leather boots and fled. The next woman screeched in anger as the slipper pressed against her toes and would go no further. Her angry squeal, along with a harsh kick to the soldier, cracked the glass. Two soldiers grabbed her, tossing her into the dirt as she screamed a flurry of foul words.

"The Prince was wise to have so many casts forged. Don't know how many slippers have been broken by this bevy of women." A soldier dropped the broken glass shoe into a box and drew a new one from the wagon. Cinderella smiled. So much effort and madness by her design. Pleasure in the day filled her.

Snickering and snorts from the huge crowd gathered around the

113

tent rose as another lady was thrown from the chair screaming. The line dwindled as the sun crossed the sky. Mugs of ale rose and fell as each new candidate sat and failed.

"Is that all?" a messenger shouted from the corner of the tent. The roped section meant for the line had emptied. Cinderella stepped forward, dropping the hood of her blue cape.

"There is one more." She stepped to the man.

"You're supposed to stay behind the rope. Should have been in line with the others."

"I was detained, and only now managed to escape." Cinderella lied with ease.

With disbelief clear in his face, he moved the rope and allowed her to enter the tent anyway.

"Name?" A soldier at a table didn't bother to look up as he waited with pen poised above the paper. A single drop of ink fell, splashing on the paper as he waited her response.

"Cinderella." She spoke with a soft voice.

He snorted. "Yeah, I've heard that a time or two today. Word travels quick, don't it? You could have saved us this trouble by mentioning it first thing this morning." He tipped his head at the seat, indicating she should move.

"I'm not certain that would have been a safe thing to do," Cinderella replied. "The ladies in that line would have demanded their own opportunity to try on the glass slipper."

The messenger looked at her and nodded. She made her blue eyes as innocent as possible, her blond curls fetching in their disarray. She could see his interest in her growing.

"If you are the prince's Cinderella, this should be an easy move." He picked up the slipper as she removed her leather shoe, revealing her slim foot. Those closest to the tent silenced as her toes slipped through the opening. The soldier looked up at her with surprise as the rest of her foot went into the glass shoe. The cast fit perfectly.

"Look, it fits."

"Her foot, the slipper isn't falling off."

"It's her. It's the prince's lady."

The murmur of voices started with those closest to the tent, rising in volume as the excited news spread through the town center. A crescendo of screams and delighted hurray filled the air.

"Bring the slipper," The messenger called to the official travelling with them.

Cinderella's eyes widened with horror, before she masked herself once again. Fury flared to life inside of her. Not only had the prince not come for her as he had promised, he'd released the glass slipper. Her hold on him wouldn't be strong.

"She's no Cinderella," an angry voice screamed.

She closed her eyes, willing herself to be patient. This scene had to play out, and then she would rectify the situation. She would not lose her prince after so much effort had gone into procuring him.

Millie pushed through the crowd and hurled herself beneath the tent. "You're not the prince's Cinderella, just trying to lie your way into a better life."

Cinderella cried out, fear ringing in her voice. The bitter hag launched over the rope.

"Worthless girl," the woman shouted as the messenger and soldiers grabbed at the crazed woman, dragging her away. Her screams rolled through the tent as she kicked and fought for freedom. "You're nothing but a base servant, listening at keyholes and spying on your betters."

The messenger slapped his hand across her cheek. "The King's decree called for every eligible lady to try the shoe. If you don't refrain yourself, I'll give you the whipping you deserve."

Cinderella watched with wide eyes as the messenger threatened and Millie wilted against the soldiers restraining her. When he returned to Cinderella and knelt in front of her, face full of concern, she made sure none of the bubbling laughter she felt showed. She held one hand to her chest. "Oh my," her voice was a whisper.

"Are you alright?" He wrapped her small hand in his, and then smiled as she nodded. He patted her hand. "You are precisely who our prince would fall in love with. I am honored to have found you." The official placed the real glass slipper in his hand. He reached for her foot and it went on as easily as the cast.

Cinderella smiled. A ray of the late afternoon sun struck her, causing the glass shoe to shoot beams of light across the well-worn ground beneath the tent. Those nearest the scene gasped at the sight. Cinderella stood, one hand on the messenger's arm for support. The blonde beauty blushed as applause started from those nearest the tent and spread like wildfire.

"Princess! Princess!" The chant thundered through the town.

Over the din, the guard looked at the crier. "Prepare a message and send the pigeon at morning's first light. The prince's bride has been found."

Cinderella pulled her packed traveling case from beneath the bed in her room at the manor. A black crow beat on the window, and she let it into the small space.

"That fool boy let the glass slipper from his sight. I will not lose my hold on him." She grabbed the bird. "You must return to Monmoore."

The bird squawked with pain, but Cinderella felt no compassion as the crow changed into a carrier pigeon. It writhed on its side. She scooped it up in her hands and set it on its feet.

"Go to him. Strengthen the spell until my arrival."

The bird fluttered through the open window. Cinderella lifted her bag and walked through the door.

23

Robert raced to the parapet housing the elevated loft for carrier pigeons. Energy brought on by the fencing matches simmered as he dashed up the twisting stairs. Fresh air dried the sweat on his face. He picked a piece of meat from the pouch provided each day by the trainers and reached for the pigeon. Everything slowed when he touched the bird. He tried to release it immediately, but his hand refused to move. Something in him fought the connection, but the image of Cinderella grew. Her eyes begged him to love her. For a moment, it was as though he held her. His heart swelled with emotion. Love overwhelmed him, rising like waves to consume him. Any thought of resistance extinguished itself. He removed the note, even though he knew what it would say.

"She is found." Robert let the note slip to the ground. "She is not a dream, nor the nightmare that plagues my sleep. She is coming."

He realized Marissa had joined him. Joy enthralled him, wiping away thoughts of fencing with his stepsister. "Mrs. Rowley must prepare the finest guest room." He walked right past her. "Everything will be perfect. I will not lose her again." Determined as he was, there was no bounce in his step as he descended the stairs.

"Does it tell who she is? Will her family travel with her?"

Marissa asked, but Robert walked past. His mutterings sounded like gibberish. What had happened? She searched the parapet and noticed a small note fluttering in the wind. With a gasp, she attempted to catch it before it could blow away. A large bird hit her in the shoulder. Screaming, Marissa grabbed the stone wall, the force of the bird causing her to lose her balance. Fear rolled through her as she glanced the ground a long distance straight down. She removed herself from the edge. The bird had disappeared. She ran to the loft, but it was empty. She shivered when she saw a black feather drift through the air to land at her feet. She hurried from the roof.

Time slowed. Hours of the day dragged. Marissa tried continuing her inventory of the attic, but a large shadow with wings crossing the window sent her to the lower floors. The large man in the cubicle watched her with tired eyes every time she crossed his path. The new serving wench touching her arm with ice cold fingers caused her to jump, spilling wine on the tablecloth. Lady DeGanne lifted a brow as Marissa slipped her hands into her lap. It wasn't until she touched the silver necklace from her father did the chill to her flesh warm.

Robert had his usual seat at the table. Marissa glanced at him. He remained pale, smudges beneath his eyes revealing troubled sleep. He focused on his food, not bothering to talk. *Fiddlesticks.* Marissa tried to enjoy her roast, but the meat lacked flavor. She pushed a potato across her plate before straightening. "Robert, come riding with me tomorrow." He ignored her. The urge to flick her fork across the table had to be tapped down. "Robert."

"Marissa speaks to you, son." King William tapped his shoulder.

Robert turned toward his father. "What?"

Marissa cleared her throat. "Ride with me tomorrow. It is still a few days before Cinderella will arrive." What food she'd managed to eat churned in her belly. "We can discuss her room, decide which prospect suits her."

"She must have the best."

"Of course. That is why I thought we could exercise the horses and talk." Marissa caught her mother's beaming smile from the corner of her eye. She turned her head to dismiss the view.

He nodded, then finished his meal in silence.

Midmorning, Marissa hesitated at the far end of the hallway. Richard straightened at his post as Abigail approached. What was she doing here? "Abigail?" Marissa called, stepping closer. The girl's dark eyes chilled Marissa, but she swallowed and gave a tight smile. "I left my riding gloves with Mrs. Haverty to mend a hole. Get them for me, please."

For a moment, Abigail's stiff posture and unwavering glare made Marissa want to wrap her arms around herself for protection. A vein in Richard's temple throbbed, but then Abigail turned away from them. His shoulders drooped. "Be careful, Miss Marissa." His voice sounded deep.

She took a step back. "Of what do you refer?"

But he returned to his post. She slipped past, keeping as much distance as she could. Once in the warm morning light, she turned back toward Richard. "If you don't see Prince Robert within the next moments, please fetch him. Remind him his promise to go riding with me."

The servant nodded. "Will you meet him at the stables?"

She nodded and turned away. The cool stable with soft light projecting through the slatted roof smelled of horse. The first waft of its stench caused Marissa to press a finger against her nose.

"Never get used to it, do you?" Robert jumped from his seat on a stall door and landed his booted feet in the hay.

"Thought we'd have to drag you from your quarters."

His lips moved in a ghost of a smile. "Sleep has been elusive."

"Fresh air will do us well." Marissa crossed to Soliloquy's stall. "Do you have your beast ready? Will only take a moment for me."

"His name is Chancellor."

Marissa swallowed the urge to giggle at their familiar scamp. "Pray he has wisdom to offer."

Chancellor was a tall, thick horse from the north with black glossy hair that moved like smooth waves onto a gentle shore. Prince Robert led him from the stall as Marissa cinched her saddle to Soliloquy. Within minutes, she walked beside Robert, their horses on either side of them. "Shall we cross the upper courtyard then take the steps to the lower fields?"

One brow lifted. "A stair challenge? Is that not how you gained a scar near your hairline?"

She rolled her eyes. "If I did nothing that risked harm, I'd have to lock myself up in the palace and never come out."

"Can't have that. The kingdom would be a lonely place without you."

There was no reason for her chest to thud at his words. "Perhaps Cinderella's coming will give me opportunity to explore more of our kingdom."

Robert opened his mouth but didn't respond. The look he gave added butterflies to her already discomfited self.

He'd never understood the phrase *warring in the soul* until now. His heart longed for Cinderella, and yet, thoughts of Marissa clouded his mind. Leave Monmoore Palace? The idea of her not being close caused an ache that did not make sense. He paused as they reached the stone Marissa used to mount Soliloquy. He waited for her to settle before pulling himself onto Chancellor using the stirrups. "We have to get past the gardens to see the guest wing."

"Lead on, sir." She waved. "If you take the stairs, I know to lean backward."

He'd had to carry her. What would it be like to hold her in his arms without blood pouring from a wound on her forehead? He shook himself, leading them between the trimmed rows of young spring lettuce. Rather than risk the stairs, he moved further afield, pressing Chancellor into a run. He could hear Marissa's laugh not far behind. They rounded the wall that divided the steepest drop from the upper courtyard to the lower. Before long, they were coming back around to the southern wing which included guest bedrooms. "Do you think she will like Monmoore?"

Marissa pulled beside him. "Who would not?"

He studied the cream-colored rock that forged the walls of the wing. "Look how the sun catches the balcony of the third window?" He pointed.

"The largest rooms are further in, but she may appreciate the long windows." Marissa frowned. "Will she be pleased with so much sunlight?"

"Her hair is golden and her skin pale." Cinderella had pressed her rosy lips against his cheek. The memory of it made his heart flutter. He faced the ridge of trees to the west. "How far are they, do you think?"

"The trees?" she asked, puzzled.

He frowned, and she blushed, an alluring color that tempted him to think of her lips against his. He looked away. "Of course, I mean Cinderella."

"She is still at least three days. Is family traveling with her? How many rooms should I prepare?"

"The missive mentioned Cinderella. No other family with her."

Marissa pushed ahead. Robert considered the line of her back and the way she held herself in the saddle. When had the little imp he'd met in the library grown into a beautiful woman? He looked at the windows of the guest rooms once more. A black bird perched on the balcony. The gleam of dark eyes sent shivers down his back. He wanted to turn and race away. Hatred and desire clawed at him across the distance.

"Robert!"

Chancellor jerked around, pulling Robert from the hold of the bird. Marissa's horse stopped beside them. She frowned at him. "What is it? Why did you not hear my call?"

"Does a bird sit on the balcony?"

She looked. "The crow?" Her lip curled with distaste. "Wherever it has built its nest, I'd like to find it and tear it down. Rid us of its foulness."

"You've seen it before?"

She nodded. "It's flown at me. Tried to knock me from Soliloquy."

There was more, some memory trying to come through, but Robert couldn't get past the image of Cinderella swimming in his mind, her large eyes glistening with unshed tears.

"We should return to the palace."

Marissa agreed. "I will get to work on preparing her room."

"Set Abigail as her waiting maid."

Marissa laughed. "Since when do you remember the name of serving girls?"

He shrugged. The name had come, yet he had no knowledge of Abigail. "The sooner Cinderella arrives, the sooner this madness will end." He faced Marissa. "I will ride out to meet her."

"Is that wise? She has all the comforts afforded royalty."

"I cannot rest until she is here. The sooner I go to her …"

Marissa sighed, then pushed Soliloquy ahead of Chancellor. He let her go. By the time he arrived at the stable, she had already disappeared inside the palace.

24

Preparing guest rooms fell to the responsibility of upstairs staff. Not this time. Marissa touched the ivy leaves of the bronze wreath on the door to the room that would belong to Cinderella until the engagement ended and she joined Robert in his rooms. Marissa opened the door, refusing to follow those thoughts further. The rose room. Crossing the space to the windows, Marissa pulled apart heavy curtains. Light spilled through the French doors leading onto the balcony.

"Marissa, this is not to be born. You are not a servant in this palace."

Lady DeGanne entered from the hallway, her protest causing Marissa to cringe. "I wanted a look at the space. Make sure it's what's best for Robert."

"For Robert? He isn't staying here."

"But the woman he thinks he loves is. As his closest friend and stepsister, it is my duty to make things ready for Cinderella."

"You would do better to put straw in her bed and clog the chimney so it smokes."

Marissa rubbed a finger through dust covering the mahogany dresser. "She has contrived her way to the palace. I doubt we can scare her away."

"You will try?"

Marissa pressed against the ache in her head as she faced her mother. "I don't know what I will do."

Lady DeGanne moved closer and rested her hand on Marissa's

cheek. "You are what Robert needs. Hear me out," she insisted as Marissa opened her mouth to protest. "I care about Robert. He has been a son to me for almost ten years. You make him happy. This other woman …" she shook her head. "If he loves her, why does he battle misery? We all do."

Marissa stepped away. "Things will change once Cinderella arrives."

"I pray they do. I will send Mrs. Rowley to you. Give her direction for what you want done. I'll not have you doing the work of a common maid." With that, Lady DeGanne swept from the room.

Marissa swished her foot back and forth. *Never could glide like Mother*. With a sigh, she turned her attention to the room. Soft hewn rose silk paper lined the upper part of the wall. A deeper hue of mauve wainscoting ended at an elevated plate rail. A trio of pictures were needed along the wall with no windows. The lounger could be situated beneath them with an ornate side table. The frames should be made of dark wood to match the thick posters at each corner of the bed.

"Your mother sent for me, Miss." Mrs. Rowley leaned on a stick as she hobbled into the room.

"You are injured," Marissa gasped, rushing across the room to assist the aging housekeeper. She wrapped an arm around her for support and helped Mrs. Rowley to a high-backed straight chair.

She sat with a sigh of relief. "Thank you, Child. I can work from here."

"Nonsense. We must return you to your bedchamber."

Mrs. Crowley wacked Marissa's knuckles. "I will do no such thing. This is the room of the intended bride for our prince. I'll not give someone else the honor of preparing it, not while these old bones are breathing." She rubbed the back of Marissa's hand as though concerned her old fingers had caused a sting. "Tell me what you want, and I will be certain everything is perfection."

Marissa pulled a stool next to the chair. "Very well. The wood needs to gleam. Have them find the orange oil." She pointed at the blank wall. "Three pictures hanging from the rail. Jelson's garden prints, I think. His colors will contrast with the rose."

"What about the border box between the bed posts?"

Marissa walked over to examine the canopy and the band around the top of the bed. Sheer curtains hung behind them, drawn back and tied at each of the posts. "The fabric is solid. No tears or sign it's been nibbled by rodents. Be sure the linens are lightly starched before pressing."

"Has the water closet been aired along with the parlor?"

"Oh, yes. Shines almost as much as my own. We do need a writing table, from the yellow sitting room, I think. Choose an upstairs maid to see to the closets. We'll need a seamstress the morning after Cinderella arrives."

"Is there a table for the balcony?"

"Have them bring a small iron set from the garden." Marissa moved to the door leading onto the balcony. At least the black crow wasn't perched, still watching. She didn't bother opening the door. She spun to face the room.

"Ah," Mrs. Rowley cooed. "It is a handsome room, though not the biggest."

"Robert thinks it has the best prospect of the gardens and woods."

"Agreed. Send me Delsea, and then nab a pair of boys in the hall. Show them the proper desk so they can bring it up." Mrs. Rowley settled back in the chair. "You may return tomorrow afternoon to review our progress."

Marissa found herself dismissed, standing in the hallway, no longer needed. The sun had not crossed its midpoint. She trekked to the lower floor for Delsea, arranged movement of the desk, and overheard Robert arguing with the king.

"My duty is to my bride. I must ride out and meet them."

Marissa knocked on the opened office door. King William waved her in, gratitude lightening the tension in his face. "Perhaps you could persuade him otherwise."

"What has she to do with it?"

The familiar sting of his words cut. Marissa smiled anyway. "We are all anxious for Cinderella to arrive. Mrs. Rowley will have her room refreshed. I will accompany her luggage once she arrives and make sure everything is set in place." Marissa took a seat across from the heavy desk. "We need something to do in the meantime."

"Like what?" King William asked.

"Tenants still need to be assessed." Not something she could do on her own. She glanced at Robert. "Together?"

His shoulders drooped. "My desire is to be with Cinderella."

"And you will be," the king reassured. "Day after tomorrow you can wait for them at the edge of our lands. Your people deserve your attention as well."

The slight reprimand had its impact. Robert nodded.

25

The mild winter had most everyone in good spirits. An older farmer with a harsh cough struggled to rise when his son brought Robert and Marissa inside their home. Marissa knelt beside him, taking hold of his hands. "Remain seated." She touched his forehead but felt no fever in his skin. "Has the cough ailed you long?"

"Much of the winter. Don't seem to bother the missus much."

"I have a jar of honey syrup. I'll give it to your son. Add a spoonful to tea with breakfast and before you go to sleep."

Robert came through the open door. "The stock of hay held up well through winter. When do the animals go to the field?"

"Still too cold at night, sir. Another month perhaps?"

Marissa grinned. "He spends too much time sparring with soldiers. Hasn't learned enough about the farms."

"Plenty of time to learn." The old man coughed.

"Get some water, Robert."

He did not question the order but stepped outside. In a moment, he returned with a metal mug filled with water. Marissa stood to the side. He handed the cup to the farmer. Marissa nodded. "Let me get the syrup."

The son, looking almost as old as his father, was outside chopping wood. Marissa lifted the satchel hanging on Soliloquy and grabbed a small jar. She took it to the son. "This should help." She handed him the jar. "Warm tea in the morning and night. Stir in a spoonful."

He nodded. "Thank you, Miss."

Robert joined her soon after, but Marissa stood beside her horse looking back at the tiny house and its growing pile of firewood.

Robert looked from her to the house and back. "What?"

"I don't know their names. What of their wives?"

"It is not your place."

"Isn't it?" Marissa gave him a hard glare. "I'm treated as a princess. Shouldn't I have a care for the people around us?"

Robert studied the farm another moment. "I attended rounds with father when I was young. He knew them. Sat and listed to tales of winter. Had gifts for them during the festivals."

"What makes us less than he?"

Robert had no answer to give, so they both mounted. The son waved. "Is everything alright?"

Marissa pulled Soliloquy around. "What is your father's name?"

"Nelman. Salter Nelman."

"Are you named for him?"

"More often called Salterson."

Robert nodded. "Speaks to the value of your father. Will you need help during spring planting?"

"We come together, my Lord. Trumpkins to the west and Penseys are north of us. Me missus is visiting her sister in that direction. Word is Ballins to the south has damage. You may want to meet with them before day's end."

Robert had a vague notion where the southernmost farm lay, so Marissa followed. Shoots of green were already marking the coming of spring.

The Ballins' property appeared deserted. One corner of the thatched roof had caved, and the front door didn't close properly. Robert dismounted but waved for Marissa to keep her seat.

"What is it?" Marissa looked around. She patted Soliloquy's neck as she felt the horse tense.

Robert knocked on the door, waited a moment, and then pushed it open. He shook his head. "The place is abandoned."

"Where could the family have gone? Shouldn't they have appealed to the king if something happened?"

"I will ask about it." He returned to his horse. "I should have done this years ago. I may have crossed paths with Ballins in town and not known him."

"You're starting now. By the time of the harvest festival, you will know your land keepers by name."

They took a different path back toward the palace. As they cut through a patch of trees, the old keep came into view.

Robert paused. "That relic looks more dangerous each time I see it. When I am king, I will tear down as much as I may without harming Monmoore.

"I would not stop you." She shivered.

He chuckled. "Still afraid of it? I thought my tour proved you had nothing to fear."

"I don't think I would feel quite as safe alone."

Thunder rumbled somewhere in the distance behind them. "Come on, before we get rained on."

LAURIE LEE

26

By the third morning, Robert was beside himself. Emotions he'd never experienced swirled like the whirlwinds that tore trees from their rooted depths. The thought of food made his stomach turn. He dressed, not bothering with the fancy knotted tie nor silver buckles on his boots. She wouldn't mind, his Cinderella.

He caught a glimpse of himself in the mirror as he hurried across his bedroom. The sight of the pale man with sunken cheeks made him stop. His eyes should have been bright with love, but the shadows in them caused the tightness in his belly to harden into pain. The image of himself faded. He was with Cinderella, dancing across the ballroom. This was love, her gazing at him as he stared down into her blue eyes. Today he would see her once more, be able to hold her in his arms again. The man of the mirror could fade away. The sooner he met up with the caravan, the better.

"Should never have let them persuade me to stay." He rushed out. The only one to meet him on his way was the strange sentry.

Richards stepped into his path. "Not a good time to be going, Sir. Fog's thick, it is."

Robert waved him away. "Fog or no, nothing will keep me from my bride." He took a step, but Richards' words made him stop again.

"Are you sure the girl here wouldn't be the better choice for you?"

Something tried to break through. The shroud that seemed his constant companion these many weeks glimmered with the thought of Marissa. There was something that needed remembering. Almost, it came to mind. He tried to think what it could be, but pain shot through his head. He wanted to tear at his hair.

"Best be going, Sir." Richards said with a sigh as he pushed Robert toward the door. "Cinderella be waiting. She's not going to let you go without a fight."

Two steps forward and the pain vanished. All thoughts aside from finding Cinderella vanished. He took to Chancellor, pushing the horse faster than he should in the fog, but he needed to get closer to his love.

The fog passed as morning progressed. Cold wisps of cloud hovered near young leaves. Robert passed through the king's lands, taking to a culvert that curved around the main road. Finally, in the distance, dust rose into the air. He stopped, breathing hard. Chancellor's sides heaved as well. He patted him. "I am sorry, my friend, but the prize will be well worth the hunt." He dismounted and crawled his way up the culvert to the road. Excitement and need caused him to quiver with anticipation.

A line of cavalry men, two abreast, marked the coming of the carriage and his future wife. An inexplicable sense of sadness welled in his chest. He shivered, and the feeling passed. Thundering hooves beat the ground as they drew nearer. Robert moved into their path. Though they slowed, the welcome was not what he intended.

"Away with you," the first soldier shouted, brandishing his sword above his shoulder.

"I have business here," Robert called back as he stepped closer.

One of the soldiers jumped to the ground, sword swinging toward Robert. "This is king's business. Step aside, or we go through you."

Robert drew his sword in an instant, and the clank of iron upon iron rang through the wooded area. A different sword blocked the soldier from a second attack as someone grabbed his arm, pulling him back. "It's the king's son, you fool." The young man snarled and jerked from his comrade's grip. Then he eyed his foe. Robert could see recognition and horror twist the soldier's face before the man knelt before him. "My Lord, I did not recognize—" the man's voice trembled.

Robert sheathed his sword and offered the terrified soldier his hand. "Far better to be prepared for an attack than to allow an enemy room to destroy."

"Forgive me."

"Forgotten. The cargo you carry is precious to me. You would give your life for her, and for that I am grateful. I must see her." Robert ran to the side of the carriage, throwing open the door.

Peace settled upon him. The young woman, though lacking in finery, was the very one who had captured his heart at the ball. Blonde hair surrounded her face. Sweet blue eyes gazed at him with adoration. She lifted her hand, and he grasped it, pressing her warmth against his cheek. The scent of her skin was a balm soothing the angst that had filled him since their parting.

"Are you well?" she asked in her soft voice.

"My world has righted itself. Welcome, my Lady, to your new home."

"We are there? We have arrived at the palace?"

"You are near the grounds. I rode to meet you."

Cinderella graced him with a gentle smile. "You found me."

"I promised I would." Robert glanced at the soldiers. "My men think I have gone mad. Come, let us finish the journey together. You must be weary of travel."

"The royal carriage is nothing compared to a market wagon," Cinderella teased. She placed a swift kiss on his cheek. "Go. I have no experience with horses, and you cannot sit with me unchaperoned."

"You won't disappear?" Fear sobered his countenance, but she shook her head.

Cinderella found more pleasure in his pale face than the warmth of his hand. Had she wondered what it would be like to love such a pup? Her lips twitched as she gripped his hand. His eyes gazed upon her with adoration. She placed a hand against his chest, pleasure filling her at the sight of Robert's devotion. "I will not disappear, I promise."

"I remain within sight of the carriage." He took both her hands, pressing kisses against her knuckles. "Nothing shall keep you from arriving at Monmoore Palace."

"I am here to stay, my love." She assured him, and then watched as he exited the carriage.

She settled on the padded bench, using the footstool to lift her feet from the floor. She leaned back with a sigh of contentment. Within the window, the sight of Prince Robert on his massive horse appeared. She waved, then said, "I am here to stay even after you are dead and gone." Excitement crept along her skin as he rode beside the carriage.

27

Robert had gone. Marissa felt the palace turn stale. The dreary view beyond her bedroom window did nothing to improve her spirit. "Nothing for it, Mars. Check Cinderella's rooms, make sure the best has been settled for her." The sound of her voice helped, even though she was alone.

The guest wing was a different part of the palace. Marissa cut through the inside hidden hallway to save time. She opened the secret door into the portrait gallery. She'd studied every one of the figures hanging on the walls. Now, the feel of their eyes watching her cross to the archway leading to the guest wing scraped against her skin. She fought the urge to turn around when she reached the other hallway. Instead, she focused on the ivy wreath of Cinderella's chamber. The bronze leaves shone. She opened the door.

The small fire in the grate took the chill from the air without making the room stuffy. Nothing caused the chimney to smoke. She twitched her lips. The scent of orange cheered the air. Woodwork gleamed, as Mrs. Rowley promised. A bowl of oranges from the hothouse sat on the desk arranged between two windows.

It was a beautiful room and the sight of it made her chest ache, making her want to cry. Marissa shivered as a chill crept across her bare skin. She pulled a pillow from the bed and hugged it against her chest.

"Are you well?"

Marissa screamed, swinging around to face the door as Mrs. Boyde burst into the room.

"You startled me." Marissa pressed her hand to her heart. Her other arm kept a firm grip on the pillow. Mrs. Boyde walked close enough to put a hand on her shoulder. She stared, searching Marissa's eyes. Marissa frowned. "What is wrong? What has happened?"

Mrs. Boyde broke her serious perusal a moment later with a happy grin. "I had the oddest feeling something horrible... but no, all is well." She patted her cheek with affection. "Don't worry, all is well." Mrs. Boyde exited the room, leaving Marissa still gripping the pillow as her heart calmed.

A new noise captured her attention, that of hooves and carriages. Her stomach turned. She closed her eyes. "This is a good thing, Mars," Marissa scolded herself. "Better to face a woman of flesh and blood rather than the illusive spirit haunting us all." Her mind whispered foe, but she refused to acknowledge the possibility. She prayed, for Robert's sake, that Cinderella would be who he hoped her to be.

The Rose Bedroom faced the back, but Marissa had no trouble imagining the greeting Cinderella would receive. Whatever luggage she had with her would be brought within minutes.

Her prediction proved correct as Derea led the small procession of a case and trunk. Marissa pointed at a far corner of the first wardrobe, indicating Derea to set the luggage there. "The modista can come this afternoon to fit the two gowns that have been hung. Cinderella must have proper apparel for dinner. As soon as you know how many helpers the mistress will have with her, make arrangements for them to stay upstairs. A workroom is already prepared in the third hall."

Derea bowed. "Yes, Miss. Have you seen her? She's a beauty, a perfect match for His Highness."

Marissa raised her brow. It wasn't the girl's place to offer an opinion. "Clear the room as soon as you can. Cinderella will desire rest after her long journey."

Marissa turned, ashamed with her sharp tone. The fault did not belong to Derea. Everyone was curious to meet the prince's mysterious lover. The sick feeling did not ease, and Marissa knew the time had come to meet the woman.

Robert did not notice the hedge of rose bushes dotting the front lawn. Nor did he notice the sea of curious servants and household members gathering outside the massive double doors of the grand entrance to the palace. With her tiny hand in his, he cared for naught but drawing his fiancé from the carriage. Her cheeks deepened to a rosy hue as he caressed her skin with his thumb.

"It is breathtaking in the daylight." Cinderella looked beyond his shoulder.

"Merely brick and stone, my dear. It is the ones we love living within the palace that matter." Robert kept her at his side as they crossed the inner ward to the undercroft. The open-air hallway ran the length of the main building to the corner tower. The murmur of voices of those gathered along the arched columns rose and fell like waves as they passed.

The ancient keep could be seen through the lowest window in the tower.

Cinderella paused. Robert placed his arm across her shoulders.

"Is it safe?" Her soft voice caused him to lean closer, and he could smell the scent of flowers clinging to her hair. He breathed before turning his attention to her question.

"The foundation of the keep is solid. It was my great grandfather who built Monmoore against the outer wall. You have nothing to fear. Perhaps you would like to explore one day?"

"Walk within those decrepit walls?"

Robert laughed at her timid reply. "There are secrets buried within the keep that have yet to be discovered. Fascinating, to walk hallways where ancients ruled."

"An adventure with you by my side?" She dipped her eyes to the scuffed stone floor, blushing. "I would like that."

Robert kissed her hand. "As would I. Come. The king waits for us." Robert led her into the main building. "This is the public area. Above us is the portrait gallery leading to the family wing and guest rooms."

Light from the open doors lining the great hallway blazed on the gilded walls and marble floor. Cinderella's golden hair sparkled when she removed the navy hood from her head. They traveled in silence with Robert mesmerized by the woman at his side. He led her into the royal meeting room. Side tables cascading with arranged blooms and greenery lined the plastered walls. A massive fireplace filled the far wall. Robert crossed the room and bowed to his father. "King William, may I present the Lady Cinderella." He placed one hand on her back while holding her hand with his other. He lifted their hands toward the king.

"It is an honor, my lady, to meet the woman who has stolen the heart of my son. You are welcome." King William accepted Cinderella's hand, foregoing the traditional act of fealty to the king.

She lifted a section of her gown and bowed with simple grace. "I am honored, Sire, beyond words."

Robert grinned like a besotted fool as Lady DeGanne stepped closer. "My Lady, may I present Cinderella."

The two women greeted each other, Lady DeGanne with a small smile and Cinderella blushing as she attempted to tidy her hair.

"Where is my stepsister?" Robert looked around the room.

"She prepares the guest room for Cinderella, insisted on seeing to it herself," Lady DeGanne replied as she motioned them to a cushioned bench.

"The room will be perfect." He smiled at Cinderella.

"You are exhausted, I am certain." Lady DeGanne sat across from them. King William stood beside the group. "How long did the journey take?"

"Many days, but the carriage is comfortable, and the accommodations—I do not believe I have ever stayed in so many pleasant rooms."

"Nothing will compare to your chamber at Monmoore." Lady DeGanne assured. She turned her attention to Robert. "Lead her to the morning room. Marissa will meet you there once she has set Cinderella's belongings in her suite."

Robert placed Cinderella's hand in the crook of his arm upon standing. They exited and took a flight of stairs to the second story landing. Cinderella, hand on the railing, gasped at the view of the grand hallway.

"Come. This is the portrait gallery that leads to the visitors' wing."

"Why does it incline?"

"We are moving from the lower ward to the upper ward. The rooms here will be on the ground level. Our chambers are upstairs. You will have a balcony overlooking the west wall down into the valley."

"Sounds spectacular. Are these your ancestors?" She looked at a life-sized portrait of a gray-haired man wearing a long black robe.

"Most of them, in one way or another. Although we did not become the direct line until my great-great-grandfather. Something about the king at that time almost destroyed the country and the keep. That monarch has all but been erased; although, I do wonder if there are trails of him in secret parts of the old castle."

"You are an adventurer," Cinderella teased. They continued their journey through the gallery, pausing for comments at the absurd garments or eccentric additions to the portraits.

"My, she is graceful. Who is she?" Cinderella stopped near the end of the hallway.

Robert gazed on the life-sized image and felt pain engulf him. "My mother, Queen Charlotte."

"Not the lady we met with the king?"

"No. Mother died when I was still a boy. A mysterious illness took her from us."

"None could save her?"

He shook his head. A strange urge to cry closed his throat. Standing before his mother, he had the oddest desire to rip Cinderella's hand from his arm. They moved on, but unrest warred within him. He felt as though claws were tearing at him, pulling him into oblivion. But the further they travelled, Cinderella planted at his side, the more the feeling ebbed, until his thoughts and desires once more revolved around her. He pointed at a hallway running in a different direction. "Our family rooms are in that direction. You will visit them during the latter part of our engagement. The guest wing is this direction." He waved at the arched opening before leading her to a different set of rooms beside the portrait gallery. They entered the first open door.

"Oh my, this is splendid."

The morning room, though more intimate in size, had several groupings of chairs and cushioned seats all covered in yellow fabrics and darker painted wood. Crown molding had been enriched with delicate carvings. A crystal and bronze chandelier hung from a round medallion. The color in the room came from soft hues of blues and greens in the Persian carpet. Landscape paintings adorned the walls. Open French doors flooded the room with light.

"It is a pleasant place to meet with family and close friends. The next room is the library."

Cinderella shook her head. "It is so much. How will I ever be worthy to stand at your side?"

"You are all that is lovely." Robert cradled her hands with his own. "Do not be intimidated by these things. You are more precious. You have the bearing of royalty, my love. People the realm over will adore you."

"They will not fear me?" Her lips twitched.

"Fear you?" He laughed. "It would be easier to fear a butterfly."

She slapped him lightly. "I hope to have more sustenance than a butterfly."

"You are grace and beauty. None who meet you could help but fall in love with you."

She smirked. "I am that enchanting?"

"You stole my heart the night of the ball. I will offer my life for yours."

She placed her hand upon his cheek. "My Robert. How long must we wait to be wed?"

"A royal engagement is forty days. Lady DeGanne will supervise the celebrations and feast."

"Of which there will be many. The days will pass in a blur." Marissa interjected, surprising the couple. She stepped back as the other woman twisted around with a harsh scowl on her face. The unsettling glance faded in an instant, and Marissa wondered if her over-active imagination had conjured the expression. She pasted a smile on her face and walked closer.

"Marissa. I did not hear your approach." Robert moved to her with his hands outstretched in welcome. The warmth of his touch caused her stomach to flop, but she smiled to hide her confusion. He held on to Marissa with one hand and took Cinderella's hand with his other. "Cinderella, my love, I would like you to meet my dear friend, Marissa."

The two women greeted each other with a nod. Robert remained impervious to the chill settling around them.

"I confess, I thought you would be older." Cinderella's soft voice wrapped around her.

"I am the closest in Monmoore to Robert's age, but still four years his junior. I have been eager to meet you." Marissa lied. She linked her fingers behind her back and took a breath to calm her muddled thoughts. "Your room has been set to rights. Would you like me to show you the way?"

Cinderella snaked her arm around Robert's. "I am tired. And a fresh gown would feel delightful."

"You will find the first wardrobe has a pair of simple muslin gowns. The modista will meet with you later this afternoon and then tomorrow."

"With me?"

"For measurements, of course. She'll fit your gown for this evening and then start a fresh wardrobe for you. She will create a divine trousseau."

"I will not know what to think or say. You will be there with me?"

Marissa nodded. "I promise. Come, let me lead you to your room."

Robert didn't seem eager to release Cinderella, but she managed to slip from his hold and move closer to Marissa, linking arms with her. "You are all that is kind. I had not anticipated such a warm welcome. My flight from the ball must have given you cause for concern."

Though taller, Marissa felt small and plain beside the delectable Cinderella. "Robert has found you, and all is forgiven. I wish you both great joy." They walked in silence up the flight of stairs to the guest wing of bedrooms. The long hallway had a series of doors on both sides, and Marissa stopped at the first room on the left. She touched the bronze wreath of ivy.

"This is how you know which room is yours. Each door has a different knocker." She opened the door and stepped aside, allowing Cinderella to enter the chamber. "There are two rooms, and a water closet. Derea will come to light the evening fire in your sitting room grate. Let her know what time you would like the morning tray delivered. They will set it upon the desk."

The small sitting room had the mahogany desk carved with roses and a padded high-back chair upholstered in apricot fabric. The entrance to the sitting area was flanked by two wardrobes of the same wood and carvings as the desk.

"The chest of drawers in the water closet contains your unmentionables. The water basin is full, so you may refresh yourself. Miss Callie will be your lady's maid."

"It is so much," Cinderella touched the amber duster on the bed.

"It is a beautiful room. I hope you enjoy staying here for the engagement." Marissa returned to the door. "The palace can be overwhelming at first, but you will learn to love it as I have. I will meet you at the second bell for dinner."

"And Robert?"

"He will meet us at the stairs and escort you to the dining hall. There is time to rest, if you like."

Cinderella curtsied. and Marissa hurried through the doorway, clicking it shut with a sigh of relief. Forty days loomed like a shadow over her. She didn't dare think of the eternity to follow after Cinderella and Robert wed.

Marissa made her way to her own room, entered with a sigh of relief, and leaned against the door. Emotion raged, yet her thoughts were too muddled to give word to any of them. A chair scooted in the adjacent room.

"It's just me," Mrs. Boyde called. "Didn't want to startle you again."

Marissa crossed to the doorway into the lounging area of her suite. Mrs. Boyde was closing a book. Her smile and steady gaze calmed Marissa.

Mrs. Boyde tucked the slim book into a pocket. Her brows lifted. "You have met her?"

Marissa groaned. "She is beautiful and sweet. Her voice is soft, and I found nothing vulgar in her manners."

Mrs. Boyde tilted her head. "You think she is likeable?"

Doesn't matter. Nothing will compel me to like her. Marissa didn't dare speak her thoughts. Why should she dislike the woman Robert selected as his bride?

Mrs. Boyde smiled. "You have worked hard today to get things ready. Have a rest. I will return before dinner and fix your hair."

Marissa groaned. "I am too wound to rest."

"That is why I provided a small glass of wine," Mrs. Boyde motioned to the table beside the bed alcove.

Marissa didn't think it would work, and yet, found herself being roused a few hours later, much refreshed. She grinned as she stretched. "Are you still here?"

Mrs. Boyde folded a thin blanket Marissa had tossed onto the floor. "I have been about my business and have returned to set you to yours."

"What business would that be?"

'A heated bath first. You have a dinner to attend. Your mother has been prodding servants all afternoon."

Marissa nabbed a robe from the wardrobe beside the water closet. "Why? Embarrassing Cinderella will do none of us any benefit."

"She thinks she is helping you."

With that, Marissa went into the bath. She did not lounge long in the rose-scented water. Mrs. Boyde had not yet returned to design her hair, so after wrapping herself in a plush towel she stood next to the door leading onto her balcony. She could just see the edge of the keep to the far left and the pond where she and Robert had learned to fish. Not the sort of thing a girl should do, but she'd been more interested in seeing how far she had to tilt the boat before Robert fell into the water. Memories of his furious attempt to toss her out of the boat while he floundered in the water lightened her mood.

"I know that look." Mrs. Boyde interrupted. "You're either remembering a bit of devilry or plotting some."

"I reminisce, nothing to plot presently."

"Yet. Have a seat at the dressing table."

The white desk with four sets of drawers held a variety of hair tools, clips, scarves, wraps, and jewels. Mrs. Boyde selected a set of silver clips and pins.

"I was thinking of wearing the necklace from my father," Marissa slid her finger over one of the clips. "Will these match?"

Mrs. Boyde brushed through a long lock of her hair, twisting it around a curling rod that had heated in the grate. "I don't think that necklace is the one to wear tonight. We are doing simple and understated."

Marissa looked at herself in the scalloped mirror. Mrs. Boyde was pinning her long hair shorter and then using the clips to arrange the curls. "Cinderella's choices are simple. Would not do for me to make her uncomfortable."

"You have a kind heart, Mars. Even if you find you cannot like the woman, I do not think you will cause her unease."

The words weren't meant as a reproach, but Marissa felt them in her heart. If Cinderella felt she did not belong, she wouldn't stay, would she? Robert would be hurt, and *that* she could not bear. Mrs. Boyde finished dressing her hair. Tawny curls framed her face.

"I will wear the brown linen." Marissa set the fancier dress back in the cupboard. The high-waisted gown had a wide silk ribbon that tied in a bow at her back. She looked pale against the darker fabric. "Will this work?"

Mrs. Boyde raised a brow. "You are charming, as you know."

Marissa scoffed. "Thank you. I doubt I will earn many compliments once Cinderella is in full form."

Mrs. Boyde pointed at the clock on the wall. "You will take her to dinner?"

"We are to meet Robert at the stairs."

Mrs. Boyde took Marissa's hand. "Take care. Do not let her rankle your peace."

Marissa squeezed. "I will be my charming self."

When she arrived at Cinderella's door, no one answered. She peeked inside and found the room empty. As she turned to leave, a flash of light captured her attention. A small mirror had replaced the middle picture. The size and shape of it were ordinary enough, but looking on it caused her to feel cold—the bitter shivery cold of a north wind at twilight. She rushed out of the room, rubbing her hands on her arms.

28

The splendor of the dining hall caused Marissa to pause at

the entrance. A string quartet played from the balcony. Towering candlesticks of wrought iron placed around the long table caused the room to glow.

"Your mother must have had servants digging through the cellars for a week." Robert teased as he leaned against the door jam. "Are you coming in or will you stand here gaping like a commoner?"

"I'm surprised your future bride is not at your side." Marissa accepted his arm and glided into the dining room. His touch dislodged the remaining chill. "I stopped at her room, but it was empty."

"So long I have waited, I could not bear to be separated longer." Robert motioned to where Cinderella listened with rapt attention to King William. "Father has her. I've heard that story more times than I care to recount. As have you, I am sure."

Marissa laughed, nodding. A glance at the table made her sigh. Five settings of complicated design in silver and porcelain arranged at each place kept the grand space from feeling empty. "I will have to thank Mrs. Boyde for her lessons on table manners."

Robert pressed her hand. "Will you help Cinderella? I cannot bear the thought of her being embarrassed her first night at the palace."

Marissa felt her heart pause at Robert's earnest gaze. Though her head agreed, her heart yearned for something different. A servant brought a tray of crystal and pewter goblets. Marissa took one, giving the red liquid a quick sniff. She wrinkled her nose. Robert lifted two glasses and crossed the room, offering one to Cinderella.

Marissa joined her mother. "The table is resplendent this evening. Unusual for a family gathering. Would that be your doing, Mother?"

Lady DeGanne barely smiled, but her eyes glittered with humor. "A fine display of royalty, do you not think?"

"More than I may find useful. What if I am the one who fails to use the proper fork?"

"You will be fine." She patted Marissa's hand.

King William stood, and the room silenced. Marissa and Lady DeGanne gave him their attention.

He raised his arm. The goblet in his hand glittered in the candlelight as he offered a toast. "To Cinderella. May your engagement bring you all the joy my son desires for you both. When the two months have passed, you will become his wife and our future queen. God save the future queen."

Shouts followed the declaration, and then the small group lifted their glasses at the King's request. Marissa sipped the wine, trying to appreciate the pretty blonde whose cheeks were red with embarrassment.

Cinderella noticed her watching and moved across the room. "I have never been so nervous before in my life," she whispered to Marissa.

Marissa grinned, bending to reply. "Your manners are above and beyond my own. I think you've had practice."

Cinderella's countenance turned pensive. "I was born a gentleman's daughter. Father was a good man." She shook her head and would say no more.

"What did you do to upset my bride?" Robert surprised them, wrapping his arm around Cinderella. The young lady rested her head upon his shoulder for a moment before straightening.

Marissa held up her hand. "I did not intend to harm. I think I said something that reminded her of her past."

"It is not her fault," Cinderella agreed. "My father, we were close when I was young. It was him and myself. Mother died before I could remember her. But then he remarried." Her nose twitched.

"My stepmother was a cruel woman with no affection. When Father died, I was left to her mercies. Which were few."

"Cruel?" Lady DeGanne repeated as she and King William joined the trio.

Cinderella's eyes widened, drawing them in. "I never understood her reasons. She worked me as a servant. After the ball, she traded me in hopes my godmother would never be able to find me." She faced Robert, adoration shining in her eyes. "I know not what she would have done if she had known of you. But you found me anyway, just as you promised."

He wrapped his hands around hers. "I will always be here for you. You have nothing to fear."

"But what of your father's family? Did they care naught for your plight?" Marissa interjected. The sight of their joined hands unsettled her.

Cinderella's gaze turned to Marissa. "I don't believe there was anyone else. Father never mentioned brothers or sisters."

"We are your family now. You will never be alone again." Robert pressed a quick kiss to the top of her head.

The dinner bell rang, and they walked to the dining table. Marissa sat beside Cinderella. Robert sat across from them next to Marissa's mother. King William stood at the head of the table until all were seated.

Marissa hinted at the proper utensil to be used with each course. The first course, roasted hare with rosemary glaze, filled the room with its pungent smell. Sugar plums and boiled potatoes dotted the edge of the plate. Marissa tapped the outside fork before she cut into a plum and lifted the silver utensil to her mouth. She closed her eyes for a moment, savoring the rich burst of flavor from the blanched fruit. She turned the fork upside down and left it overhanging the plate. She smiled as Cinderella mimicked her actions.

A page dressed in white presented the second course, eliciting a round of applause from the diners. Upon a large oblong platter sat a huge turkey. Its feet had been dipped in gold. The tips of feathers remaining on its wings had been painted blue and yellow. A lawn had been created beneath the bird, using wild greens from the garden. Radishes cut into roses, carrots carved into leaves, and a fanciful bird fashioned from melon decorated the greenery.

Cinderella placed her hand on Marissa's shoulder as she leaned forward for a better view. Marissa shivered. She stopped herself from rubbing the spot once Cinderella released her. A queasy sensation burned her stomach, and she picked at the delectable selection of food from the platter. A sorbet dish replaced the platter, and Marissa fiddled with the spoon. She moved her hands to grip her fingers in her lap when she noticed her mother's frown.

"You are so kind to me," Cinderella leaned to whisper to her.

"We are soon to be sisters." Marissa stared at the uneaten scoop of sorbet decorated with fish-shaped jellies. "I have never had a sister before."

"You must have met all manner of interesting people growing up."

Marissa shook her head. "Quite the contrary."

"But you live in a palace. There must have been nobles and princes visiting from other countries." Cinderella stared.

Marissa laughed. "Little girls weren't allowed to attend royal functions." She shrugged her shoulders. "I'd rather spend my time fencing or galloping through fields and woods on Soliloquy."

"Not I," Cinderella shook her head. "I want to wear beautiful gowns and dance with royalty." Her nose wrinkled with self-derision. "Foolish daydreams."

Lady DeGanne stood, disturbing their conversation. "Shall we retire to the drawing room?"

Two servants held open the doors on the far side of the room. Lady DeGanne led the way, and Marissa allowed Cinderella to take her place behind her mother.

"She is enchanting, my boy, as you described." King William held a crystal tumbler with brandy toward Robert.

Robert dragged his attention from the sway of Cinderella's gown. "What?" He shook his head, fighting against the cloud now residing in his mind. He had little memory of the dinner except images of Cinderella. His desire to go with her drew him to his feet.

The king pressed a hand against his shoulder with a laugh. "You've enough time to follow, son. Allow the ladies time to talk. She has no knowledge of castle life. Lady DeGanne and Marissa will help her adjust."

Robert felt a semblance of calm at his father's touch. "I am a stranger to myself."

The king nodded. "Love can do that. I remember when I first met your mother. I came alive the moment we touched."

"Did you feel bound to her?"

"Bound?" He shook his head. "Free is a better way to describe... her love loosed everything that kept me from who I was meant to be."

Robert frowned. Free? He felt bound to her... to Cinderella. *Marissa's the only one who's ever made me feel free to be myself.* A faint touch brushed against his forehead. The wayward thought flew into the dark, and his focus remained with Cinderella. Desire for her pulsed, and he gripped his glass. "What of the engagement period? Was it hard to bear?"

"I struggled, I will not lie. But I also understood the expectations and obligations I had to my people." He met Robert's gaze. "Our people."

"I understand," Robert said with a sigh. "I wish I could marry her tonight."

"She is a beauty, no doubt, but no passion is worth jeopardizing the power you hold, nor your place of honor as Prince Regent. Our people deserve time to adjust and prepare."

Robert finished drinking his brandy. "Have we given them enough time?"

The three women sat in the parlor, their dark dresses contrasting with the soft fall tones of the setae and chaise lounge. Cinderella sipped her sherry as she looked at Marissa. "The king is a delightful man."

"Mother chose well. I couldn't imagine a more caring stepfather." Marissa glanced at her mother.

Lady DeGanne shrugged. "We made a choice for the good of our children. You needed a father in your life."

Cinderella sat up. "Soon he will be my father as well."

Instead of the intense dislike she'd experienced earlier,

Marissa's feelings toward Cinderella warmed. She watched the young woman pluck at the fabric across her lap, as though she pulled a long, very thin piece of thread. She tilted her head. "How did you end up at the king's ball?"

"You wouldn't believe me. I don't believe me, except I'm here. It had to have happened." Her eyes widened, inviting them into her confidence. Marissa couldn't keep herself from leaning forward.

"I have a godmother. Someone I never knew about. She argued for days with my stepmother before agreeing to pay her. I don't know how much, but it must have been a great deal."

"You left in such a hurry." Marissa interrupted. "If you were under the protection of a benefactor, why?"

"I had four hours. Four glorious hours dressed as a princess, dancing in a ballroom. I never intended to meet Robert. But I did, and oh, how time flew. Before I understood what had happened, I had to leave."

"What woman would limit you to four hours at such an event? Tell me her name."

Marissa startled at her mother's harsh voice.

"No, do not be upset." Cinderella hurried to lay a hand on Lady DeGanne's arm. "I agreed. When the night was over, I had to return home. The enchantment was gone, but I had hope. Hope that Robert would find me. Imagine my surprise when word of the glass slipper spread. I had no idea where I lost it. It is a sign that Robert found it."

"A miracle." Marissa agreed.

A knock at the door marked the arrival of the king and Robert. Robert all but ran to Cinderella's side when the door opened. Marissa turned her head rather than watch him pull Cinderella close. Cinderella hid a yawn behind her hand.

Marissa agreed, the night had gone on quite long enough. She caught her stepbrother's attention. "Robert, our guest tires. I will show her to her chamber."

The gentlemen stood first, and then Cinderella looped her arm with Marissa's.

"A peaceful evening to you all," Marissa offered her farewell and stumbled as the two of them exited the parlor. She walked in silence as Cinderella chatted.

Cinderella pointed at a painting. "Odd dresses to wear. They do not appear at all comfortable. We would need a barrage of maids to prepare us for the day. Have you explored the keep? Robert showed me from the lower hall. Do you think it is dangerous? Would there be ghosts?"

Marissa was grateful to see the corridor turn ahead, leading into the guest wing.

"I cannot believe I shall one day be queen of Monmoore." Cinderella whispered as they moved through fixed stares of ancestral portraits.

Marissa glanced at the image of Robert's mother and found courage to talk with Cinderella. "What manner of legacy would you wish to leave your people?"

"Legacy? Me? I would whisper words of peace in the king's ear."

"There are a great many things a queen can do for the betterment of her people."

Cinderella's eyes narrowed. "Is peace not a worthy cause?"

"Peace saves lives but for what? What do we do with those who no longer need to fight wars? What do we do with those who no longer make weapons? We have to give life that will survive in peace, not just war."

Cinderella stopped and focused on Marissa. "You would make a fine queen. Why not take Robert for yourself?"

Marissa shook her head, ignoring the thump of her heart. "Robert and I are friends. He has been my older brother and my confidant. I adore him, but my feelings are nothing compared to the bond between you."

Cinderella offered a pretty smile. "Your honesty is refreshing."

They stopped at the doorway with the knocker of intertwined leaves. Cinderella traced the swirl of leaves with her finger. "I really am here."

Marissa backed away, a fresh breath of air sweeping across her pale cheeks. "Rest well, tomorrow will bring its own circumstances." Marissa walked away.

The dim hallway crept with shadows. She felt them sweep against her bare arms, and shivers raced through her. She moved away, not caring to look back to see if Cinderella watched from the open doorway of her room.

Cinderella watched from the doorway as Marissa ran down the hall. Unlike the others bending to her will, this girl somehow fought the spell. "Not just you, is it? Something else is working here?" She whispered her questions at the receding figure. Thick webs hung unseen throughout the palace, but not everywhere. A little challenge? She stretched up and plucked a silvery web running along the ceiling. "Come to me, my pets."

"You require more than I?" Crow wrapped his arms around her, pulling her into the room.

Cinderella turned, smiling up at him. "You are not a pet, dearest. I must have eyes throughout the palace."

"What do you expect to see?"

"The source of what troubles me most." She narrowed her eyes. "Have you not noticed opposition to the spell?"

"Light will always war against darkness."

A knock sounded at the door and Cinderella stepped out of his arms. "Let them in."

Crow obeyed her bidding. When she turned, Abigail stood in the room. "Where is Richards?"

The younger woman shrugged. "He keeps away from me."

There is something here. Cinderella walked into the sitting room. "My maid will arrive soon and neither of you can be here. Keep watch and let me know the moment you see or hear something suspicious." She waved Abigail away. "Crow, I want you to lead the prince's stepsister into the keep. If you can get her to the ramparts, you know what to do."

"I've frightened her, to be sure. Do you think killing her this early is wise?"

"You won't kill her, not yet anyway. We must drive her away." She took hold of his hand. "Fly."

Muscles in his face knotted as the shift from man to bird started. Cinderella relished the feel of his pain. She released him, and the black bird left through the window as a soft knock sounded from the ivy wreath against the door.

29

Marissa rested her forehead against the cold wood of her own door before entering the chamber beyond. Candlelight flickered from bronze sconces lining the walls in both rooms. The linen pattern of ivory and blue above half-wall paneling created a sense of calm, easing the unsettled feelings coursing through her. With a sob of confusion, she sank into a chair in front of the large mirror at her dressing table. She rubbed two fingers against each temple, but the stuffy feeling in her head did not ease.

"Are you well?"

Marissa opened her eyes and offered a wan smile to Mrs. Boyde's reflection. "What's not to be well?"

"Dinner appeared spectacular."

"The walls have eyes?" Marissa's smile brightened.

She returned her head to her arms as Mrs. Boyde picked up the ivory-handled brush and began sweeping it through Marissa's thick tresses. She heard the ping of tiny pins hitting the desk as they were pulled from her hair.

"Is Robert's intended as he described?" Mrs. Boyde asked as she continued working the brush through Marissa's hair.

Marissa smirked. "She is beautiful. And charming."

"With a sad tale to tell."

"Walls have ears as well."

"Secret passages were built for a purpose. How else would we know what goes on? I know a certain young girl spent her share of time exploring many of Monmoore's secret places."

"Can't keep anything hidden from you, can I?" Marissa sat taller, her heart lighter. Mrs. Boyde continued dressing her hair for night. Marissa tilted her head as a white cloth was wrapped around a braid. She inspected her mirror image, moving her head from one side to the other. "She is beautiful." Her heavy sigh caused a wayward wisp of hair to tickle her ear. "I always wanted hair the color of sunlight."

"Yours is cocoa mixed with cream. It is as God intended."

Marissa's smile showed white, straight teeth. "I am perfectly made."

"In God's eyes and your family's. If not your own."

"I have been blessed in my family, especially in you."

Mrs. Boyde's gray eyes turned serious. "You are sweet, Mars. Do not allow Cinderella's power to change that."

Marissa bit the edge of her fingernail, an idea taking shape. "Cinderella's tale is a sad story. I remember how I felt losing Father, but Mother did not choose a horrible replacement. King William cares for me."

"Cinderella was not so fortunate?"

"Her stepmother was a wicked woman, taking her from the privilege of being her father's daughter. She knows nothing of his family."

"A horrible fate for any orphan."

"What if we found them for her?"

Mrs. Boyde's bun loosened as she shook her head. "That endeavor would be dangerous."

Marissa huffed. "Better than remaining here."

"She bothers you that much?"

Hands raised, Marissa tried to explain the anxious edge of her feelings, but no words came out. She dropped her hands to her lap with a sigh.

"You are tired, my dear. Rest. Tomorrow is a new day. Let us consider the idea then."

An hour after Mrs. Boyde took her leave, Marissa stared at the swirl of light and dark across the ceiling as she lay beneath the silken blue spread. The alcove surrounding her bed hid most of the single lantern flame that remained lit by her door. She frowned, trying to recall events of the evening, but her thoughts were a blur. *What happened?* It wasn't until Mrs. Boyde brushed through her hair that her mind cleared.

Marissa closed her eyes and let her mind drift. Cinderella was different than she imagined. They had much in common. Fathers who died when their daughters were young. It had been too long since Marissa had thought of her father. He liked to smile and laugh. Even when he tried to be stern, usually in the presence of Mother, his eyes would twinkle. What color had they been? Lighter than hers. A memory surfaced.

Father crouched in front of her, hands on her shoulder. Dark brown hair blew across his forehead in an afternoon breeze. "Are you going to be a great rider someday?"

Marissa nodded, sending her seven-year-old pigtails flying. "I will Father, promise."

"You've seen the saddle your mother uses. Makes her sit sideways on the horse? You'll never be able to gallop in that seat. Won't get to feel the wind tugging on your tails." He pulled one of her pigtails, causing her to giggle.

"Is there a better seat to use?"

"We'll get you a real saddle."

Her heart leapt. "Like yours? I'll be able to race across the fields? Jump fences?"

"No fence jumping, young lady." He held her arms. "Too dangerous. If a horse knocks his hoof on a post, he'll be lame."

"I would never hurt my horse, promise."

He kissed her forehead. "You're a good daughter, Marissa. Nothing like Cinderella. Don't believe in her."

Marissa jerked up in bed, heart pounding. Oddly real, his telling her. Desire to escape the palace grew. She hadn't expected to care so much. Her cheeks were damp, whether from memories of Father or the woman that had come to the palace, she could not tell. Candlelight glowed in the next room. The soft light calmed her until something struck the window.

LAURIE LEE

30

Elizabeth Boyde tossed the web-twined brush into the library's burning fire. The hiss of evil rose like a ghost through the chimney. She bowed her head.

"Elizabeth."

The intruder's voice calling her first name pulled her from prayer. She frowned at the man standing inside the doorway. "Nicholas." She acknowledged Captain Standish. "What are you doing here?"

"Darkness sits heavy this night." He crossed the room with long strides. Shoulder-length hair of dark gray and silver stilled as he reached her side.

She returned her attention to the green flame struggling against the fire. "You know what has arrived?"

"The witch is powerful." He tossed a handful of willow bark into the fire. A hissing scream blew past them and the green dissipated.

Mrs. Boyde knelt in front of the fire, using the iron to spread the coals. She raised her eyes to Nicholas. "Marissa needs to leave. She is in danger."

"And Robert?"

"Cinderella has thirty-nine days until the wedding. She will allow no harm to come to him until the deed is finished."

"Marriage is the Master's plan."

"She will use it to gain what she desires." Elizabeth jabbed at a log. "Until then, Robert remains deep within her spell."

Nicholas shrugged. "Perhaps not as deep as she would like. He fights it."

Her brows raised. "Are you certain?"

He nodded.

Elizabeth accepted his assistance to stand. "He is in love with another." *Did Robert care for Marissa as much as Marissa cared for him?* Joy flooded her heart. "Cinderella will haunt his steps and her evil will invade Monmoore. This is not the danger Marissa's father feared, but he was right to set a Guardian with her."

Nicholas shook his head. "I am no longer a Guardian."

"The sword Marissa found in the attic belongs to you. You will protect the prince with your life."

He agreed with a nod of his head, and then looked over her shoulder at the window. "What is that?"

Elizabeth turned her attention to where he pointed. The window showed the stone of the keep bathed in moonlight. She doused the lights in the room.

"Light moves in the keep." Nicholas' voice reverberated with urgency.

They watched. Mrs. Boyde's breath tight in her chest. "There." She pointed to a figure in white passing a thin window. "Marissa." She shoved Nicholas toward the door. "Wake Robert, he will know how to get to her." She followed him from the room.

Robert struggled for breath, but he refused to slow. The ancient stone of the keep had been used to form narrow staircases leading to the highest tower. Captain Standish's urgent call had pulled him from a shadowy nightmare. The cold touch of air dried his dampened skin, but fear lingered. He could barely hear the patter of feet far above him. Marissa feared the height of the tower. What drew her in the dark of midnight?

Black sky surrounded the open causeway at the top of the tower. Moonlight shown over the scene as Robert burst through the doorway from the stairs. Marissa stood at a low rise looking into the field. One arm linked a stone high rise, yet she leaned into the empty space before her.

"Marissa?" Robert kept his voice soft, stepping closer. "What brings you so near the edge of the tower?"

She gave no response, merely bent a little further. Robert felt his heart squeeze into his throat. He moved closer, not wanting to startle her, yet fearful she was but a moment from plummeting to her death.

"Marissa," he called again.

"Robert," she whirled around. "Did you see it? Is that why you are here?"

"See what?"

Marissa looked over his shoulder with a gasp of fear.

A dark shape buzzed past him, ramming Marissa in her right shoulder. She teetered, her arm swinging wildly. Robert grabbed her waist and jerked her from the edge. Her scream muffled against his chest as she fell into him.

She pulled away a moment later. Robert stared at her, heart pounding. Seconds passed without a word between them. Her face flushed, and then she turned and ran for the stairs. He started to follow when a loud squawk nabbed his attention. He spun. A large black crow bounced across the mottled rock of a high rise. It squawked again. The air in his lungs sat heavy on his chest. Robert tried to pull away, but his feet remained rooted to the cold stone. The bird hopped once more, its shrill voice calling him forward. He fought the desire to move closer. He could feel the touch of evil clinging to the air. He tried but was helpless to ward against it. A shroud descended through his mind, driving thoughts of Marissa into a forgotten realm. His thoughts as he descended the stairs were of Cinderella.

LAURIE LEE

31

Marissa raced down the stairs, cold stone pounding against her bare feet, bringing tears to her eyes. Fear continued to course through her. What had caused her to behave so? She screamed when someone grabbed hold of her as she hurtled through the broken doorway of the keep into the upper courtyard.

"It is I."

The familiar sound of Mrs. Boyde's voice shot relief into her. With a sob, she stumbled into the older woman's embrace.

Not much later, Mrs. Boyde placed a warm mug of creamed tea in her shaking hands. Sitting on a lounger with candles burning in their sconces throughout her bedroom, the past hour seemed more like a jumbled dream. She sipped the brew, inhaling a whiff of cinnamon.

Mrs. Boyde drew another chair close. "What caused you to enter the keep?"

Marissa looked at the window. "I was sleeping when something crashed against the glass. I thought it part of the dream."

"You opened the window?"

She nodded. "A bird flew into the room. It landed there, on the towel bar near the water closet." Her thoughts raced. *How had something that huge settle in such a slim space?*

"What did it do?" Mrs. Boyde encouraged her to continue.

"I…" She paused, wrinkling her forehead. It couldn't have talked to her, it must have squawked. "And then it flew through the opening above the door. Just as though it knew the direction it was going. I had to follow it." She could tell Mrs. Boyde wanted to say something, but the kind woman kept silent. "Robert found me on the tower roof. He saved me from falling, but what of him? He walked past us without a word when he came down. Is he angry with me?"

"Anger is not his problem, I fear. Perhaps your idea of finding Cinderella's family is a good one."

Marissa glanced at Mrs. Boyde over the rim of her cup. "Do you think there is something peculiar about her?"

"Whatever do you mean?"

"I'm not quite sure. Monmoore feels strange having her here."

"There are stranger things beyond the protection of the palace walls. Are you prepared to face life outside the curtain wall?"

"I feel I must. How difficult can it be? We ask Cinderella for the name of her father's family and track down her missing relatives. We invite them to Monmoore."

"And if her stories have been lies?"

"The truth is better than what we have now." Marissa placed her mug on the side table and stood, agitation visible in her short, tight stride. "Robert behaves like a besotted fool. If this is falling in love, I want none of it."

"There is much you do not know, but now is not the time. Are you prepared to sleep? I will remain in the sitting room, so do not fear being on your own."

A yawn gripped her, and then Marissa laughed. "Real sleep would be a blessing."

Morning light showed through the crack in her curtains, and Marissa rose from her bed. Twisted sheets glimmering with sweat revealed her struggle throughout the night. The chambermaid had not yet arrived when she sat at her dressing desk. She reached for her brush, but it was not resting upon the marble top in its usual place. Instead, she placed her chin in her hand and leaned closer to her reflections.

Her hair was a few shades lighter than cocoa. Her skin looked soft, smooth, and pale as expected of a royal lady. Her eyes were a cross between brown and green. She pursed her lips. A memory of

Robert's arms around her rose to mind, and color suffused her cheeks. She looked away.

Feet pattered across the tiled floor, reminding Marissa of Mrs. Boyde's promise to stay the night.

Mrs. Boyde grinned. "I thought you would have slept longer."

"Thank you for staying. I feel rested." Marissa laughed as Mrs. Boyde yawned. "You could not have been comfortable. Go, get some sleep."

"What of your plans?"

She shrugged. "Find a way to convince Mother I am ready to go into the world on my own."

Mrs. Boyde shook her head. "Not on your own. I will go with you."

"Are you sure? It may not be an easy journey."

"Your father charged me with your care. There was not an age limit. I will be quite content as your travel companion."

"Then go rest. Once permission has been granted, we will not have much time until we are on the road."

"I should at least help you dress."

"I think I can manage." Marissa shooed her from the room and then breathed in the quiet. *Can I do this?* She looked at her reflection in the mirror. *For Robert?* It wasn't how she'd imagined going out into the world, but it would be better than having to live through the engagement of Robert and Cinderella. She didn't push herself to think why that was.

Marissa selected the simplest dress she could don without assistance. *I can join Mother for a cup of chocolate in her rooms.* She exited her chamber. The knocker on her mother's door was a wreath of roses. Rather than the bronze like most of the other doors, this wreath was red and green. She knocked twice, her usual habit, and entered.

While Marissa's rooms were well-supplied, Lady DeGanne's apartment reflected her high honor of being the king's wife. The ceiling was twice the height of the other bedrooms. Great tapestries countered the pale-colored walls. Golden cherub frieze looked down from the coffered ceiling. The main room had a sitting area with white couches on a blue rug woven in silk and wool. A breakfast table draped with a white cloth was set with morning tea. But her mother was not sitting at tea. Marissa was surprised to see her staring from the long window, shoulders drooped.

"Mother?" Her voice sounded hollow in the large space. Lady DeGanne did not move. Marissa crossed the room. She placed her hand on her mother's shoulder to gain her attention. She looked older with darkened skin beneath her eyes. Marissa grabbed her hand. "Did you not sleep well?"

"What?" Lady DeGanne turned. It took a moment to focus her eyes, and then she offered a slim smile. "Good morning, Marissa."

"You're pale. Is anything amiss? King William is healthy?"

"Everyone is fine, dear. Just slow getting moving this morning." She moved away from the window to the table. "Fix the tea. I'll take mine black."

"Yes, Mother."

Lady DeGanne sat, arranging the skirt of her robe so her pink slippers peaked out. "What did you think of last night's dinner party?"

Marissa shrugged then placed a thin porcelain teacup in front of her mother.

Lady DeGanne patted her arm. "You did well, Child. I must say, I also thought Cinderella handled herself with aplomb." She took a sip, closing her eyes. She frowned, returning the cup to the table. "That's odd. Cook forgot to add something for flavor."

"No flavor? I thought I caught a hint of orange." Marissa took a sip. Though still hot, she could detect orange. "It is."

"Can't taste much of anything through this fog I'm feeling. I hope everyone else is fine. I would hate for Cinderella to feel poorly her first day in the palace."

"You liked her?"

She nodded. "More than I expected. Robert has made a wise choice."

The change in her mother frightened Marissa. Ten years of badgering her daughter to marry a prince could not have reversed overnight. Should not. *What's happening*? "I'm glad she feels at ease with us," Marissa said, then sipped her tea. "The story of her family is disturbing."

Lady DeGanne pressed a hand against her chest. "I cannot imagine the distress the poor girl has had to endure all this time. You know what it is to lose a beloved father. I did what I could to protect you. Poor Cinderella had none to see to her needs. She couldn't have been much older than you at the time."

Marissa took a deep breath before speaking, and then, her words were running over each other. "I want to find her family. Cinderella's father's family that is. It was wrong of her stepmother to separate her from those who would care. I think I shall find them and bring them to the palace in time for the wedding."

"But she has us now, why would she need…"

"If Father had relatives," Marissa interrupted, "I would want to know them, to have them in my life. It wouldn't change how I feel about you, or the king."

"But you would have to leave, go out there." She waved in the direction of the long window beside them.

Marissa laughed. "You mean go into the world, not just read about it? I would take Mrs. Boyde. We can travel to the Belton province."

"Perhaps it would be good for you." Her mother's slim chest rose and fell with a heavy breath. "Yes, go if you must. I am sure Cinderella will want you to go."

Marissa stared at her mother then gulped her tea to cover the sick feeling beating in her chest. *Mother never acquiesces to my plans. She should be listing reasons why my plan's foolhardy and dangerous.* She forced herself to finish the tea and stood. "I should find Robert and King William. See what they have to say. Robert, at least, should know enough of her to get a family name."

Lady DeGanne smiled, but it looked more like a wan grimace. "You have a good mind, my dear. No doubt you will be successful. Less than two months to bring them here. Speak with Robert, he will explain how to use the birds to communicate with us." She picked up her cup of tea and stared out the window without taking a drink.

Marissa felt dismissed. She stood. Lady DeGanne didn't acknowledge her departure. Tears burned her eyes as she left the apartment. *What must I do to quell this madness?* There were no answers for her silent question.

Cinderella heard the quiet knock on her door as Mrs. Belling finished hemming the second gown. The russet-colored undergarment complimented her pale skin and blonde hair. The overdress was patterned with browns and cream as well as the russet. She swished back and forth, admiring the way the fabric moved against her skin. "Would you get that?" She asked with a kind smile.

Mrs. Belling stood, pressing pins into a cushion attached to her wrist. "Of course." It took a moment, and Abigail trailed the dressmaker into the dressing room.

Abigail curtsied. "I have news."

Cinderella glanced as Mrs. Belling. "This will do for now. I will see you later?"

"Yes, miss. Lady DeGanne has ordered a full wardrobe for you."

"Of course, she has." She walked to Abigail. "You heard something?"

She nodded. "I heard the mistress and her daughter this morning. The daughter seeks approval to search for your father's family. She wants to bring them to the palace in time for your wedding."

"Does she?" Excitement swirled. Cinderella crossed to the table with the morning tray and poured a cup of tea. "What do you mean?"

"They spoke about you, how your father died and stepmother treated you horribly. The young lady is certain your father must have family and wants to find them in time to attend the wedding here."

"Indeed." Cinderella curled a bit of blonde hair around her finger. *Marissa wants to get away from the palace? For my benefit or because seeing Robert with me pains her? Cinderella smiled. Does it matter?* "Did you hear much of her plan?"

"She went to find the king, or prince, and get their permission."

"Where is Robert?"

"His servant said he'd be practicing arms this morning. In the fencing yard."

"Very well. Continue your watch." *You did well, Crow. Let's see how quick I can have her gone.*

Abigail removed herself from the bedroom, and Cinderella stared at the mirror. "Once she has passed the lands of Monmoore, everyone here can forget her." Marissa could disappear into the world and no one would care. "Robert will not want her to leave. I must be there to persuade him." The new dress fluttered as she spun away.

32

Marissa's simple silver gown swished as she walked the carpeted hallway. She sought Robert. His approval was integral to her plan. Besetting him alone would provide the opportunity to quell any refusals. The sound of metal upon metal rang through the skinny arched window as she walked the upper alley. Her hand brushed against familiar stone as she wound her way down the stairwell toward the weapons courtyard. The blade of the fencing master flashed toward Robert, and Marissa gasped as the prince parried with a clever twist. She continued to watch from the arch at the base of the stairs. Sweat drenched both men as they fought for an advantage over the other. Robert's shirt clung to his muscles as he countered another move, his feet dancing across the cobbles.

Marissa felt her breath catch and she wished for her fan. Her mind cleared, becoming resolute. Taking the journey wasn't just about finding Cinderella's family. It was about truth. Analyzing her feelings for Robert would be part of that truth. She stepped into the morning sunlight as the fencing master called quits.

"You've been holding back for me." Marissa smiled as she walked closer.

Robert stood in place, his chest heaving for air. "Your speed is a real challenge. It wouldn't be right for a prince to best a whelp of a girl."

Marissa moved closer, encouraged by his easy smile. "No fear of that."

"Why did you come out here this morning? Did you want me

for something?"

Marissa felt her cheeks warm at his innocent words. He must have noticed, for his smile faded and his eyes remained fixed on her.

But then a veil slid into place and his eyes turned cold and glassy. Fingers from a dainty hand spread across his arm. Cinderella came into view.

Marissa took a step back and fixed a smile on her face.

"Is it true?" The soft voice dripped with sweetness. "Oh, Robert," Cinderella looked up at the prince. "Have you heard? Has she told you?"

"What?" Robert turned his head from Cinderella to Marissa. "Told me what?"

"She has promised to seek my father's relatives. To reunite me with my family. It is wonderful."

"No." Robert's firm protest surprised them both.

"Yes."

The one word from Cinderella sounded harsh to Marissa, but Robert bent his chin to the earth, providing approval.

The exchange happened so fast, Marissa wasn't certain what she had just witnessed.

"Cinderella is right, Marissa. It is a fine idea. I am eager to meet them. But you must have an escort."

"Mrs. Boyde will be with me."

"Not your companion, Mars. Soldiers. Men who know how to protect."

Marissa shook her head. "Is our country a dangerous place?"

Robert waved at the fencing master as he replied. "There are always dangers, especially when you haven't travelled beyond the orchards."

"Sir?" The fencing master acquired Robert's attention.

Cinderella turned toward Marissa with a sweet smile. "You never know what might befall you in the wilder regions of the world."

Marissa felt an evil shiver. She faltered. "I…I'll see you at breakfast." She fled, certain she could hear Cinderella laughing at her retreat.

33

Marissa refused to give in to the threat of tears clogging her throat as the carriage rolled from Monmoore. Robert had wrapped his arms around her, allowed her a moment to rest her head against his chest. His heart beat against her cheek, but then Cinderella joined them, and he withdrew. As he had since Cinderella's arrival at the ball. The cold emanating from his fiancé caused shivers down her back. It felt good to leave, and yet, here she sat wanting to cry.

Trees whipped past the open windows as they entered the wooded route of the king's land.

"I remember when you were twelve," Mrs. Boyde drew Marissa from her musings with a chuckle. "Bouncing from window to window."

The memories made her smile. "Driving Mother mad."

"Now here you are a young woman. I would have chosen different circumstances for your first visit into the world on your own."

"Last night you thought the idea ill, yet here we are today. I have never prepared for anything so quickly."

"She did magistrate the endeavor with speed." Mrs. Boyde offered a wry grin. "I wonder at her purpose."

"Cinderella?" Marissa grew serious when she noticed Mrs. Boyde flinch. "You do not believe she is what she appears?"

"I do not." Mrs. Boyde dropped the knitting needle into her bag, and Marissa felt her full attention.

"How do you know?"

"Because I am not what I seem."

"Not?" Marissa couldn't help but laugh. "I have known you my entire life. You are as dear to me as my own mother. How could you be naught but my Mrs. Boyde?"

"Your father called on me to protect you. Now, do not misunderstand. I love you as a daughter and will give my life for yours if need be. Within the confines of the palace there has never been a need to reveal more of my story. But the world is dangerous." She leaned closer. "Cinderella is dangerous."

Marissa wrapped her arms around herself to ward off a sudden chill. "She remains in the palace."

"Her reach stretches beyond the walls of Monmoore. To what purpose, I know not, but my heart trembles with the knowledge that she seeks to destroy you."

"Destroy?" Her eyes widened. "You mean kill? Me? But why? What harm am I?"

"There is more to her need for Robert than love, and you distract his affections."

Marissa shook her head. "But I have never sought Robert's affection."

"Would you deny your feelings for him? Allow that woman victory without a fight?"

Marissa turned to the window, but the whirl of passing trees wouldn't distract the question now reverberating within her mind. "I swore to my mother in this very carriage all those years ago that I would never fall in love with the prince. I would not marry him."

"Words of a precocious child. Will you allow the child to control your heart now?"

"Robert chose Cinderella." Her voice sounded harsher than she intended. Unexpected anger gave her pause. She looked down at her clenched fists.

Mrs. Boyde placed a hand on her arm. "He did not choose. It is by witchcraft and evil design he has been forced to play her puppet. But he struggles against her. Because of you, Marissa. That is why we are leaving. There is something between you and Robert that Cinderella cannot control. It is by your death that Robert will be completely in her power."

Fear clenched her throat. "Can you protect Robert?"

Mrs. Boyde shook her head with a frown. "It is not within my power to do so."

"Then I shall make it my purpose to protect him. We will learn the truth about Cinderella and find a way to release her hold on Robert for good." Marissa wanted the vestiges of sadness and anger to fall away, but how was she to discover the truth? And how could she release Robert from Cinderella's spell?

The clack of wheels along the well-used path lulled Marissa into a dream state. The trees parted, allowing them access to an ancient path. Deeper and deeper into the forest they journeyed, the afternoon passing into dusk and darkness drawing around them. Lights flickered beyond the open windows of the carriage. Some grew brighter as they drew near, while others flared then disappeared among the twisted trunks. A wing covered with glossy black feathers flapped through the nearest light, creating a shower of sparks that sprinkled through the air. The stench of rotted meat wafted through the window as the wing stretched toward her like fingers.

She jerked awake, heart pounding. Mrs. Boyde glared out the window and then looked to her. Marissa gulped. Afternoon light filled the carriage.

"What is it, Child?"

Her heart continued to thud as she rubbed her arms and shrugged. "A dream. A silly dream." She shook herself. "Too much time sitting here without form or focus."

Mrs. Boyde offered a sweet smile, calming the lingering feel of anxiety. "You have grown in grace and beauty, my dear, but you are still full of energy."

Marissa couldn't contain a mischievous smile. "I continue to fail to sit and wait as a proper lady ought. There is always a more interesting plot to perpetrate."

"Not here, Marissa DeGanne. There is no way to know what trouble is afoot."

"I will do my best to resist all adventure." Marissa frowned, pressed the back of a hand to her forehead, and gave a dramatic sigh.

Mrs. Boyde laughed. "I am here to prevent adventures and mishaps. Our goal is to learn the truth of Cinderella and act accordingly."

Marissa grimaced and said no more.

34

The carriage rumble changed pitch as the vehicle turned onto a graveled courtyard. "Where are we?" Marissa asked as she turned her gaze from Mrs. Boyde to the darkening window.

"I surmise we have arrived at the Crescent Inn."

Marissa reached for the door handle, but Mrs. Boyde pulled her back. She sighed and rolled her eyes as the handle twisted from the outside.

"We've arrived at the inn, my lady."

Marissa looked around but didn't see her mother. She could feel heat coloring her cheeks as the lanky livery servant watched her. "Yes, of course. Thank you," she muttered as she accepted his assistance to disembark the carriage. She heard Mrs. Boyde plod down after her, but her attention focused on the crowded activity across the yard. Within the palace walls, she had seen soldiers and workers, but here a mix of stations mingled. Voices raised above the noise of animals filled the air with a buzz of energy. Marissa felt the hairs on her arms tingling.

The young servant clacked his heels together. "The captain has ordered you a private sitting room, my lady."

Marissa dragged her attention from the bursts of color and peals of laughter and allowed Mrs. Boyde to guide her across the yard. She side-stepped globs of manure and turned her head from their heavy smell of decay. A burly chap, with an ugly scar cut through his right cheek, eyed her, causing her to stumble across an uneven patch of ground. More eyes seemed to fix upon them as they made their way into the inn. Its sign swayed in a soft breeze as she stepped beneath the arched entrance.

Mrs. Boyde's familiar arms swept her through the common room where an oversized fire blazed. The sound of dishes clanking and ironware scraping bits of meal added to the cacophony of voices. Swirls of color rushed by as she was heralded into a quiet, bland space. The captain bowed and slipped from the room, closing the door. Silence reigned within while beyond the thick wood of the door murmured the liveliness of the unfamiliar inn.

"Don't even ask." Mrs. Boyde raised her hand before Marissa could squeak a sound. "We've garnered more attention than is warranted. I would prefer not to stay, but dark roads are far more dangerous."

Marissa flopped with a disappointed grunt into a padded armchair.

"Manners, my dear. We will enjoy a meal and then retire to the rooms the captain has procured for the night. I dare say a few nights' rest and early starts can have us in the Belton province before the week is out."

"Greetings, ladies. A good evening to you." The door creaked as it opened and a round woman stepped through. Marissa offered a wide smile, drawn to the little lady with a friendly twinkle and rosy cheeks. "My husband runs the inn, and I runs the kitchen. I'm delighted to fix whatever fits your fancy."

Marissa watched as Mrs. Boyde fell into conversation. She eyed the open door and the hub of activity beyond. Her journal, laying on the floor in the carriage, came to mind. She edged closer to the door and stole a glance across the room. Neither woman paid her heed. *Just for a moment, out and in again.* She slipped through the opening. Without the gaggle of soldiers, she crossed the common area with nary a turned head. She stopped a lad beneath the arch for directions to the stables. He nodded across the yard. Lanterns had been lit to stave off the night, and she could see the building across the way. She crossed the distance and entered the stables. The mingling scent of leather, horses, and hay caused her eyes to water. Wooden planks creaked beneath her feet, unsettling the quiet. Somewhere behind her, a booted footstep followed. She gazed down the long hallway of horse stalls and the open carriage area beyond. Someone continued to follow her, and she gulped. "Choices, Mars."

She muttered, before swirling around to face her fears.

The older man laughed, closer than she had anticipated. An orange scarf hung down his well-patched open coat. "What have we here?" His voice grated like sandpaper across an old rusty chain.

"Go about your business and stay out of mine." Marissa stretched herself as tall as she could as she searched the area for a weapon.

"But you are my business, Princess."

She backed away as he stepped forward. "You're a rabble-rouser with too much drink in his belly. You'd be wiser to sleep it off."

His laugh sent shivers coursing across her skin, but she refused to show weakness.

He moved quick, nabbing her hair.

Marissa gasped against the boorish smell emanating from him. She raised her foot and stomped down on his, but her dainty shoe glanced off his leather boots without harm. He shoved her, and she fell to the ground, scrambling out of his way. "All I have to do is scream and that bevy of soldiers out there will come in here and tear you to bits before you can even beg for mercy."

"You got a mouth, I'll give you that. Will be my pleasure to teach you some better ways to use it than screeching like a harpy."

"Lay another hand on the lady and you'll screech like a stuck pig when I run my sword through you."

Marissa gasped at the familiar voice of Captain Standish.

"Mind your business bloke and let me mind mine." The stranger growled without letting his eyes move from Marissa.

She shuddered as candlelight flickered in them.

"She is my business."

The sound of a sword being drawn from its scabbard roused the drunk. He turned with a growl, but then faltered. Marissa couldn't blame him. Standish held his weapon with ease, and though his wavy hair was streaked with silver, there was no doubting his strength. Marissa almost felt pity as the stranger's shoulders drooped and he stumbled out of the way.

Marissa grinned at Standish and raised her hand for assistance, but he scowled at her, eyes dark with anger.

"What were you thinking? You waltz in with your royal carriage and soldiers and then go off on your own? Did you honestly not expect to get accosted?"

She drew her hand back as though he had slapped her. "I came to get my journal. I didn't think I required protection for a two-minute errand."

"You are not safe alone, Lady Marissa. There are dark forces working against you."

"She was not alone, Nicholas." Mrs. Boyde stepped into view.

Marissa lowered her face and picked straw from her skirt.

"You were aware of the danger?"

Marissa peaked to see Captain Standish glare at Mrs. Boyde.

"I meant for her to receive enough to learn a lesson but not so much as to be harmed. I am aware of my charge, Nicholas. What are you doing so far from yours?"

His charge? Marissa looked at him closer. *What did they mean?*

"I am not a Guardian, and Robert insisted I follow the two of you. Since you agreed earlier that Robert's life is not the one in danger, I allowed him to persuade me. Seems like the princess may need more than one Guardian watching over her."

"I'm not a princess." Marissa interjected, then turned away as they both glared at her. "Well, I'm not." She muttered, dusted herself, and pulled herself to her feet.

"Your service will be required no longer tonight, Nicholas. I will see Lady Marissa to her room and make certain to lock her door."

"I'd check the windows as well," he chuckled, and feigned a cough at Mrs. Boyde's glare.

"You know Captain Standish?" Marissa asked as they stomped across the yard once more. She didn't like feeling as though she were a scolded child.

"We have crossed paths on occasion."

"His name is Nicholas?"

"You will address him as you always have. Do I need to reprimand you further for your actions this evening?"

"I promise I won't go off on my own again. I did not realize the attention we garnered with our royal entourage."

Mrs. Boyde's warm hand on her shoulder offered comfort, though her words remained firm. Marissa shook the feel of unease as they reentered the parlor room. Mustering courage had not prevented fear souring her stomach. She ate little before retiring to their sleeping quarters. Mrs. Boyde remained at her side until the door closed and Marissa turned the key in the lock. She thought the events of the evening would prevent sleep, but she drifted soon after touching her head to the feathered pillows.

35

Soldiers led them along the main highway from the inn toward Anglesworth, the largest city in the southern region of the kingdom. The king's carriage rode well, so there was little to do but sway with the motion of the wheels. The trees were in the distance and open fields passed in a blur. Marissa leaned her head against the side of the carriage. She couldn't quite let herself fade to sleep. Memories of the old man and the beat of large black wings hovered too close to the surface. *What is Robert doing? Is he with Cinderella?* Her mind turned to the final dance when Robert had twirled her in his arms. To where she'd stood with him in an alcove. Where his lips moved against hers. *What if I stayed instead of ran? Would Cinderella have lured him anyway?*

"It's no use wondering. A witch has her way. She's laid a foundation, years in the making."

"How do you know she's a witch?"

"I am a Guardian. It is my place to know such things."

"You said Father hired you."

Mrs. Boyde smiled. "He called for me. There is a difference. Your father was a merchant, an honest man. When he refused to bow, threats came against the family. Against you, though you were but babe-in-arms. I was sent to protect you."

"When the threat ended, why did you remain with us?"

"A Guardian makes a lifetime commitment. I cannot protect you from all ills, but I will give my life to save you from the worst."

"Can you banish Cinderella?"

"It would take more than one of us to defeat her. If we can find the source of her spell…" Mrs. Boyde tightened her lips as she looked out the window.

Marissa turned to look. "It's Captain Standish. You don't like him?" The captain noticed their attention and gave a tight salute before pushing his horse ahead of the carriage, out of sight. "He carries the sword I found in the attic."

"It belongs to him."

"How could he get a fine blade—oh, right. He's a Guardian as well."

Mrs. Boyde sat straighter. "His story is not mine to tell. Keep watch," she nodded at the window. "They say Anglesworth appears at the rise of a hill. The entire city has been built across a valley."

Marissa looked. There were hills, and deep gray along the horizon. "Will we reach the mountains tomorrow?"

"They will consult the Crestor in the morning. If no storms are forewarned, we should take the mountain pass and reach the village of Havenswold."

They reached the top of the hill, and Marissa leaned closer to the window. Mid-afternoon sun lit the pitched roofs piled one on another. Chimney stacks rose to varying heights, and bits of color showed through gaps in the roofs. Like a sea, the village spread across the valley.

Entering Anglesworth was not as pleasant as viewing it from afar. The close houses meant people, lots of people, carts, carriages, and wagons crowding the streets. Unpleasant smells wafted through the open windows.

Marissa wrinkled her nose. "I hope we don't have to stay longer than tonight."

"A good rain will clear the air. You saw the clouds moving up the valley. There will be rain tonight."

Mrs. Boyde's prediction proved true. The splatter of rain could be heard outside the window. The sun set in colors of gold and crimson as lightning flared in the bank of clouds further south. The black silhouettes of tree trunks stood out in the last vestiges of light, then a shadow moved. A tall, slender figure slipped closer to the inn. Marissa moved to the side of the window, hoping the shutter would hide her from view. Her heart thudded in her chest. Was this going to happen everywhere? Was the slinking shadow brought on by the presence of soldiers and the king's carriage? Or was it something altogether different?

Mrs. Boyde's arrival less than an hour later did not help the unsettled feeling in her chest. "What happened?" Marissa looked up from the thin book she'd been trying to read.

"A man from a neighboring village, seems he wanted a souvenir." Mrs. Boyde sat in the wicker rocking chair across from Marissa.

"Why risk foolishness? Is there need here?"

"What did you notice when we came through town?"

"Fire through the markets. Would make selling and buying of goods a challenge. Have they appealed to the king for help?"

Mrs. Boyde shrugged. "Not an easy task."

Marissa took to her feet. "If Robert were smart, he'd set a center of rule somewhere further north, easier to reach for our subjects. There could even be a second location beyond the mountains."

"You do have a good head on your shoulders." Mrs. Boyde grinned. "Wasn't always certain during your years of lessons."

"Father said I'd have a head for business."

Mrs. Boyde gave her a look. "Or for a queen?"

Marissa sat on the edge of her bed. "Not one of my choices."

"Not at present, but free Robert from the enchantment …"

Marissa remained silent for a moment, focusing on the dark beyond the window. "What will happen to the man?"

"There are dungeons for such as he."

"Give him what he needs and let him return home."

"Now that would not be so wise. He broke the law. Let it go unpunished and reward his arrogance … havoc will follow."

"Then tell them not to hold him too long once we've gone. If he is otherwise an honest man, his family will need him."

"If he is not?"

"He will get what he deserves in the end."

Mrs. Boyde nodded. "That is true. No matter how strong Cinderella is now, she will fail."

"But will it be soon enough to save Robert?"

LAURIE LEE

36

"Do you know what you will wear tonight?" Lady DeGanne asked as she scooped from her soft-boiled egg.

"Mrs. Billings delivered an apricot gown with a blue sash. Should that please the king's friends?" Cinderella tilted her head. *Not that it matters, I could wear black and you would be pleased.*

"Perfect choice. I will send Attilee to set your hair. The king will order up a tray of sapphires." She turned to Robert. "Will you wear blue as well?"

He smiled at Cinderella. "I have been assured our clothes will compliment. Fitting for our first engagement gathering."

"I am beside myself with excitement." Cinderella dabbed her fingers in lemon water and motioned for a footman to pull back her chair. "I will rest and look through the cards again. I do hope I remember their correct names."

Lady DeGanne patted her hand. "You will be fine. We haven't had this much excitement in so long. I am glad Robert found you. Have your rest. Would you like tea brought before you bathe?"

Cinderella stood. "Lovely thought." Instead of leaving, she stood beside the door of the morning room and watched the trio pick at the remains of their breakfast.

Lady DeGanne sighed. "Like the daughter I never had."

Robert frowned.

Cinderella could see a thought trying to form, a contradiction to what she wanted him to think. "Crow." Though her voice was a whisper, the demand that could not be ignored coursed through the palace. When Cinderella arrived at her suite, Crow waited for her. Despair and desire etched lines in his face. She opened the door. "The time has come to finish her."

"She is all but forgotten." Crow moved into the room.

"Robert does not think so. I will not have him distracted from my purpose. Find the girl and kill her."

"You have the mirror. Can it not do your bidding?"

"We are able to see where she has been, not where she presently is. Someone with her is protecting her. Follow their trail and wait until she is alone."

Crow paled. "You will send me through the mirror?"

"Oh, yes." Memory of the servant's pain made her heart flutter. Would Crow suffer such a transport? Cinderella caressed the frame of the mirror. Glass dripped and spread until the mirror was large enough for someone to step through. "Where is Marissa?" Cinderella spoke, and the reflection of her and Crow in the rose bedroom faded into a cloudy shroud. She had a sense of the image shifting backward until it settled on a town with an inn on Front Street butted up against a row of shops.

Cinderella kissed Crow. "Go, my dear. Complete your task and bring me a token."

Crow touched the mirror, his black skin contrasting the silvery light of the mirror. His hand dipped through. Cinderella held her breath as the rest of him was drawn. In a moment, he was through, no terrifying pain to be witnessed. She rubbed her fingers upward on the mirror's frame, and the mirror returned to its previous size.

Cinderella glanced around her chamber. Alluring as it was, she didn't desire to remain within its walls for hours until preparations for the engagement gathering would begin. Traveling through the back halls, she crossed paths with a familiar servant. The large man blanched when he turned and saw her. Cinderella narrowed her eyes. "What are you doing here?"

His chest moved up and down. "Minding my post."

"As a guard? That is not the job I set for you."

He frowned. "I don't know what you mean."

Cinderella touched his arm, then hissed, pulling away from him. Her fingers tingled as though scratched. "I don't know what has turned you from me, but it will not protect you forever."

He shook his head. "My purpose is to stand guard at the door."

"For now. Once I have what I seek, your journey through the mirror will be a walk in the garden."

His face hardened. "I'm going to trust that light will return to this place."

She smiled, tossing her blonde curls. "You do that. I look forward to watching your flesh turn to ash." She continued on her way, taking a dim corridor that led onto the easement. A few steps, and she entered the ancient keep. She dragged her fingers along the cold stone wall. Doorin walked here. The mirror had been forged in this place. Where had his power come from? Who sealed it away? She walked the empty halls, enjoying the touch of shadows, whispers of the past. The trail of her finger on stone marked her way.

Exploring the keep ate away at the afternoon. Cinderella returned as her maid arrived to draw a bath. Cinderella washed her hands in the basin. "I would like tea before bathing. Have Abigail bring it to me."

Derea nodded. "As you like."

Cinderella sat at the window, waiting for the younger servant to arrive with a silver platter. The tea carafe and plate of scones clattered when Abigail set them on the iron table. Cinderella slapped her. "If you are going to serve, you must learn the proper way of it."

"Yes, my lady."

"I saw Richards today. You did not tell me he is turned against us."

"I stay away from him."

Cinderella grabbed Abigail's wrist. The servant gasped with pain, but Cinderella did not release her. "You are here for my purpose. Who released him?"

"I don't know."

Her grip tightened, and the girl cried. Cinderella tugged at the memory of sand ripping through Abigail. "Is that what you want? Locked within the mirror? Never to escape. If you fail me, or turn from me, your death will be as a torment for ages."

"No, my lady, never! I serve you." Abigail fell to her knees as Cinderella released her.

"Your ability to serve must improve. I will request better training for you. Tonight will be a start. You may go."

Abigail ran. Cinderella poured her own tea and looked across the field to the woods beyond. "Where are you, Crow? Have you found them?"

37

"Why would he think he could get in?" Marissa glared at the broken bench beside the door and the pale scrawny thief lying beside it. In four days of travel, she'd been accosted twice and now a burglar.

"A hundred soldiers wouldn't make a difference, not when wine and rash friends heckle you to go where you don't belong." Captain Standish led her to the sitting area.

"Don't encourage her, Nicholas." Mrs. Boyde stepped across the rubble and entered the room. She pressed her hand against the thief's neck. "Alive. Best send for a guard."

Marissa leaned closer to Captain Standish. "The king's carriage is naught but trouble. We'd be better off without it."

Mrs. Boyde scoffed. "How would you expect to travel, my dear? By foot?"

Marissa rolled her eyes, earning a laugh. She went as far as the doorway and leaned against the jam. "How do normal people go about their business?"

"You are the king's daughter," he raised his hands to forestall her argument. "For all intents and purposes." The captain followed her. "You should be protected."

"We arrive in Belton province in a couple of days if the weather holds. Who will speak to us if we arrive like this?"

"You are a lady of privilege," Mrs. Boyde interrupted.

Marissa huffed with frustration. "I am not a fragile flower. Yes, I have been blessed, living in the palace as I do, but I am certain I can survive with less pampering." She stomped her foot. "In fact, I mean to. Captain Standish, I order you to return to Monmoore with this ridiculous pomade."

"Absolutely not." Mrs. Boyde burst out, but Captain Standish shook his head.

"I am not part of that regalia, Lady Marissa."

"It matters not, Nicholas, no one is returning to Monmoore."

He stepped closer to Mrs. Boyde. "Obviously, she isn't. Her life is in danger."

Marissa plopped into a chair and watched the pair square off. Mrs. Boyde looked her usual put-together self, but a rosy hue to her cheeks and flashing eyes made her appear lovelier than usual. Captain Standish seemed just as intent, and the two of them glaring at each other caused a smile to tug at her lips. Neither seemed to remember she remained in the room.

"If Cinderella is what we suppose, we need the soldiers to protect Mars." Mrs. Boyde placed her hands on her hips for emphasis.

"And how will you inquire into Cinderella's life? Who will speak to you?"

"We are heading into the witch's lair."

"Are you certain? Cinderella laid claim to this province, but how can you know? She has every reason to lie,"

"Something is here, Nicholas. Do you not sense the air?"

Marissa stood with a growl. "Since neither of you need me here for this conversation, I am going to find the leader of the guard and speak with him."

"Not by yourself." Both turned in an instant and screeched at her.

Though taken aback by their vehemence, she remained steady before them. "The soldiers go back, and the carriage with them. We rent a vehicle that will blend. With the two of you, I will be safe."

With hands on her hips, Mrs. Boyde frowned her displeasure. "Do you know what a stagecoach feels like? We will need more time, and you will be black and blue before we arrive."

"I can do it for Robert, if it saves him from her. From her vile enchantment."

"Fine." Mrs. Boyde huffed. "The two of you have convinced me."

Captain Standish frowned. "You intended to allow it all along."

Her lips twitched. "She is willing to encounter hardship for his sake. Why do you think that is?"

Marissa groaned, throwing her journal at Mrs. Boyde. The older woman caught it, laughter easing the tension in the room.

LAURIE LEE

38

Mists shrouded the courtyard as Robert stood at an open window in the upper reaches of the tower. What brought him there he could not recall, but the feel of wet wind upon his face cleared his senses for a moment. A rattle came from south of the main gate, and though he could not see, he heard wheels rolling across gravel. Curious, he took the stairs two at a time. He reached the courtyard as soldiers faded into the mists. A captain and carriage master remained.

"Are there plans for travel this day?" He asked as he approached the pair of men. The captain gave him a quizzical glance.

"Plans? We've only arrived. I hope there are no plans for a few days at least."

"Just arrived?" Robert placed his hand on one of the white horses. Its coat was slick with sweat. "From where? None of the vehicles should have been out this morning."

"Lady Marissa ordered us to return, sir."

"Marissa?" The name sounded familiar. "One of the courtiers? Why would she have the king's carriage?"

"A courtier? You jest, sir. Her ladyship would cut you down fine hearing talk like that. You sent us with her a week past, and she ordered us to return."

"Where is she?" Robert pulled his hand through his hair. A memory was trying to break free.

"She remains in the northern provinces, sir. Refused to return

191

to the castle with us. Captain Standish is with her, but we … Sir?"

Pain stabbed through his head, searing yet brief in its intensity. From it flowed the memories of Marissa. He gasped and staggered to his knees. The captain of the guard grabbed his arm and held him firm.

Heart pounding, he stared at the carriage. "How could I have forgotten?" The fog in the courtyard seemed to clear with his head. "Where is Marissa?"

"We left her four days' journey south of Belton Province. By public cart, four days." He shook his head. "Don't know what she was thinking."

"You left her unaided?"

"Captain Standish remained, and her maid. She was determined to go forward without the king's emblem. She'll have trouble without it, mark my words."

Robert rubbed his eyes. He had to go to her, bring her home. "She will find trouble, I have no doubt."

He left the courtyard and strode to Marissa's quarters. His hand trembled as he reached for the latch. Thoughts bombarded him, urgent needs pulling him from opening the door. Fencing. Moving maps in the king's study. Arranging a painter for Cinderella. He took a step back, then halted. Intending to move forward but wanting to fall back. Confused by his behavior, he pushed through the door and entered the bedroom suite.

A fine layer of dust covered everything, as though the room had been unused for years. "How long has she been gone?" He tried to think, but he couldn't remember the words of the captain. He touched a box centered on a dresser, wiped what looked like gray ash from its surface. Beneath, rich wood tones appeared. The sudden color revealed the dinginess of her rooms. A memory stopped him as he moved toward her sitting area. He had seen her off, kissed her cheek before she entered the carriage. He held her in his arms. How could he have forgotten? How could they all have forgotten?

The chime for breakfast rang as he returned to the hall. He pressed his hand against the wreath of daisies. "I won't forget you, not again."

The quiet of the breakfast room seemed oppressive. Robert paced while King William sat across from Lady DeGanne, pushing a pile of eggs across his plate.

"I must go to Marissa, foolish girl." Neither his father nor stepmother seemed to know of whom he spoke, but Cinderella rose from the settee to stand in his way.

"Go to her? Why would you bother, my love? Marissa is exploring the world. Give her this time to spread her wings. She does not need you to ride to her rescue."

A cold sense of dread crept through him as he stood before Cinderella. She remained the young woman he'd fallen in love with, and yet, he wanted to back away from the warm glow of her blue eyes. "Someone has convinced her to throw away her protection. She is defenseless in the world and her life is in danger. I am sure of it."

"Oh, Robert." She touched his arm, but he jerked away. "What happens to us if you leave?"

"Nothing changes. I love you, Cinderella, but Marissa is dear to me as my own sister would be. I could never forgive myself if something happened to her. A fortnight is all I need to return her to Monmoore. The wedding is more than a month from now."

"I don't want to lose you, Robert." She reached again for his arms, and this time he did not push her away. "Send someone else. Soldiers, let them drag her back kicking and screaming. Or let them remain with her as she travels. What harm is there in that?"

His chest ached, heart drawn in two directions. He wanted to stay with her, with Cinderella. But he needed to go to Marissa. "We'll be fine, I promise. Stay and make plans for the wedding. I will return before you realize I am gone."

"It won't be the same." Tears choked her voice. Cinderella walked away from him.

39

"I'm not sure which is worse, three days of rain or one day bouncing back and forth on the cart boards." Marissa groaned as she pulled herself from the public carriage. Had the royal seat been that much softer? She winced as tiny steps forward caused her backside to ache.

Mrs. Boyde stretched beside her. "At this rate, it will be another week before we arrive in Eglin."

"Belton province is that far?" Marissa's insides groaned.

Captain Standish jumped to the ground beside them. Marissa narrowed her eyes at him. He could bloody well pretend to be sore like the rest of them. The two of them. She looked around the muddy lot leading to the inn. No unwanted attention. Her drab green gown gave no indication of royal connection. Something good at least. She stepped to the side. Mrs. Boyde caught her arm, linking the two of them together.

"Just a precaution, my dear." Mrs. Boyde matched steps with her.

Marissa smirked. "You need a hand, don't you?"

Mrs. Boyde slapped her knuckles. "If I wanted assistance, Captain Standish would be a much better choice."

"Then I wonder at your choosing me."

The banter continued as they entered the inn. The name on the sign had long since worn off, but above the huge fireplace hung a plaque which read *Holmes Inn*.

Mrs. Boyde rubbed her hands together. "I'll have Captain

Standish order a sitting room for us."

"Not tonight." Marissa grabbed her hand. "We should remain in the common room—a table near the hearth. Wouldn't that be pleasant?"

"My dear girl—"

"We're nothing special now, just like everyone else who came in on the four-twenty cart."

"You are special, hard seats won't change that."

"We need to speak to people. With the captain watching over us, nothing untoward should happen."

"Your propensity for trouble …"

Marissa gave her no further time for arguing. With Mrs. Boyde's hand in her own, she dragged her toward a table recently vacated. The fire did feel good, and although her rump complained about sitting, her stomach rumbled at the smell of roasted venison.

Mrs. Boyde plopped beside her. "Very well."

The evening passed without trouble. An older couple traveling to visit their daughter took seats beside them. Mr. Corly, a large man with an exuberant laugh, talked them into a game of Sevens. Marissa took to the game within a few hands, and their shouts filled the room more than once.

"It has been a pleasure, Dear." Mrs. Corly hugged Marissa as the late hour drove them to their rooms.

Mr. Corly pulled the drawstrings on the pouch and held it out to Marissa. "No need to worry, got more sets than one. This'll give you something to do on the rest of your travel."

"Thank you, Sir. You are kind."

He shook his head. "Kind is you hanging out with the likes of us when you're clearly our better."

Marissa laughed. "You're good people, Mr. Corly, you and your wife. Safe journey." The older couple turned down a different wing of the inn. Marissa continued another flight of stairs, Mrs. Boyde a few steps behind.

"Still a bit sore? I think I've got something that can help with that." Mrs. Boyde followed Marissa into their room. A pair of beds left little space for walking around. A small fireplace glowed beneath a crate. A crock on the crate gave off a rich scent.

Marissa leaned toward the fire, closed her eyes and took a deep breath. "How did you manage that?"

"Captain Standish."

Most of the soreness had worn off, helped with a glass of mulled wine. The tied bed creaked as Marissa settled into it. *Different than what I'm used to, but not awful.* Her eyes drifted closed.

The next five days flowed much the same. *Nothing much to do, and yet I'm weary to the bone.* Marissa sighed as she stared at her reflection in the window of the moving carriage. Wings and a man's face appeared in the window, causing her to jump back with a screech. Her heart pounded, and her hand shook as she gripped the fabric of her jacket. The toddler across from her began to cry, his mother scowling in her direction.

Mrs. Boyde placed an arm around her shoulder. "What happened?"

Marissa shook herself. "I dozed. Saw someone standing outside the carriage." She laughed, swallowing her fear. "Ridiculous. The vehicle is in motion, no one could stand at the window."

"No, probably not." Mrs. Boyde hugged her anyway.

Too many days to find her. Too many paths to follow. Smart, changing like that. Oh, they thought it worked, that would be his advantage. Kill the girl and return to Cinderella. Hate for the witch bubbled with love. What would it be like to be rid of her, once and for all? Never stand by her side again? He couldn't bear the thought. With a mad howl, he changed forms and followed the troublesome stepsister.

LAURIE LEE

40

Marissa felt tears gather in her eyes as the streets of Elgin rumbled beneath wagon wheels. Her body ached. Weariness pulled on her. She wanted a bath, a bed of feathers, sweet smelling oils for her hair. She grinned at her own pettiness. *I have grown as a woman blessed with privilege. Thank you, Lord. May I be ever grateful when such things are restored. If ... No. That wasn't to be thought. We will succeed.* An image of Robert came to mind. *We must succeed.*

Their conveyance stopped outside a brick-faced inn, The Lucky Lady. The township of Eglin bustled around them. Unlike the stopping posts along the travel route, Eglin was a city. Cobbles had been laid in the road, causing the clatter of horses and carriages to add to the bustle of people going about their business. Across from their accommodation stood an archway barred by an iron gate. A myriad of shops could be seen beyond the fence.

"I wonder when the market opens." Marissa commented as she lifted her valise.

"Matters not. I don't think such a place would be safe for us."

Marissa rolled her eyes but was too tired to argue. Food and sleep, and no need to rise before the sun. That was all she required at the moment. Other plans could wait for the morrow.

The sun was well into the sky the following day before Marissa stretched and rolled over in the bed, a wider bed with a slim mattress. Luxury, after so many nights with ropes. She tucked her arm beneath her head and watched as lazy shadows of tree limbs danced on the ceiling. *We're here. We could discover Cinderella is as she appears.*

Robert's love could be real. Why did the thought terrify*? Or we could find her lies. Would knowing the lies be enough for Robert to break the engagement? What if he didn't? What if Cinderella is as horrible as I think she is, and he marries her anyway?* "He can't, he mustn't." She didn't dare dwell too long on why he mustn't or why she felt she couldn't breathe.

Marissa jumped to her feet. Sleep had done her well, her body protested little at the sudden movement. Breakfast and then what would they do for the day?

Nothing. Mrs. Boyde insisted on a day of rest. On the second day without doing anything, as night settled over the inn. Mrs. Boyde stretched with one hand against her back. "I could use more mulled cider."

Marissa grinned. "Is Captain Standish available?"

"He is not," Mrs. Boyde gave her a pointed stare.

"Then you can get it."

"I do not want to leave you on your own." She shook her head.

Marissa grunted. "This is our second night. There has been no sign of ill will or trouble. I will be fine."

Mrs. Boyde put her hands on her hips. "You'll stay here? Not try to run across to the market?"

Marissa chuckled. "It's dark and I have no desire to climb an unfamiliar fence." She walked to the window and opened it. The ground was a long way down. "I don't think anyone will come up this way." She closed it most of the way.

Mrs. Boyde grabbed her pouch. "I will not be gone long."

Marissa lay on the bed, one hand resting against her chest, the other on the linen cover spread across a coarse sheet. The hum of crickets broke through the cracked pane of glass. A drunken din washed into the quiet room. Waiting, Marissa stared at the crisscross pattern of beams on the ceiling. A patch of light would dance across them. No heavy brocade curtains to block the light or quiet the noise covered the windows. No fresh scent wafted from beeswax censors. The room smelled like meat pies and human sweat. She wrinkled her nose and shut her eyes.

Noise and smell continued to assault her senses. Now what? She tried to roll to her side, but her body refused to move. Marissa thrust her eyes open. She had fallen asleep, that was all. She blinked. The room was dark. What happened to the lantern? Had Mrs. Boyde returned, and she not notice? Noise from below crept through the broken windows. She glanced down. Her arm remained across her chest. She could see it, could feel the soft woven fabric of the thin blanket covering her lower body. Why couldn't she move her arm? Her fingers wouldn't wiggle. Her other arm remained at her side. What was happening? She could barely make out her feet, toes refusing to bend. Anyone who saw her would assume she slept soundly. Peacefully. *Wake up, Marissa.* She must be sleeping, dreaming. But her eyes were open. She could see the ceiling, the play of light and shadow dancing.

But something more than shadow lingered. Something thicker. Marissa felt her heart pound, yet still her body refused to move. A thin leg tapped the white-washed section between rafters. Hairs rippled as it slid out from a corner, moving bent legs to follow the first, and creeping against the rough edge of a wooden beam. Something crossed toward her side of the bedroom, toward her bed.

It couldn't remain in the shadows. Pale light skittered across its legs, for a moment illuminating its thick fur-draped body. Marissa strained against the lethargy holding her in place. Breath gasped in her throat, and yet her chest moved little more than the natural breath of sleep would cause it to move.

An eye gleamed at her. It knew she was trapped. Knew, and its slow creep from the darkest corners mocked her fear. An intelligent will laughed at her struggle.

A sliver of silvery cord dropped above her. A breath of air caused it to flutter as it drew closer like a thin finger stretching from the menace grasping the ceiling. She sucked in her breath as the cord touched her arm. Cold spread from the barest touch of the web. Marissa could feel sobs shaking her insides. How could her body remain lax? Betrayal. The creature stretched, release its grip on the ceiling and swung onto the web. With its head toward her, it hovered. Eyes gleamed. Mouth stretched. It wanted a kiss. She could read intent and tried to shake her head. Its legs moved and the creature drew closer. Screams shouted in her mind, but the room remained eerily silent. It waited, close enough that straightening its leg would bring it in contact with her arm. Eyes stared at her, full of emotion.

"Go away!"

But it laughed, its mouth opening. The eyes spread, its face stretching until it resembled something more human than not. A man hovered over her, or rather, the shadow of a man.

Marissa could barely breath, fear and something more gripped her. She closed her eyes and sang the first thing that popped into her mind. The simple nursery rhyme barely sounded through her lips, but she immediately started another. She squeezed her eyes closed, trying to sing, all the while expecting to feel that thing…

The door banged open. Marissa jerked up from the bed, eyes wide. Light filled the room. Not just the lantern she thought had gone out, Mrs. Boyde seemed to radiate, thrusting away shadows and things that lingered within them. A moment later, the room returned to the yellowish cast of the lantern. Mrs. Boyde hustled to Marissa. "Here, drink this."

Marissa didn't question, she still shook.

"That was a nasty bit of work. I am sorry. Trouble seems to find you even when you are incognito."

"It was horrible."

"Drink."

The warmed cider stilled her shaking. She breathed the apple smell rising from the cup. "I think apples will always be my favorite."

Mrs. Boyde sat beside her on the bed. "A good night's sleep is what we need."

Marissa trembled. "I don't think I can."

"Oh, you will. Those memories will not linger."

Indeed, what had scared her so badly was already fading away. She looked at Mrs. Boyde with a frown. "Something happened."

Mrs. Boyde patted her leg. "I know. Nasty dreams, but the good Lord gives a way to forget them." She glanced around their small room; her bed stood out on the opposite wall. "Not what you're used to."

"I walked around the servant quarters once. Their rooms were about like this. They could use a rug on the floor. Some curtains."

"You will be the mistress someday, somewhere. Experiences like this will guide your actions." She finished her own drink. "I am ready for bed, I believe."

"And then tomorrow, maybe we can do something?"

"We will see."

The third day, Saturday, dawned, and Marissa glared at the activity across the street. The iron gates were open, peddlers were bringing their wares to market. Smells wafted through the open window. Foreign smells. Delicious scents that made her stomach grumble, broiled beef and pastries. Her mind longed for conversation. Interactions. Shopping.

Marissa huffed, but Mrs. Boyde remained sleeping beneath a flowered quilt. An hour passed as she waited for her to wake. People walked through the market. Marissa stepped across the room, away from the window, but the noise of the market breezed through the open window. She couldn't stop herself from going back for another look.

"Wearing the floor is not going to help your restlessness." Mrs. Boyde spoke from her bed, eyes shut but a grin on her lips.

Marissa's shoulders slumped. "I am not a princess, at least I don't look like one." She flicked the heavy fabric of her skirt. "Remaining indoors is dull. Can we not go to the marketplace?" She worried her bottom lip with her teeth as she slid a glance toward her chaperone.

"I knew once you were free of the castle, the draw of life in the villages would be too great to resist."

Could she mean to let her go? She felt her heart leap with hope. "I promise I will not leave your side." Marissa pulled Mrs. Boyde to her feet.

Mrs. Boyde laughed. "Don't make promises you will be unable to keep, young lady. Be ever watchful. Cinderella will not know what to make of the return of the guard. She will seek your whereabouts and do harm if she may."

Marissa sobered. This was but a respite in their search for the truth.

Mrs. Boyde clapped her hands. "Enough. We want to visit shops before the sun is overhead." She grabbed her arm and gave a tug. Marissa shook the feel of dread and nabbed a shawl as they exited the room.

Standing in front of the hotel, they paused for a moment to

absorb the strangeness. Mrs. Boyde touched Marissa's shoulder. "Should we become separated, return to our dwelling immediately. Do not linger in the market on your own." A mingle of smells swept across the thoroughfare from the marketplace. The thick scent of broiled meat wandered through an apothecary's aromas. Marissa tried to take a step closer, but Mrs. Boyde held her back. "Your promise, Mars."

Marissa wrapped the worn shawl around her to keep the bluster of cold wind at bay. "I promise. If I lose you, I come right back here."

With a nod of acceptance, Mrs. Boyde allowed Marissa to pull her across the street. Morning fog clung to the wooden gate marking the opening of the marketplace. A horse and wagon rolled past, the rumble of its wheel splashing her foot with wet mud. She jumped to the side, bumping against an elderly man.

"Sorry," she muttered, watching as he rearranged the shuffle of hats.

Noise assaulted her from every direction as more and more merchants and peddlers jostled with the growing crowd.

Mrs. Boyde tugged on her sleeve. "Come this way," She pointed at a vendor selling dried bread.

Marissa freed herself from Mrs. Boyde's arm for a moment. The throng of people jostled her, and soon she was alone. No mother. No guards. No Robert. Why should the last one cause the most distress? She could just make out the top of Mrs. Boyde's hat.

"A lovely rose for the lovely lady," a woman with a high voice hollered as she waved a handful of wilting flowers in the air. Marissa laughed.

A rotund man with hands stained brown waved a wrapped package toward her face. "Gel, wut yew needs es thistle, good fer yew blood, thet." He grinned, revealing a gap where his front teeth should be. Marissa shook her head, then became alarmed that the crowd of people moved her forward.

A flash of black flew past, and Marissa felt someone bump her from behind. "Sorry, Miss." The deep voice caused a shiver, and it took a moment to realize someone pressed her toward a building with a hand on her arm.

"What are you doing?" She tried to pull away, but the hand tightened. "Have off," she struggled, but could not loosen his grip.

No one seemed to notice, and she soon found herself in a shadowed alley, alone, save for a slender, dark-skinned stranger.

"You are fair, fair, fair." His hand lingered an inch from her cheek, but he did not touch her face. "Such a pity she has to want so much."

"Who? Want what?" Marissa frowned, trying to pull away.

He didn't reply, but threw a sack over her head, binding her before she could twist from him. She kicked with her foot. His hand pulled her hair and drew her close. "You fight, Little Miss, and I hit you until you no longer move."

Her heart thundered, and her head felt light. *Would he?* She yelped as he tossed her onto his shoulder. Caution warned her not to try him.

41

Marissa pounded her fist on the heavy old oak door hard enough to rattle the iron hinges, but the door remained shut. With her throat raw from screaming, she rested her head against the door. How foolish of her to be caught. Why had she removed herself from the safety of the inn and gone into the market?

Shy beams of light peaked through the rafters and dotted the floor. Marissa looked at her dungeon. Weapons? Nothing but empty boxes littered the corners. Determined to find something, she ran her hands along the walls. There had to be a window somewhere. Boarded, but a way out if she could break through. She worked her way around the small room. The walls were smooth. Returning to the door, she sank to the ground. Now what?

Something scurried across the floor and she pulled her skirts close, shivering at the thought of a mouse. Mrs. Boyde would know she was missing. She would go to Captain Standish. *They can find me, can't they? Something about being guardians?*

The door rattled. Marissa scooted out of the way. *Had he returned?* Something hit the jamb. Not the stranger, then. He'd had a key. Marissa moved to the stacks of boxes. It could be Mrs. Boyde, but how had she managed to find her so quickly? She crouched, teeth nibbling at her thumbnail, as she heard another hit against the jamb. The door creaked open.

A whispery voice called her name. She frowned. *Why did that sound like…* The door pushed further. "Marissa," his voice called a bit louder.

"Robert?" Her mind fooled her. She stood and peaked over. A sob choked her. The weapon he'd used to break through fell to the ground as she leapt into his arms. Oh, to hold him, to be held. She didn't want to look, afraid it couldn't be possible, but the arms that pulled her close were familiar. His scent was familiar.

She raised her head from his shoulder. "How is it even possible?"

His hand touched her cheek. "You manage to find trouble everywhere, don't you?" His voice sounded odd, as though emotion clogged his throat.

A sob of relief shook her body, and she pressed her forehead in the nook between his neck and shoulder. "Trouble found me. He nabbed me and brought me here. Locked me in without a word. I don't know where he went or when he's coming back." She shook, but fear seemed more distant.

"I saw. I followed quick as I could. Had to search for an ax, not knowing if he'd harmed you, or worse." His arms tightened around her, and she swore his lips pressed against her hair. "My dear girl, what were you thinking, releasing the soldiers from their duty?"

He swept her up in his arms, causing her to squeal as she tightened her hold on him. "Robert," she kicked her feet, "I am unharmed, let me down."

"Stop squirming. I want to be removed from this place before your captor returns."

Marissa settled, thoughts of the stranger setting her on edge. *Be honest Mars*, she scolded herself, *you don't mind being in his arms anyway.*

She stayed where she was, watching the number of people increase, until they had returned to the bustle of the market. Captain Standish appeared a few paces behind them. Marissa smiled at him, then felt her cheeks warm as his brows raised. She turned her attention to Robert, who seemed none too winded for carrying her a distance. She tapped his shoulder. "Let me down," she hissed, "Captain Standish is behind us."

Robert didn't seem impressed, so she tapped a bit harder. "Mrs. Boyde will be close as well, Robert. It isn't appropriate, you carrying me unnecessarily."

"I'll carry you to Monmoore to keep you safe. Which residence holds your accommodations?"

"There." She pointed toward the brownstone with her foot. "And here is Mrs. Boyde, just as I surmised." Looking none too happy, Marissa noted. "He's already lectured me about getting into trouble," Marissa blurted as the others drew close enough to hear. "Not that this was my fault, a madman grabbed me off the street."

"Are you injured?" Mrs. Boyde placed her hands on her hips.

"No." They both answered. Marissa rolled her eyes at Robert's look.

"She is fine," Robert assured them. "I did not wish to risk losing her myself."

Maybe you shouldn't have fallen in love with another so easily. Marissa pressed her teeth against her lower lip. She couldn't very well deny feelings for the prince when her heart thudded in her chest and being held in his arms felt … right.

The four of them stopped in the street. Marissa watched others slow as they passed, heading into the market. "Perhaps we should remove ourselves to the residence."

Carrying her hadn't been a burden and setting her on the sofa of a private parlor left him with a sense of loss. He paced from one window to another, searching for the dark-skinned scoundrel.

"You'll wear the floor, Robert. Why are you here?" Marissa's tone sounded confused. Hopeful.

He faced her, noting Mrs. Boyde seated beside her and Captain Standish near the door. "The soldiers arrived without you." *No need to mention his memory loss.*

"Traveling with them seemed to cause more of a ruckus than not. We sent them home and continued using the stagecoach. Should have arrived a week past, but rain slowed our journey."

Was she daft? "Public?" *Scoundrels, lower classmen—what manner of person used public transport?*

She ignored his concern. "You still have not answered the question. Why are you here?"

"To take you home to Monmoore Castle."

"We have yet to find Cinderella's family."

"I arrived as a strange man pulled you from the street. You are not safe here." He took a breath. "Relatives or no, it is time to return home."

Marissa crossed her arms. "I am not returning to the palace." Her brows furrowed, and her lips firmed.

He knew that look. "It is where you belong."

"Belong? As what?" She stood and walked to the window.

"You are stepdaughter to a king. Whether your status is wanted or not, you warrant the privilege of a princess of the realm."

Her eyes darkened and she jerked around, facing the window. A moment later, she turned away, pressing herself against the wall. She had palled. Robert walked to her side. He searched the street and the grounds but saw nothing familiar.

Her hand grasped his. "I saw him, but I do not think he noticed me."

Mrs. Boyde stood, clearing her throat. "None of us are going anywhere today. Marissa will rest in her room, and we will meet at dinner." She looked at Captain Standish. "Have you acquired rooms for the prince?" He nodded, and Mrs. Boyde offered a smile. "Good."

Robert squeezed Marissa's hand. He did not want to release her. Did not want her out of his sight.

She gave a lopsided grin. "We'll argue some more at dinner."

He let her go.

42

She dreamt of snow. Large flakes drifted around her, among the trees. A hush settled across the glen. She looked at the sky. The feel of flakes melting on her face made her smile. She stuck her tongue out to catch a few, twirling with her arms out. A strange, real dream. A house stood across the way. Most of the windows were boarded by shutters. A large front door stood ajar. Curious, she crept across the road and up the uneven cobbles. The room to which it opened was dark. She pushed against the door. A great screech disrupted the quiet of falling snow. She pressed herself against the wall, not wanting to be seen by whatever must lie within. Deep within the house, a flurry of wings beat then settled to silence once more. Nothing else stirred. She slipped inside.

It took a few moments for Marissa's eyes to adjust to the dark.

An old woman sat in a corner, rocking as she twisted a pair of knitting needles around about each other. The squeak of the rocker stopped as she looked across the room, squinting. "Is that you, Ella? Have you returned? I went to town asking for you, but no one's seen you." The old woman pushed herself from the chair and hobbled across the rug. Her smile turned to a frown as she drew nearer. "You are not my Cinderella."

Marissa felt herself jerk awake, a heavy hand pushing on her shoulder. Mrs. Boyde leaned close, a lantern in her other hand. "Not dreams as you should be dreaming."

Marissa gulped. Had it been real? It seemed real. "Can't be." She looked at Mrs. Boyde. "Cinderella worked at a manor house.

Sold there by an evil stepmother."

"What did you see?"

"An old woman, asking if Ella was come home. But it was real."

"Or so you are meant to think."

She rubbed her eyes. *Think, Mars. What did it mean?* "We know Cinderella is not the young woman she wants us to believe. The old woman could be her mother, or grandmother. No stepmother at all. No drudgery or ill treatment. She invented it all as part of her tale."

"Perhaps she did. That is what we have come to discover."

"The old woman said she went into town and asked if others had seen Ella. We ask where the old woman lives."

"This town or another? This is what she wants, to confound your progress. She planted the dream to influence your actions."

"We'll find a way to use it to our advantage."

Mrs. Boyde nodded. "We will try."

Marissa twisted a lock of hair. Mrs. Boyde's worried stare did not help dispel the unease in her stomach. She glanced out the window where late afternoon sent long shadows across the yard. "We should dress for dinner."

Mrs. Boyde agreed, first closing the shutters and lighting a lamp on the dresser. Marissa folded her arms across her chest and tapped her foot. Mrs. Boyde struggled not to grin, but Marissa noticed her twitching lip. Finally, left alone, she rubbed her hands through her hair. Dirt smudged the dress, probably from crawling around on the floor. She pulled it off, unmindful of the sound of tearing fabric. "This dress I will be glad to burn." She kicked at the pile on the floor then moved to her closet.

Drab was the first thought as she looked at the slim selection of dresses. *I should have kept a flowered dress.* Marissa chewed her bottom lip as she tugged on one lackluster gown after another. *Not having royal garb hadn't mattered 'til now, and it still shouldn't matter. Robert remains engaged to Cinderella. There were how many engagement days remaining? At least twenty. A forty-day engagement wasn't long enough, not by half.*

With a grunt of frustration, she grabbed a dress and slammed the wardrobe shut. Robert showing up confused her. *I care because we're close, the way siblings ought to be.* "Liar." She narrowed her eyes at herself in the mirror. *At least he's here. Not at Monmoore and not with her. He's having his evening meal with me. Us.* She pulled the sides of her hair to the back and secured them with a simple clip, and then made a face. *Best remove myself from my own company before I think something truly awful.*

For all her edgy nerves, dinner was uneventful. Robert had calmed down. Captain Standish and Mrs. Boyde spent most of their time picking at their food instead of adding to the conversation. Marissa kept her glance traveling among the three. They had acquired a private dining room, so there would be no other entertainment for the evening.

"How many days remain for your engagement?" Marissa dropped her fork against her plate and leaned forward. She ignored Mrs. Boyde's huff and focused on Robert.

"Engagement?"

"To Cinderella. How many days remain?"

He seemed pale for a man eager to wed. "Twenty-four? If I haven't lost track of the number."

"As long as you insist on remaining with me, uh, us." She looked at the others. "As long as you insist on remaining with us, we have at least two weeks before we need return to the palace."

Mrs. Boyde placed a hand on his shoulder. "You still wish to marry Cinderella?"

"Marry? Of course, I intend to marry."

He didn't sound as convincing as he should, Marissa noted, ignoring the smug feeling in her chest.

His eyes glittered as he returned his attention to her. "Returning to the palace is the most prudent response to what happened this morning."

"There are four of us if you remain. No need for anyone to be on their own. We stick together and complete our task."

"Which is what?" Robert dropped his fork on the plate. "Cinderella has no need of family, especially those who have had nothing to do with her for more than ten years."

"Do you notice anything different?" Marissa glared at him. *Thick-skulled nimrod. How could he not notice a difference without Cinderella hanging on his arm?*

"What do you mean?"

"Marissa," Mrs. Boyde gave a dark look. Captain Standish

seemed no less pleased with the question.

She ignored them. "Do you feel different here than you did at Monmoore Palace? When did you leave, a week past?" His eyes shuttered. She saw it. Something was different. "You *have* noticed something."

"Marissa," Mrs. Boyde tugged her arm. "Now is not the time."

"He needs to know."

"I agree, but how do you intend to prove your point?"

"Prove what? Tell me what?" Robert glanced from one to the other, his eyes turning deeper green in color. "What don't I know?"

Marissa straightened in her chair. She folded her hands in her lap and ignored the two older guardians. "You have noticed. There is something about Cinderella that isn't quite right."

"Not right? Cinderella is my intended. I have made a vow to her, a pledge. I wouldn't have done that if something wasn't right with her."

Why can't I shake sense into him? That would feel more satisfying. "Have you ever met anyone who threw your world into turmoil from the first moment?"

"Aside from you?" His eyes were blazing with anger, but something else lurked in their depths. She could read him. He knew, even if he didn't want to admit it to himself.

"This isn't about me."

"Isn't it? You've always wanted the world to revolve around you. Now it doesn't. Another woman will stand in your place at the palace."

His words were biting, and Marissa tried not to let them hurt, but this wasn't going as she had planned. "I've always known someone else would become mistress. This isn't about that, it's about Cinderella and her hold on you. It isn't natural."

Robert jumped to his feet. "I never would have taken you for a jealous woman."

He left before she could refute his claim.

Captain Standish stood. "I will go. Give him the night to sleep on it. He may come easier to reason in the morning."

Marissa looked at her lap, tucking hair behind her ear. "I didn't mean to upset him."

Mrs. Boyde chuckled as the captain left the room. "He's a man, Marissa. He'll need to be hit over the head with proof before he sees the truth."

Marissa propped her elbows on the table and rested her chin against her fists. "I want to be the one to hit him."

"I think you just did."

She couldn't stop her lips from twitching. "Then I want to hit him again."

LAURIE LEE

43

It wasn't only the loss of memory. Robert stood near the window of the third floor hired room. Moonlight broke the darkness, illuminating the town. Marissa's words struck a nerve. He rubbed his eyes. Perhaps he should drag her from slumber as well. Something wrong with Cinderella? Her sweet face hung in his memory. If he closed his eyes, he could almost feel her standing beside him, an arm about his waist. She was dear to him, had been from the moment they met. That didn't explain the sickening cramp in his gut. It didn't explain the shadow that hovered.

A slender man walking in front of the market captured his attention. Robert moved closer to the wall, out of sight but still able to have a clear view of the street. It could be the man who nabbed Marissa. Any sense of a shadow lifted as he spied on the stranger. The man stopped, leaned against a wall. A smaller man ran to him. The two exchanged words. Money changed hands, and then the boy faced the inn and pointed up and a little to the left of Robert's window. In the direction of Marissa's room. The nauseous feel in his gut intensified.

Robert closed his lantern and watched until the two faded into the night. He couldn't say for sure the direction the taller man had taken. It was as if he melted into the dark. Robert tapped his finger on the edge of the sill. Mrs. Boyde would keep Marissa safe. They had selected the upper floor, but what if there were a way through the windows? Would Mrs. Boyde know to keep watch? His thoughts whirled until he wanted to hit his head against the wall. The urge to go to Marissa's room didn't lesson.

Self-recrimination clenched his chest as he crossed the hallway. He should go back. Sleep. A deeper part of his mind urged him to ignore the contrary voice and go on. The carpet runner on the floor muffled his steps. Gold light of oil lamps on the walls flickered, simulating movement of things that weren't there. He stopped at Marissa's door. Uncertainty gripped him, but the man in the alley had been real. He tightened his jaw and knocked twice. Easy knocks, not meant to cause alarm. It took a moment for Marissa to open the door.

Robert felt his breath catch in his throat. Maybe this wasn't a good idea. Her feet were bare. Hair fell around her face, across her shoulders, and down her back. Her brows lifted in an articulate question. What was he doing here?

Her eyes were the color of a fawn's coat speckled with gold. Color seeped into her cheeks and she turned from him. "The hour is late. Why are you here?"

Marissa's flat tone calmed the odd thoughts churning with feelings he shouldn't have. Not considering his engagement to Cinderella. "I saw a man in the street, like the one who nabbed you."

"We are three flights above the ground. Captain Standish will not allow a stranger to climb."

Something struck the window across the room from them.

"Stairs were not my concern." He pulled her behind him as the window casing flew open, striking the wall, back to the window, and then slowing to a halt. Marissa's hand gripped his arm as they stood together. A black creature with wings and beak broke into the room. It stumbled to the wood floor, Marissa gasped, and Robert grabbed for his sword. But his side was bare, his weapon remained in his own quarters.

The creature shifted. Among the night beyond the dim glow of a candle, something unfolded, stood, and faced them. Marissa stepped closer, pressing against Robert as her fingers dug into his arm. The man standing before them had skin the color of tea. Thick, black hair tied back resembled the gloss of feathers. His dark eyes pierced with a determined hatred.

"What foul devil are you?" Robert glanced to the left. A fire poker lay against the fireplace. He stepped closer to it, never taking his eyes from the creature while keeping Marissa behind him.

It laughed, the throaty sound of a man out of humor. "Devil, perhaps. Cursed more likely."

Marissa pressed iron into his hand. Smart woman. He shifted it to his right, raising it between them and the foul creature.

It shook his head. "You think that can stop death, if death is meant to join us this evening?" It moved further from the window, still on the other side of the bed.

"Stay where you are." Robert lifted the poker higher. "Better yet, return your cursed self to the night where you belong."

"Where I belong? What of you? You are caught as well, surely as a fly in the spider's web. Her poison will destroy us both."

"Her? Who?"

"Robert, don't talk with him," Marissa gripped tighter.

It smiled, teeth gleaming white in the candlelight. "Whose image presses your mind? Urges you to her side?" It stepped closer. "You can leave here. Return to her as you should. Let this other woman remain with me."

Cinderella needed him. For a moment, Monmoore seemed more real than the inn. But no, Marissa stood with him. She needed protection. Now. From the creature that had taken her once already. He shook his head, clearing the other thoughts.

"No. My duty is protecting Marissa."

The stranger grasped his head with a howl. "Do you mean to defy her? Cause me to defy? This woman dies."

The door to the room slammed open. Marissa screamed.

Mrs. Boyde raced in front of them, putting herself between them and the evil creature. "Fly, foul beast. Return to the witch. Let her know your failure and hers."

It screamed again. "This is not yours, Guardian."

"You will meet more than one, cursed man. Be gone, ere you face your destruction this night. Warn her she is known, and her foul deeds will not remain unpunished."

It shook, whether by anger or fear, Robert could not tell. Hate chilled the bedroom. With a final cry, it fell into wings and feathers once more, bursting through the window and into the night. Robert dropped the poker and wrapped his arms around Marissa. She shook, her head buried against his chest. But he shook as well. His mind whirled with questions he didn't dare set in words. He stood, Marissa in his arms, as Mrs. Boyde walked to the window, pulled the sash and locked the shutters in place. The woman he'd seen countless times as nobody special spoke softly while holding her hand against the closed window. Silver glimmered, and then the light in the room brighten.

Marissa loosened her hold on him.

When Mrs. Boyde faced them, she offered a smile. "That was not wholly unexpected."

"What do you mean, not unexpected?" Robert pulled a hand through his hair.

Marissa slipped away, though not so far she didn't keep a hand on his arm. "Come, sit," Her voice shook as she pulled him toward a bench. He sat but grabbed her hand when she tried to move elsewhere. She slumped beside him.

"What was that and why was it expected?" Robert looked from one to the other. Marissa's eyes were large, fear cooling, but he could read uncertainty.

Mrs. Boyde slid a look at the window. "In order to answer questions, you have to be willing to face the unpleasant truth of your fiancé."

This didn't make sense. "What would any of this have to do with Cinderella?"

"That man is hers."

Robert scowled. "He is no man …"

"He belongs to a witch, a powerful witch that twists him into whatever form serves her purpose. As a bird, he covers distance and spies with keen eyes. In his human form, he fulfills her bidding."

"A witch?" It wasn't possible. "You want me to believe the future queen is a witch? To what purpose?"

"Control of a country has its privileges, but to be honest, I cannot see her true purpose."

"If you suspect her of harboring ill will, why wait? Why not expose her sooner?"

Marissa scoffed. "Have you been able to see her as anything other than what she wants you to believe?"

Doubt lurked. Robert stood, but pacing the breadth of the room did little to alleviate his confusion. "I've been tricked, fooled by a beautiful young woman?"

"Snared." Mrs. Boyde assured him. "Caught in a web. Her reach is strong. Even now, you fight against us."

"Are we close to finding her home? Is that why that creature wants me dead?" Marissa crossed her arms.

The threat to her was real. Robert shuddered. What if death… "If Cinderella is what you think, why would she allow me to leave Monmoore?"

"Sit, Robert. You make me dizzy." Marissa covered her eyes.

Mrs. Boyde stood near the window. "The fact she couldn't prevent your leaving infuriated her. Killing Marissa is the way to gain complete control of you—of the future she desires through you."

"I'll break the engagement and put an end to her schemes."

"So easily? This is not a young woman with a hard heart. She is a witch wielding dangerous powers."

"But her youth, how can she be pure evil?"

"You see as you are meant to see."

He didn't want to believe. The urge to curse them both, Mars resting with her head against the wall and Mrs. Boyde keeping watch at the window, made his throat close. Hate burned, but why? He'd witnessed the man change into a raven.

"Can you stop the lies?" His voice sounded like a husky whisper and his nails bit into the palms of his hands.

"Not completely. You are far enough away from her to weaken the hold."

"But not break her hold?" The steel edge eased, helping him breath once more.

"How to break the spell remains hidden from me."

"We continue our search for her home," Marissa spoke without opening her eyes. "The answer must be found there. Now, if you both don't mind, I wish sleep to put an end to this horrid day."

He didn't want to leave, but Mrs. Boyde patted his shoulder. "I will remain with her. Return to your room. Captain Standish will meet you in the morning. We can plan at breakfast."

Marissa opened her eyes and offered a small smile. Her face looked pale against her dark hair, eyes tired. Yet there was beauty in her face, high cheek bones and lips the color of autumn leaves.

He raked his hand through his hair. "Until tomorrow." What was he thinking? Her lips were the color of autumn leaves? Even worse, the memory of her lips against his came to mind. He needed sleep as well.

44

Though she promised to remain with Marissa, Elizabeth found sleep elusive. Marissa had no such problem. After a mug of warm milk and assurance that the shutters had been sealed across the windows, the young woman curled on her side beneath a light blanket, fast asleep. The creak of a floorboard in the hallway turned Elizabeth's attention. Nicholas walked nearby. She met him at the door. "I desire to go to the parlor; will you keep watch?"

He nodded. "I will be certain they sleep undisturbed."

"Is Robert sleeping?"

"Not yet." Nicholas leaned against the wall. "He blames himself. He does not yet realize this danger has been within the palace long before he could do anything about it."

"The death of his mother?"

His features darkened. "I should have realized."

She reached for his arm, his flesh warm beneath her fingers. "I understand the death of your charge hit hard. You required healing. You could not have known what coming to Monmoore would entail."

A sparkle in his glance caused her to withdraw her hand. "You enquired of me?"

Elizabeth straightened, permitting a faint grin. "Our paths were going to cross. I thought I should know a thing or two about you."

"I will share any part of my tale." He bowed. "When we have secured victory for our charges."

"Agreed." That she wanted to know him better surprised her.

She looked back at Marissa. Tonight, Elizabeth had a different purpose.

"Go." Nicholas tilted his head toward the stairs.

She managed the stairs without a sound. A low fire burned in the grate of the main room. Elizabeth heard noises from the back, staff washing up, but no other patrons remained. She crossed to a smaller room with a long table in the center, a sofa against the back wall, and a few chairs near the large windows. The windows were long enough to be doors, one could step over the lower lip to be in the garden surrounding the front of the inn. No lights in the room allowed her to see outside. A moon not yet full hovered at the edge of the long casement window.

Elizabeth first searched the night, but the foul creature could not be sensed. He had come into their room from the street side, but any passing of the magic needed to hold a changeling would leave a trail. Cinderella would leave a trail if she indeed lived in the region. Elizabeth closed her eyes. "I need more than myself."

"Our charges sleep."

She turned to find Nicholas standing at the far end of the darkened room.

She reached her hand toward him. "The paths are muddled. Will you aid my sight?"

"I am not a Guardian."

"My dear Nicholas, you are as you have always been." She crossed the distance between them. "Your hand, sir."

Nicholas wrapped her hand with his. Never one for being half-hearted, his touch was sure and true. Elizabeth pressed back, and the world darkened. They moved through the window. Paths made of the passing of dark magic lit, glowing like embers. With Nicholas' help, the jumble of paths cleared, and she could sense the power of the witch. Cinderella's strength lay to the west.

Vision of the paths could not endure. Embers dimmed as darkness lifted. Elizabeth could feel Nicholas' hand around hers, but her head grew faint. He caught her before she could stumble.

"I'm fine." She insisted, but he carried her to the sofa anyway.

"Fine and foolish." He placed a thin pillow beneath her head and brushed hair from her cheek. "What good is it to tire your strength?"

"That vile creature and the spirit she holds must be stopped."

Elizabeth moved her hand to push against the back of the sofa to sit up, but Nicholas pulled her hands down to rest on her chest.

"The paths cannot be followed tonight. You think you will find a weakness if you journey to her lair? What is to stop her from detaining you, or worse?"

"I pray for revelation. There has to be a way to free Robert and save Marissa." He was right, sleep tugged at her. She relaxed against the firm cushions.

Nicholas frowned. "If we can't save them both?"

Elizabeth looked at him, his eyes gleamed with doubt and past pain. She patted his cheek. "Guardians aren't perfect, but we serve a good Master. He will guide our way."

"Your faith surpasses my own."

"Yet here you are, doing the work of the Master."

He shrugged.

Elizabeth fought to keep her eyes open, but the expenditure of energy to see the hidden paths cost her.

Nicholas laid his hand across her forehead, rubbing his thumb between her brows. "Sleep. I watch over you this night."

She settled deeper into the cushions and allowed her mind to wander.

45

Marissa shot up on her bed as light splashed into the bedroom. Memories from the previous night made her hands shake, but she forced herself to stand. She looked at the locked shutters over the windows. Not a dream. It didn't take long to complete her morning ritual. She peaked into the hall. No dark strangers. No cold fingers stretching through the air. She made her way to the first floor.

Robert stood in the open door of the inn looking inward. Light from outside kept her from seeing his face. She rubbed her hands against her dress. *What is this flurry of excitement and nerves?*

"Good morning."

His voice swept over her and she wanted to be nowhere else. "Looks to be a beautiful morning." She managed to glance around him. "Weather cooperates for a day's journey."

"Are you sure this is what we should do?" Robert crossed his arms over his chest. "We could return to Monmoore and face Cinderella. Demand the truth."

"Would she offer it? Give us enough truth to believe her words?"

"I know I can't have it both ways." Robert shoved his hands in his coat pockets. "To be so easily duped." His downcast head shook.

Marissa placed her hand on his arm. "Not duped. You were taken in by an evil spell. Even now, this far from her, you fight against it."

Robert didn't move from her touch. He trailed a finger from her temple to her jaw, making her insides quiver. Then he withdrew, bending as he fisted his hand.

"Mars." A moment of pain reflected in his eyes. Cinderella's hold on him, though weak, was still present.

Determination straightened her spine. "We have work to do." Somehow, they would free him. She linked arms with him, and they walked to the parlor.

Mrs. Boyde sat at the table, a cup of steaming tea in front of her. Captain Standish stood nearby.

Marissa frowned at her friend. "You seem pale."

She waved the concern away, but Captain Standish placed his hand on Mrs. Boyle's shoulder for a moment. Was there something between them?

"We will need to travel west today." Mrs. Boyde dropped two cubes of sugar into her tea and stirred.

"Travel? I thought we searched here for Cinderella's home." Marissa sat across from Mrs. Boyde. The door to the kitchen creaked open and a serving girl brought a platter of eggs, ham, tomato, and mushrooms.

"I'll have toast for you in a moment," the girl spoke with a local accent and offered a quick curtsy.

"Smells delicious." Robert sat beside her, grabbing the platter. He pulled a plate from the center of the table, plopped a ladle of the breakfast grill on it, and passed the plate to Mrs. Boyde. He served Marissa next, then took a heaping spoonful for himself. Captain Standish took what remained.

For all Robert's appetite, Marissa couldn't feel the same. She moved food on her plate but didn't feel like eating. "What have you found out?"

"Her paths lead west. There are two possible routes. I asked the innkeeper. Captain Standish and Robert will take the trail to the north and west. We will follow the trail along the river. We meet in Atwood and discuss what we see."

Marissa snuck a glance at Robert. "Is separating wise?"

"The alternative is to travel back and forth."

Captain Standish offered a stern look at them all. "The single purpose today is to travel the roads. Report what we see when we meet in Atwood and devise further plans."

Robert pushed his empty plate out of the way. "We may find

more than one possibility. Or nothing."

Captain Standish nodded. "If that is the case, we figure out what to do next when we meet up in Atwood."

Mrs. Boyde seemed satisfied, and that was enough for Marissa. She agreed, and the others nodded.

Robert and the captain located two carts for hire. Marissa settled to one side of the first and watched the men enter the other cart. Unease made her chew her bottom lip, wanting to call them back and insist going together.

Mrs. Boyde patted her leg. "Just taking a look. We'll be back with them by the end of the day."

They followed the others a few blocks, past the shops and buildings that seemed to lean on one another. They passed beneath an archway through the town wall before Robert's vehicle turned toward the northwest. The rumble of wheels increased as the quality of road declined. Hours passed, and Marissa bit her lip to keep from complaining. She turned to the window, and the view captured her attention. Groves of trees gave way to sprawling green hills dotted with sheep. A large manor home with field workers nestled against a hill. Low stone fences formed paddocks field markers.

Marissa grunted and held onto the seat as they crossed a rougher patch. Mrs. Boyde rocked back and forth, pressing against the side of the carriage to keep from slipping off the seat.

"We need better roads." Marissa wanted to rub her back side.

Another patch of trees went by, and then the burgeoning vista made Marissa gasp. There was a meadow with a few trees in the distance and a pond of water where cattails bent. A country manor came to view as they turned the corner. There wasn't snow, but the shape of the land, the house itself, they were from the dream. She banged on the wall behind the driver. "Stop!" She looked at Mrs. Boyde. "There it is," She grabbed her hand, and then nearly slid from the seat as the cart jerked to a halt.

"Wot's the problem?" A deep voice yelled from the driver's seat.

Marissa stared through the window, wanting to be sure. The sun shone on the spring day, yet the large house appeared cloaked in shadows. Quiet hung in the air. The slow breeze brought the smell of decay and age.

Her heart pounded. "This is it. This is what I saw in my dream."

"Purty, but not an inviting place," the driver mumbled. He made to grab the reigns, but Marissa protested.

Mrs. Boyde frowned. "Are you certain?"

Marissa agreed. "There will be an old woman waiting in the manner house."

"We continue to Atwood and return with Robert and Nich--"

"We've not come this far to turn back now, have we?" Marissa reached across to open the carriage door. The urge to stay and explore, to seek the truth, burned in her chest.

Mrs. Boyde tried to grab her. "We mustn't."

She slipped from her reach. *What does this mean?* Marissa wondered as she stepped down. The land had an air of abandonment, the manor as though it had been closed for more than a season. If an old woman lived in the house, the poor thing could be dead, and no one would know. Had Cinderella been raised in such a place? Her heart stirred with compassion.

"Be on your guard," Mrs. Boyde pulled her shawl tight around her shoulders before motioning for Marissa to follow. "We see as we are meant to see."

"It's not real?"

"Enchantment upon enchantment." She shivered.

Marissa studied Mrs. Boyde. Her guardian's silvery blonde hair remained coifed as usual, pins in place. But her blue eyes were wary, lines between them spoke of anxiety. She still looked tired.

She meant to follow Mrs. Boyde on the path to the main house, but the sparkles of light across the water invited her to investigate. Ripples from a slight wind caused the water to lap at the edge where tiny fish darted among the reeds.

Something struck between her shoulder blades. The momentum threw her forward, arms flailing, into the water. It was deeper than she'd thought. Her heavy skirts dragged her down, and the weeds tangled her arms, her legs. She struggled, trying to keep from breathing water into her lungs. She couldn't free herself. Her vision began to fade, and darkness pressed against her mind.

Marissa jerked to a sitting position. This wasn't the Belton

Province countryside where she'd been a moment ago. Her heart pounded. She was indoors, inside a stone-hewn hallway flickering with torch light.

"You think you can defeat me?"

Marissa hissed, pressing herself against the wall as a man with a slim gold crown was dragged, struggling, between two men. Three ladies walked behind them. None seemed to notice Marissa.

"Derilla loved you. You didn't have to kill her."

"I didn't mean to."

"You play with powers beyond your control."

He struggled harder. "I am king. Who are you to tell me no?"

Marissa followed. This was the keep but not Robert's father. How could she be witness to something of the past?

"Renounce the black art. Free yourself of its hold." They led the king into a room. Fire had been set in a fireplace. The women who followed walked to a shelf above a desk. They pulled the books, carried them across the room, and tossed them into the blaze. The flames hissed, burning colors not of wood. The king screeched. One of the men pulled something from a pouch and tossed it on the fire. The flames licked higher, and the books burned. The men released the king.

The woman nearest the fire faced the king, her eyes shining with tears. "My sister, Derilla, begged me to help you, and I will." She took a step closer. "If you are willing to turn from this destructive path."

The king looked at the empty shelf above his desk, and then faced the fire that poured heat into the room. He rubbed his eyes and then pulled his hands through his hair. "I can't."

The first words Marissa couldn't hear, but then his voice shook the room.

"Curses have you, I won't." He turned for the door, stepped over the threshold, and froze.

It was as if something invisible caught him. Pain etched onto his face, and although she couldn't hear him, his mouth opened to scream. His skin began to pucker. Marissa threw herself against the wall, curled up, and buried her face in her arms. Fear shook her body. How could she get out of this? Wind blew across her, whipping her hair, and then settled once more.

She heard shoes scuttle on the stone floor, and managed to lift her head enough for a peek. The doorway was empty.

Derilla's sister knelt beside the door and took hold of the crown. She looked at the others in the room. "We must find whatever remains of Doorin. His things need be destroyed. "

One of the men nodded. "These rooms will be sealed. Camden must be fetched from the battlefront."

"A new line of kings. They will need Guardians. If an offspring of Doorin were to be born with his talents …"

"Pray we find him, train him in the ways of the Master."

Marissa's head spun, her chest tightened as though something pulled her back.

"Marissa!"

Mrs. Boyde's fist beat on her back, and Marissa coughed, splattering water from her throat. She lay on the ground, body shivering with cold. She was outside. The walls of the keep were gone, its hallways gone. Air struggled in her chest and another round of coughing hurt.

Marissa closed her eyes and gulped. Shivers continued. She needed to move, heat her body. Her muscles protested as she turned and tried to sit up. Another fit of coughing took her.

When it passed, Mrs. Boyde crouched beside her, holding her shoulders. "You're freezing."

Marissa pushed herself to sit up. She was cold, and the sun seemed powerless against it. "We should go to the house." How could she explain what she'd seen?

"No." Mrs. Boyde's firm refusal surprised her. "The closer we are, the more fowl things become. We should never have traveled here. Her power is too strong. How could I have been so blind?"

Marissa shivered as a chill brushed across her soaked skin. She rubbed her hands on her arms. "I saw something, when I fell into the water."

"Something? Like what?"

"A vision, I think. They were Guardians, like you."

"Where were they?"

"In the keep. A king died horribly. He'd worked with black

magic, like Cinderella."

Mrs. Boyde looked at the manor house. "She is linked to him. Did you hear his name?"

"Doorin." Wait, they had said something important. Something useful. Marissa grabbed Mrs. Boyde's arm. "His things needed to be destroyed. The things in the keep that gave him power."

Mrs. Boyde placed an arm around her shoulder and helped Marissa stand. "Say no more in this place. This is the witch's lair. I have no doubt of it. There is no old woman, no family to seek. Cinderella has set this place to her will. We are not safe."

"Do you mean give up? Let her win?" A wet braid fell across her face. She pulled out the pins and twisted her hair, letting water drip on the ground. "What of Robert?" Marissa forced herself to her feet, though her legs felt rubbery. She stumbled and Mrs. Boyde caught her arm. They walked to the horse and carriage.

It wasn't until they were settled and a few minute's journey from the manor that Mrs. Boyde resumed the conversation. "What do you think you learned from the vision?"

"It's not just her. Cinderella uses something to strengthen her spell. It's how she kept power over Robert while he searched for her, before she came to Monmoore for the engagement period."

"The glass slipper."

Marissa nodded. "The first morning after the ball, I was with him. He changed when he saw it, forgot I was there. That must be it. The glass slippers are linked to the spell she has over him."

"Don't forget Crow. He is bound to her will."

"Is there no way to save him?"

"He would have to choose it for himself. I do not know if he could."

"We need to return to Monmoore."

Mrs. Boyde nodded in agreement. "But destroying the slippers may not be enough."

"What else is there?"

"A stronger bond than one forged of dark magic."

"A stronger bond?"

"Love."

They continued on the road leading to Atwood. Marissa stared through the window, though she did not notice trees zipping past. The thought of drowning didn't frighten her. Regret that Robert would never know … what? *I promised myself to accept the truth. What is the truth?*

Did she love Robert?

She did. She closed her eyes and allowed the words to flow. She'd been fighting herself, wanting and not wanting. But just saying the words offered so much freedom. She could admit it—to herself. To Mrs. Boyde. To the world, even. Something inside broke, as if a great weight released itself. She loved Robert. Adored him. He called her his dearest friend; he was hers as well. "I love him. I love Robert." The words parted her lips with ease. Flew from her heart. Laughter shook her. "I do." She wanted to grab Mrs. Boyde and twirl in the carriage, but neither of them could stand up. She settled for gripping her hands tight, shaking with excitement. "I love him."

Mrs. Boyde pulled her close. "Of course, you do, child. Probably from the beginning, you're just that stubborn."

"Ha, look who speaks." She sighed. "I love Robert." She flopped against the seat, heat from her heart warming through the cold brought on by evil waters. How could the words be so easy to say? How could she not have said them sooner, when her body pulsed, knowing her love for him was strong and real. Her love was true.

LAURIE LEE

46

The carriage stopped at The Swan. Marissa could not wait for help with the door. She flung open the handle, stepped partway through, and looked back at Mrs. Boyde. "We must return to Monmoore. What say we hire the private dining room and plot with the boys?"

Someone grabbed her from behind, lifting her off her feet as she squealed. "Dining with us?" Robert had her. He placed her on the dirt and rubbed his hand across the still damp sleeve of her dress, frowning. "Why are you wet?"

"A story we shall share at dinner. Be a dear and save the parlor for us? Order something hot to drink, I'm cold through and through." She pulled away, offering a hand to Mrs. Boyde. "We both are."

"Elizabeth."

Marissa turned to find the captain running toward them.

"Captain Standish," Mrs. Boyde's brows rose with her firm voice. She offered a slight smile. "You will join us as well?"

His eyes sparkled. "Seems like dangerous company to keep. Every turn and trouble finds you."

"I can't argue with that. We shan't be long, gentleman. A fire and warm cider beckon."

Marissa and Mrs. Boyde walked to their room in silence. Mrs. Boyde entered first, pausing long enough for Marissa to bump into her.

"All is well," Mrs. Boyde assured.

Marissa wasted no time in pulling fresh under garments and clothes from her travel bag, grabbing a towel as she went behind the screen. She rubbed her skin after pulling the damp cloth from her body. She hung the wet stuff from hooks on the back of the screen.

"You think it's a good plan, returning to Monmoore?" She asked once she was dry and warm.

Mrs. Boyde took her place. "There may be great pain for you, in returning."

"I know." She stood to the side of the window looking out into the busy yard. Late afternoon sun caused long shadows. What would happen if Cinderella ruled the land? She'd been willing to kill for that power. She shuddered at the thought of what she would do with it. "She must be stopped. Cinderella must never be queen."

The private parlor had a cracked door that dulled the roar of the tavern to a buzz. There was a long seat covered with faded fabric, images of flowers and shrubs still showed. They sat at the wood table. For all its grimy dirt, the inn provided a decent tray of supper. Roasted lamb, stewed vegetables from the winter garden, and mugs of warmed spiced cider were offered to ward off the chill. Marissa served Robert a portion of lamb, leaning close enough for their shoulders to touch. She breathed his scent, reminding her of earth and wind.

Captain's Standish's wink caused her cheeks to heat. He plucked a potato from his fork and turned to Mrs. Boyde. "You found something on the river road?"

"Cinderella's home. The attack came close to achieving her goal." She shared the ill adventure that had plagued the afternoon.

Captain Standish glared at Marissa. "We had a plan."

"I couldn't help myself. Something drew me from the carriage."

"Your own innate sense of curiosity."

Marissa wanted to deny it, but the captain's blue eyes bore through her façade. She lowered her head.

Robert took Marissa's hand.

"Do you believe us?" She peered at him. "Do you believe Cinderella is not the woman you think her?"

"I struggle to think of her as a witch, but I cannot deny—" he released her, grabbing his fork to toy with the food on his plate.

She wanted to wrap her arms around him. "The raven man. He's been held by her for an age, forced to her will. Would you suffer the same fate?"

"But what is to be done? How do we stop her?"

Mrs. Boyde straightened in her chair and placed her mug on the table. "We return to Monmoore. She has woven a deep spell around that place, and that is where it must be broken."

Robert knew what going back meant. Here, free of Cinderella, feelings for Marissa raced through him. Feelings that were stronger than he believed possible. Going back would take those feelings from him. He studied the woman at his side. She hadn't taken time for her hair, allowing it to fall except for the front pulled back in a braid. Her eyes glowed, though death had tried to claim her that afternoon. He knew every imperfection. The scar on her forehead. Freckles across her nose because she hated bonnets. He shook himself and focused across the table. Mrs. Boyde and Captain Standish ate in silence, but both had interesting smiles on their faces.

"Maybe returning isn't the best choice. There has to be another way."

Mrs. Boyde gave a stern look. "Prince, I'm going to ask something bluntly, and I want you to think before you respond. Cinderella's spell is strong, and yet she struggles to keep you in her control. Is it possible you love another?"

"Love? Of course, I love others. Father." He looked at Marissa. "Do you love Marissa?"

"She is my dearest friend, the sister I never had."

Marissa's face drooped. She pushed her chair from the table and stood. "I am ready to retire. The events, this afternoon," she glowered at Robert, causing him to frown. "We can plan further in the morning." She rushed away before he could stop her, before any of them could make her wait.

Mrs. Boyde stood to follow, but Robert held up his hand. "I will go. We need to talk."

He took the stairs two at a time, reassured to hear Marissa's steps not far from him. She had unlocked the room when he caught up with her.

She gave him a glance and then stood in the doorway facing into the room, her back to him. "I'm tired."

"Liar." He knew her, could feel emotions rolling from her.

Her arms crossed. "I almost drowned. I think I'm permitted to be a bit tired."

"We've grown up together, Mars. I know you're angry with me."

"I'm not angry. You said what I've always wanted you to say."

Little curls hid in her hair. He couldn't resist sweeping his hands beneath it and letting it run across his fingers. "I cut a bit of your hair, once. When you were sleeping."

She twirled around. "You did not."

"Did. I wanted to see if it was the same color as the cocoa made by the monks."

"Cinderella's hair is prettier."

He shook his head. "Pretty, yes." He twisted a lock of Marissa's hair around his finger. "You are beautiful." He kissed her. Not a chance meeting of lips, this. He wove his fingers through her hair and pulled her close. His lips covered hers. She leaned against him, moving her lips as he moved. He wanted to pull closer, this gentle exploring more than he had dared.

Breathless, they both took a step back, her forehead resting against his. He could feel the brush of her breath on his face. "I love you, Mars. It has nothing to do with growing up together, and everything to do with spending my life with you. Cinderella's spell buried it, but she could never erase my love for you."

"Oh, Robert. I love you, I do. That's why we need to return to Monmoore."

He shook his head. "I will be dragged into the spell once more."

"Don't you see, as long as the spell exists, we will never be free of it. Free of Cinderella. Our love is stronger than it's ever been. We can break the spell."

"You almost fell from the tower of the keep. I will be lost forever if something happens to you."

He wrapped his arms around her. Never had he allowed himself the feel of holding her. Now, with her soft body pressed against his,

his blood heated.

"It appears things have taken a turn for good." Mrs. Boyde's laugh rolled through the hallway.

Robert realized they remained in the doorway, and Marissa didn't seem to want to release him.

"Come now, dears. We need rest. Ten days' journey by coach to return to the palace." Mrs. Boyde stopped beside him, patted his cheek. Marissa pulled away with a sigh.

"We will join you and Captain Standish at the carriage in the morning. Have a safe, peaceful night. We can plan more as we travel." Marissa kissed his cheek, and then Mrs. Boyde pulled her away, closing the door between them.

LAURIE LEE

47

Seven days they journeyed, and Marissa basked in his attention. They were never alone, yet he found opportunity to touch her arm, her hand, to brush against her as the carriage rocked. They watched the kingdom fly past, arguing the riches of land and people.

But the eighth day his demeanor changed. He slid further away, passed hours in silence as he stared at the corner. On the tenth, he stretched his torso through the window. "Are we near?" He cried to Captain Standish riding on the front bench of the carriage. "My Cinderella awaits, and I am eager to see her."

Marissa pressed her nails into the palms of her hands. She knew the spell wove its will over him. She knew in his heart he loved her, not Cinderella. But to see such eagerness in him for another—her eyes burned with unshed tears. Mrs. Boyde brushed her hand through her hair. Marissa leaned against her.

The sound of the wheels changed as they crossed the moat, and then they were halting, standing still in Monmoore. The familiar castle did not feel as it should. She leaned close to whisper with Mrs. Boyde. "Are you sure this is the right choice for us?"

Mrs. Boyde kissed her forehead. "Have faith, child."

Robert burst out of the carriage as a woman's cries disrupted the courtyard.

"I thought you lost," Cinderella flew into his arms.

Though he did not twirl her with lighthearted joy, he held her close. Too close, Marissa thought, judging by the lump in her throat. Cinderella looked as she ever had. Long blonde curls, sweet innocent face. Her cheeks were damp as she pressed her lips against Robert's face. Marissa rolled her eyes.

"So few days remain," Cinderella whimpered. "We've heard nothing. I thought for sure an ill fate had befallen you."

"Yet he is safely returned." Marissa spoke as she climbed from the carriage. "We all are."

Cinderella turned, keeping herself in Robert's arms. "You?"

"When Robert found me, he insisted we return."

"Did he? I am glad to see you."

Of course, she was. Marissa noticed the gleam in Cinderella's eyes. It was like seeing double. The innocent young woman, beautiful and in love, and the strong-willed woman with jealous eyes and covetous hold on the prince.

"I'm exhausted," Marissa held Mrs. Boyde's arm, "as is my companion. Robert moved us at a trying pace; he was eager to return."

"As he should." Cinderella gave him a brief kiss. "You know where your rooms are, I'm sure you can make your way there."

Already taking control? Where are the king and Mother? Marissa harrumphed and plodded across the lawn, Mrs. Boyde in her wake. Captain Standish followed, arms loaded with their traveling boxes.

48

"I'm not sure what you plan to achieve, returning." Cinderella stood in the doorway of the library.

Marissa turned from the window. "Achieve?"

"Is it so horrible," Cinderella asked as she stepped into the room, "to want love? To desire security?"

Marissa shook her head. "Not when those things come naturally, in the course of one's life."

She wrapped a blond curl around her finger, tilting her head. "You don't think my love for the prince natural?"

"Birds come to the lake after winter's chill." Marissa nodded at the window. "Spring is upon us, and yet the lake remains undisturbed."

Cinderella laughed, "You think I have power to keep birds from their natural habits?"

"The palace is not as it should be. Silence weighs upon it, as though something smothers us."

"An insect caught in a web?" Her eyes sparkled, chilling Marissa. "Why return? Why not remain free?"

"Love doesn't allow that. If there are foul works afoot, our duty is to fend them off."

"Indeed." Cinderella stretched her arm forward, moving her hand back and forth so that the large diamond-crusted ruby glittered in the light. "It is a good thing the forty days are coming to an end and we can wed. Once you see our happiness, perhaps your fears will fade." Her tiny smile and sparkling eyes chilled Marissa. "Or not."

"Why not allow him to choose?"

"But he has chosen. The ring is on my finger, not yours."

"I've not wanted his ring on my hand…"

Cinderella interrupted, pulling closer. "Haven't you? Isn't that what this is about?"

"There you are, Marissa." Mrs. Boyde burst into the library. "The housekeeper is in a dither. You must show her where the trunks are meant to be stored in the attic."

Though the smile remained the same, Cinderella lowered her voice. "Robert is mine. Your Guardian cannot save him, neither can you."

Marissa walked across the room, then paused at the open door. She turned around, facing her enemy. Cinderella stood, a smile of victory on her face. Marissa shook her head. "You're wrong. I can save him. Love can save him." She stiffened her back against Cinderella's icy glare.

Mrs. Boyde pulled her into the hallway. "Now, now. No point giving too much away."

She shivered. "She's evil."

Mrs. Boyde nodded. "Tomorrow is the final day of the engagement. They can be wed after the stroke of midnight."

Marissa hurried her way down the corridor. "I must find Robert, break the spell before that can happen."

"He spars with Captain Standish in the morning. Find him there. But first, there is something else you must retrieve." Mrs. Boyde handed Marissa a sack woven with gold and lavender linen. "Find the slipper."

Marissa shook the bag. Something was already inside. "What are these?"

"Extra copies the prince made. No need to let Cinderella know what you are up to before tomorrow."

"She would keep it near him. I can check his offices and quarters."

"You have to get her to leave the palace first. It would not do to try something while she is near."

Marissa thought for a moment, then smiled. "I have a plan."

The day crawled. Cinderella managed to cross Marissa's path often, Robert at her side. He kept an arm around her. Pressed kisses against her blonde curls. Lunch brought them together at the smaller dining room. Marissa gasped at her first sight of King William and her mother. The king's hair had turned gray. His pale cheeks were no longer smooth, but wrinkled, deep shadows beneath his eyes. Lady DeGanne's hair, also more gray than not, had been pulled into a loose French twist with strands jutting unevenly. Her eyes had dulled. She glanced at Marissa but said nothing.

"Do you not care for the soup?" Cinderella asked.

Marissa moved her spoon through the butternut squash brulee. She didn't bother to respond. Defeat pressed against her shoulders. If she closed her eyes, she'd feel the sweep of webs across her skin. But then she noticed Robert held one hand fisted on the table beside him as they waited for the change in course. It wasn't a gentle fist; his knuckles were white. He struggled, and so must she.

Marissa straightened in her seat. "Do you have plans for the afternoon?"

"Why do you ask?" Cinderella placed her spoon beside her empty soup bowl.

Marissa shrugged. "There were clouds hovering in the distance. I thought perhaps we could play a game in the library."

"That would be pleasing." Cinderella leaned back as a servant removed her dish and replaced it with the lunch plate. She placed her hand on Robert's shoulder. "But you wouldn't want to stay cooped up inside, would you dear?"

His smile seemed real enough. "What would you suggest?"

"How many days did you sit inside the hired carriage? Your horse has returned. Wouldn't you like to take a ride?"

Marissa protested, "But the rain, you could catch a chill."

King William pointed with his spoon, dripping thick yellow drops onto the white tablecloth. "Your friend makes a good point, Cinderella dear. Wouldn't want you uncomforted with the wedding so close."

"What do you mean, her friend? I'm your daughter." She

gulped. "Stepdaughter."

He didn't hear her. Her mother looked, a frown bringing wrinkles between her brows.

Marissa could feel Cinderella's pleasure like waves of heat pouring across the table. She faced the witch. "Why have you done this?"

"Would have been better for you to stay in the world beyond the palace, but you are here now." Cinderella gave a satisfied grin. "Witness to all that is to be, come tomorrow night when the wedding bells shall peel. So, no, I don't believe we will join you in the library for games. I think it best Robert keep from your company, until it is too late for you to do anything but weep."

The remainder of the meal passed in silence. Marissa managed a few bits of tenderloin. Cinderella and Robert would be gone for several hours, enough time to search for the real slipper.

Marissa excused herself to her suite. She slammed the door behind her. "Vile, evil woman."

Mrs. Boyde crossed the room and engulfed her in a hug. "I'm sorry for what you have to endure."

Marissa used the warmth of the embrace to bolster her courage. Through the window, she watched as Cinderella and Robert walked their horses toward the woods. She pulled away from Mrs. Boyde. "They are leaving. I must find the slipper."

Marissa stepped into the hallway and came face to face with Abigail. Marissa pulled back. "What are you doing here?"

"Cinderella asked me to remain with you. I am to see to your every need."

"I am capable of making my way through the palace. I do not need you."

Abigail stepped closer. "My duty is to follow Cinderella's orders."

Mrs. Boyde stepped around Marissa. "Indeed? Following Cinderella's orders?"

Abigail's face darkened when she saw Mrs. Boyde. Before Abigail could react, the Guardian blew a silvery powder over her.

Marissa backed away as Abigail twisted with pain.

Mrs. Boyde grabbed hold of Abigail's hands. "She holds you with fear. Let it go."

"I can't, you don't understand what she can do."

"Child, the way of Light holds more power than darkness ever can. Be free of Cinderella."

Abigail fell to the floor, crying, her body shaking. Mrs. Boyde stayed with her, looking up at Marissa. "Go," she whispered.

Marissa fled. She went to Robert's suite first. There was little challenge in finding the glass slipper. The deep blue dressing room had a slender table draped with a soft yellow cover that went to the floor. A pedestal in pewter sat upon the table, and the glass slipper rested upon the pedestal. Marissa had no desire to touch the original slipper. She pulled a hanging shirt and used it to place the slipper inside the bag. She retrieved the false slipper and placed it on the pedestal. The false slipper did not gleam as the original, but with so short a time, it couldn't matter much.

She returned to her bedroom. Neither Mrs. Boyde nor Abigail were there. Marissa dropped the bagged shoe inside a corner closet. Unease struck her. Cinderella had worn two shoes. Could the other be in the palace as well? "Should we destroy them both?" There was no one else in the room to offer guidance. She walked to the windows, but there was no view of Robert or Cinderella. A little time remained to see what she could find. Marissa made up her mind and strode from her bedroom.

She used the hidden passageway to cut through to the guest wing on the other side of the portrait gallery. The ivy knocker looked the same, but standing in front of Cinderella's room made her sick. Her stomach broiled, and it took all her concentration to keep from bringing up what little she'd consumed at lunch. She pushed into the room.

She expected to find dark and dreary, but the Rose Room remained cheerful, light from the windows brightening the space. The mirror nabbed her attention. It was the same mirror, Marissa was certain of it. But instead of the small, hanging mirror, it was now long enough for a person to step through. *How is this possible?* The glittering reflection drew her closer. She reached her finger to touch the glass, but fell into it instead.

She fell through the glass, falling to her knees on hard cobbles of stone. She gasped with pain. A man standing at a large table froze, looking in her direction. Marissa couldn't move, but his glance passed over her as though he could not see her. It was King Doorin.

Marissa skirted back until she touched the wall. It was a large room with lots of books. Piles of books spread across the table except where a large empty picture frame lay. There were vials of things as well. Glass containers with dark liquids were stored on shelves beside a fireplace. A few stools sat beneath the table. King Doorin pulled one to him, sitting as he drew his finger across lines of writing in an oversized book open in front of him.

What am I doing here? Marissa looked around, but there were no Guardians. A young man entered holding a tray with three containers of sand. Marissa knew it was sand, and yet, it was unlike sand she had seen before. Faceted sides of each grain glittered, even though there was no source of light. Marissa watched him drop the tray onto the table.

"Watch yourself," Doorin rested a hand against a jar of sand and then backhanded the young man. The boy staggered back and made as if to turn and leave. Doorin caught his arm. "Pour the sand into the frame."

The young man had to climb on the table to reach the large frame made of white oak. He knelt beside the frame, picking up the first large container of sand as he looked to Doorin. "Just pour it?"

"Fill the inside of the frame with the sand." Doorin remained at the end of the table, watching. The young man poured the sand from the container, moving back and forth. When he emptied the first container, he picked up the second. When he finished with the third container of sand, Doorin moved. The young man was still stretched over the frame, reaching across to fill the last few spaces on the far side with sand. Doorin pushed, and the young man fell, elbow and forearms dragging through the sand.

The grunt of complaint stopped in an instant. There was silence, but Marissa could feel tension growing throughout the room. A high-pitched screech emanated from the young man as the sand took form and oozed over him, burning with its touch. The glittering particles turned red. Marissa wrapped her arms around her head, curling herself as small as she could get. Her body shook.

The scene changed. A woman wearing a yellow gown crouched beside her. Reaching through to touch her cheeks, the woman lifted

Marissa's face. "You do not belong here. Withdraw from Cinderella's room in the palace this instant. Search no further. You have what you need. Now go."

Marissa was standing, staggering back from the mirror which had turned black. Still shaking, she lifted her skirts and ran.

Mrs. Boyde caught her up. "My dear girl, what were you thinking?"

Marissa couldn't speak. She wrapped her arms tight as she could around Mrs. Boyde, sobbing.

"Come, let us get away from this space." Mrs. Boyde led her through the portrait gallery.

Marissa halted in front of the image of Robert's mother. The woman's sweet face brought calm. Robert had her eyes. She stared into them. Mrs. Boyde remained at her side. Marissa drew a deep breath, wiping her cheeks with the back of her hand.

"King Doorin was evil."

Mrs. Boyde kept an arm around Marissa's shoulders. "Is that what you saw?"

Marissa nodded. "It was a room in the keep. He killed a man. More than one. The mirror—"

"Don't speak of it here. I called to the Guardians of the past, and they pulled you out. Cinderella will not know you were in her room."

"I thought we needed the other slipper as well. It was the most logical place for it."

"If the other slipper remains with her in the palace, Cinderella would have known as soon as she laid eyes upon a fake. No, we have the one that works against Robert. And we have you."

The anguished voice of the man pulled at her, making Marissa want to hide.

Mrs. Boyde moved them along the corridor. "What you need is rest. I can ease your memory, but you need strength to break the spell against Robert." They kept to the main hallway, even though it would take a bit longer to get to the family's quarters. Marissa didn't mind. Shadowy places were not where she wanted to go.

Evening ended, and Marissa sank exhausted onto her bed.

Mrs. Boyde disappeared for a moment, then brought a glass of wine. "Drink this. You will sleep in peace."

"What happened with Abigail?" Marissa took the glass, hating to see her hand shake.

"She has been deeply wounded. I have provided her with a few days of sleep without dreams. Cinderella will no longer have control of her, but she will have to decide to heal. Now drink. You need your own time to heal."

"How can I help Robert if I sleep?"

"Cinderella will keep him from you. We know he is to work with Captain Standish tomorrow morning. You will find him then."

Marissa didn't have it in herself to argue. She drank the wine, then laid back. Restful sleep carried her away. There were no nightmares.

49

Robert did not show for his fencing match.

"Where could he be?" Marissa stood in the yard rubbing her arms as she faced Captain Standish.

His look was grave. "I received no note, and the soldier I sent round to his quarters reported his rooms empty, bed unslept."

Marissa looked up at the colonnade. "She has him somewhere. I revealed my heart." She stomped her foot. What had caused her to say so much? Her fist tightened on the bag she had brought with her.

"Noon is here, you have twelve hours to find him."

"Can you not?" She turned to her companion. "Mrs. Boyde?" Marissa blinked tears from her eyes. Not now, with everything at stake.

"I should, but I have no sense of him. The spell is heavy upon us."

Do not allow fear to reign, Mars. She closed her eyes and breathed. "Now is the time to break it."

For hours she searched, wandering the halls and smaller rooms of the castle. A glimpse of a man riding in the fields beyond the grounds sent her to the stables. More than an hour wasted, searching the nether-reaches of the king's land. When she returned to the stable, all the horses were accounted. Had he slipped past unawares, or had she been fooled? She dipped her hands in the cool basin of water kept near the entrance to the stable and rubbed her face. Foul deeds, indeed. She should be hungry, but her stomach turned at the thought of food. She had to find him. The sun was sinking toward the west.

Glimmers of light broke through the cords of gray clouds across the sky. Marissa paused, leaning against the door jamb. "Lord, help us." No sooner had the words been spoken, the keep came to mind. Marissa ran to the undercroft, catching herself on one of the stone arches. In the dim light of evening, massive walls of the keep cast a dark shadow across the lawn. No light shown in any of the slim arrow holds, but Robert was within. She was certain of it.

Searching, ever searching. Her voice faded from crying his name. Foolishness, Cinderella probably heard each one and managed to keep ahead of Marissa. A bit of moon rose in the east. One room in the keep which did not show the years of decay, as most of the rest, had been lit with torches. A large box shape like a church alter covered with red cloth stood at the front. Like an altar, or like a coffin? Marissa moved the pair of candlesticks, a goblet with wine, and a book of verse from the top. She pulled the cloth away, but it was a table. Nothing hid beneath. No sign of Robert. This was where Cinderella planned to hold the wedding. Marissa ran from the room.

She went up. The stairs to the roof of the keep taunted her fears. The first stroke of midnight rang out, louder in its urgency. There was no time for fear. Marissa grabbed the wall at the bottom of the spiral stairs leading to the parapet. She lifted her skirts and ran, using the rope handrail to pull herself faster. But the old stone released the hold of the rail and she fell to her knees as the second bell tolled. Ignoring the pain, she pushed herself to her feet and continued. She knew the number of stairs, but she dared not think of it, or despair would overwhelm her.

She struggled on, stumbling onto the roof as the fourth bell of midnight struck. "Robert," her scream surpassed its ringing. Stars glittered above, the moon a distant cold light. Yet, in the bits of light, she could see a large shadow standing beside the bird pen. She raced to his side. "Robert."

She fell into him, he was here. The fifth bell sounded. He did not move.

Marissa touched his face. His skin seemed cool, but his eyes were open, staring beyond the cage where birds were kept. Another chime, the moment of midnight half gone. "Prince? Why are you here? It is not a safe place to roam in the dark." More bells rung, but he did nothing. She shook him, sobs choking her. "Do not leave me, my love. Not here, not like this. Not for her." She kissed him as the final toll of midnight struck. For a moment, he remained as he was. Then as the final ember of sound stilled, his arms moved, his hands creeping along her sides. Gaining strength. Warming.

He kissed her, pulling her tight against him, but she didn't mind. With a shout of joy, he lifted her in his arms and twirled them around. Her head spun as he returned her to the ground.

50

A screech echoed across the rooftops. Robert and Marissa dropped to the ground beside the roosting house.

"Do you think you can upset order with chaos? Really, little girl, you think you can defeat me?" Cinderella's voice screamed through the blackness. It was not the voice of a woman in love, but an angry witch seeking revenge.

With Robert's arms around her, Marissa drew strength, though she remained silent.

"I have waited long for this moment. I will not be thwarted. The secrets of Doorin's rooms are meant to be mine." Cinderella's voice drew closer.

Robert pressed his forehead against Marissa. She curled her hand against his cheek. "We must stand against her together." With his precious face a breath from hers, she could see him nod. A quick kiss, and Marissa twirled, standing to face Cinderella. Robert stood behind, his arm around her waist.

Cinderella's eyes burned with hatred as she shook her head. "You think you have won? You are but insects caught in a web, struggling in your death throws."

Marissa touched her father's necklace that lay unnoticed on her chest, feeling him with her, then she pulled the sack she kept at her side throughout the day. "Your spell will not last without the aid of this." She dropped the sack to the stone floor, the sound of glass breaking sweet to her ears.

Cinderella shrieked. "How? When—"

"You were intent to keep Robert from me, it never occurred to you to keep me from you." She took a step closer. "Every stair climbed, every doorway entered and exited, every passage." She opened the edge of the sack and turned it over. Shards of glass fell to the ground. "You have no power here, Cinderella of Belton Province."

Cinderella snarled. "I should have destroyed you when I had the chance."

"That's just it." Robert stepped in front of Marissa, protecting her. "You tried and failed, time and again. Real love is stronger than your spells and webs."

Marissa gripped the sides of his tunic. "Be gone, witch. Take your evil arts beyond the borders of our lands."

Cinderella laughed, a chill sound that caused shivers. "You think it that easy to banish me?" She drew a sword. "I had hoped to find pleasure in the arms of a young prince, but an aging king will do just as well."

Robert reached for a weapon at his side, but he carried nothing. The two of them backed up a step.

A large black bird flew between them as Cinderella lunged. The caw of Crow turned to the screams of a man as her blade pierced his side. Cinderella cried out as huge wings beat against her. Marissa gasped, curling against Robert.

Cinderella railed her arms against the cursed creature, but they were too close to the edge. Her feet slipped in the pile of glass. She grabbed the injured bird, but it was changing into the dark stranger. Her sword clanked against the keep as they fell, screams mingling together, until silence stretched into the night.

It happened so fast. Marissa caught her breath as she clung to Robert. Cinderella had been standing there, and then she was gone. A trick? A ruse to beguile them yet again?

"Careful." Robert held her as they inched closer to the edge. They stepped around the pile of glass debris. Darkness hid most of the scene from view, but blonde hair splayed across the lawn could not be hid. Marissa buried her face in Robert's shoulder. He moved them toward safety.

"It's over." His voice rattled. "I'm free. We," he lifted her, "are free."

Marissa laughed as he spun. Free to live. Free to love. It did not matter if they were royalty or common, as long as they remained together.

51

Elizabeth and Nicholas remained in the shadows as the broken form on the ground changed. The black man's unseeing eyes dimmed. Skin pulled taut across his face and his hand that could be seen. Cinderella's blonde curls darkened, her features aging even as her chest rose and fell with breath. She reached a hand upward, but neither Elizabeth nor Nicholas could tell what she reached for.

Cinderella's breath rattled. Whatever she had hoped for did not materialize. She struggled, but eventually, her chest lay still. Long fingers dug into the ground, then stilled.

Elizabeth felt something brush against her side. They were no longer alone. Other silent Guardians kept witness beside them. As the glimmer of life faded from Cinderella, they set fire to the bodies. Flames of blue and orange whipped across the ground, consuming the corpses. Charred earth remained once the fires dwindled.

Nicholas took Elizabeth's hand. "Her rooms remain to be purged."

Elizabeth felt joy ease the knot settled beside her heart. "The palace can be purged."

A Guardian with golden hair tapped her shoulder. "Your charges are coming. We will clear the palace and remove what remains in the witch's quarters. See to them."

Elizabeth didn't mind the directive.

Marissa refused to release Robert's hand as they walked down from the tower side by side.

"I should see to the bodies," Robert sighed as he squeezed her hand.

"No need." Mrs. Boyde greeted from the bottom of the stairs. Nicholas joined her.

"But is she dead?" Marissa tried to see past them.

"We no longer need to fear Cinderella or her purpose here."

"Tomorrow will be busy turning away wedding guests." Nicholas suggested they retire for the remainder of night.

Robert looked at Marissa. The glow of his eyes made her stomach swirl. "The wedding need not be cancelled." He pulled her closer, taking hold of both her hands. "I have no doubt you will bring trouble, but there is no other woman I want by my side."

"Me? Trouble?" Marissa's heart bubbled. "You brought a witch into the palace and nearly ruined everything."

He grinned. "Can't help if I'm irresistible."

Marissa tilted her head. "Perhaps I should resist. At least long enough to make you realize the value of what you are getting."

"I am aware of your value, dear heart."

The warm tone of his voice made Marissa blush.

"Adorable, both of you." Nicholas interjected, nodding as Mrs. Boyde pulled Marissa from Robert.

"Before your banter turns into an argument, are you willing to wed on the morrow?"

"Yes." Marissa jumped at the offer.

"Good, that's settled." Mrs. Boyde linked arms with Marissa. "We will see you in the morning."

Marissa took a few steps with her then turned back. "But not that room in the keep."

"The real chapel is in the palace." Robert nodded. "Where my parents wed."

Marissa could have stayed with him, but Mrs. Boyde had her walking across the dark path leading to the palace. Tiredness following in the wake of emotional upheaval muted the excitement of marrying Robert. Mrs. Boyde wrapped an arm around her shoulders as they walked, and Marissa leaned her head against her. "Will Mother and King William return to themselves? They looked ill when we saw them yesterday."

"The evil of Cinderella is being cleared from Monmoore and the keep. Memories of what transpired will fade."

"I hope so."

"We serve a good Master."

Marissa yawned.

Dawn brought light into the palace. Surfaces that had been covered in gray ash now gleamed. Air, sweet with morning, moved in the hallways. Marissa closed her eyes and breathed. Darkness had passed. The white gown swished against her bare toes. Her wedding gown. She wanted to pinch herself. Could it be real?

"Beautiful, daughter."

Marissa turned toward her mother.

The older woman blinked moisture from her eyes. "Your father would be so proud."

"Because I marry a prince?" *Was it the right choice?*

Her mother placed her hand on her cheek. "Because you marry for love. As I shared with your father. As the king shared with his wife."

"I never thought … Mrs. Boyde was right, I allowed a child to control my feelings."

"No longer. You best get shoes on your feet. You and Robert insist on a morning wedding."

The midnight hour to now had been long enough to wait. Marissa ran for her slippers. Woven slippers not quite as pristine as her gown.

It took all her energy to not sprint from her mother's side. They walked at a sedate pace through the gallery then down to the lower court where the chapel stood. Its ornate oak doors stood open. White and yellow flowers with bits of greenery decorated the small space. Beside the round alter stood Robert. Marissa thought her heart would burst. *Dear man.*

The king drew close, holding his hands to her. His arms about her brought tears to her eyes. He cleared his throat. "This is what I had hoped with the engagement ball. All those women of the realm, Robert would realize none were more precious than you."

She swallowed the lump in her throat. "I am the hardheaded one. It took losing him for me to realize the depth of my love."

"That is all I ask. Love my son. Be his helpmate. Stay by his side no matter what."

"I will." She glimpsed the man waiting for her. "I do."

Lady DeGanne patted her shoulder. "Those are words to say before the priest." She kissed her cheek, and then her mother and the king walked hand in hand into the chapel. Marissa turned her attention to Robert. Her dearest friend faced her, the smile on his face welcoming, the gleam in his eyes causing her stomach to tumble with excitement. Love shone through him. She didn't count the steps to his side. It was the feel of her hand in his that mattered most. He didn't wait for the priest's permission. He kissed her. Marissa kissed him back.

They lived happily ever after, Marissa and her true love, Prince Robert of Camden. The kingdom had never known such joy and prosperity. When their time to rule came, King Robert and Queen Marissa faced every peril together, loving each other to the end of their days, which were many.

It was their children's children who faced the peril of the mirror once again. But that is another tale altogether.

Laurie Lee is taking her first steps into fantasy with a twisted fairy tale. Her inspiration comes from the likes of the Brothers Grimm, Tolkien and Lewis. Learn more about Laurie Lee at her website: www.laurieleefairyland.com.